John Hulbert Glover

Kingsthorpiana

Researches in a church chest, being a calendar of old documents now existing in

the church chest of Kingsthorpe, near Northampton, with a selection of the MSS.

John Hulbert Glover

Kingsthorpiana
Researches in a church chest, being a calendar of old documents now existing in the church chest of Kingsthorpe, near Northampton, with a selection of the MSS.

ISBN/EAN: 9783337251598

Printed in Europe, USA, Canada, Australia, Japan

Cover: Foto ©Andreas Hilbeck / pixelio.de

More available books at **www.hansebooks.com**

KINGSTHORPIANA;

OR,

Researches in a Church Chest.

BEING

A CALENDAR OF OLD DOCUMENTS NOW EXISTING IN THE
CHURCH CHEST OF KINGSTHORPE, NEAR NORTHAMPTON,
WITH A SELECTION OF THE MSS., PRINTED IN FULL,
AND EXTRACTS FROM OTHERS.

EDITED BY

J. HULBERT GLOVER, M.A.,
Vicar,

FORMERLY FELLOW OF CLARE COLLEGE, CAMBRIDGE.

Common Seal of Kingsthorpe.

LONDON:
ELLIOT STOCK, 62, PATERNOSTER ROW, E.C.

1883.

PREFACE.

THE documents presented in the following pages were found some twenty years since in a promiscuous heap in the Church Chest of Kingsthorpe, much mutilated, injured by damp and mildew, and likely in a short time to perish altogether. From this fate (though perhaps no living interests are concerned in their preservation) it seemed a duty to rescue them and to secure future safety by making a calendar, with a description of the contents and condition of each, so that reference might be easy, and the integrity of the collection at any time readily ascertained.

More than this was certainly not necessary. But upon examining the documents for the above purpose there seemed to me a possibility that the inhabitants of Kingsthorpe and its neighbourhood, perhaps even a wider circle, might find in these papers matter of interest. The references to historic names of men and places might perhaps be useful.[1] The notices of events of local importance—such as the great coney question, referred to so often in the following pages—though beneath the regard of history, might not

---

[1] In questions of date, for instance. Thus in No. I. William of Wykeham is styled Chancellor at the date 34 Edw. III. (1361), though the date usually assigned to his appointment is 1367.

be without their use to the historian in enabling him to form an estimate of the condition and character of the people at a certain date, to mark the rising force of public opinion, and the national advance towards a day of liberty.

The allusions to manners and customs, the circumstances and ideas of our village ancestors, may be thought worth preserving. We see, for instance, how the bailiff of Boughton rides out of Northampton with his crossbow hanging at his saddle-bow, prepared for a chance shot at a coney on the way to Kingsthorpe. The chauntry priest of Boughton, an arrant poacher probably, is assailed at his own chauntry door by the underkeeper on a charge of coney-hunting. The pious people are unable to attend High Mass on Sundays and Holydays at Boughton Church (the old one, of course, now in ruins) for fear of stumbling into a coney burrow, even the bones of the dead being unearthed and exposed to view, to the great scandal of Christian people.

We see also the yeomen of Kingsthorpe, stung into resistance to an oppressive game-law, combining to meet with ploughs and horses to break up the infested grasslands, and thereby subjecting themselves to an indictment for riot. Then again there are the curious laws and ordinances by which the inhabitants of the royal manor, meeting under their bailiff at the Court Leet, were permitted to govern themselves and to exercise something like the summary power of our magistracy. These ordinances appear to have been stringent enough ; there was no scruple about sending the 'myster[1]-woman,' who was unable to support herself, out of the town, and prohibiting her return, and 'impotent folk' must stand outside the town to beg, and change their domicile before such and such a feast, under a penalty.

The drinking habits of the time are suggested by more than one incidental notice. The strange custom of brewing ale for the profit of the Church, which had for a certain time

---

[1] *Vide* Ordinances (1547).

the monopoly of sale, must have a pernicious moral effect, and helped to strengthen the hold of that habit of intemperance under which the country still so deeply suffers. We find also reference to the office of the May King and Queen, which seems to have been compulsory on the person elected. The 'cucking stool,' moreover, was thought to be a necessary implement of government in those times.

Then we see the three commissioners for the town riding up to London on the burning question of the conies; how they travelled from Northampton to Stony Stratford, thence to Dunstable, to St. Alban's, to Barnet, and so to London, where they retain as their counsel Master Morgan (probably of the Morgan family of Kingsthorpe), to plead for them at the 'Ster Chamber;' the fees they are constantly giving, which are suspiciously like bribes, to the servants; how they went to Istylworth (Isleworth), so as to be within easy reach of Sheen, where the Lord Protector (Somerset) was at that time living, and who apparently had much to do with the settlement of their 'hundreth matter;' then their engaging the help of 'Mr. Sessyl' (the future Lord Burghley[1]), and going with him in a 'boyt' to the 'Towre' to get the copy of Edward III.'s grant of freewarren—doubtless the identical paper marked No. I. in this collection. One of the most noticeable features in the journal kept by these persons is the regular mention of their 'drynkynge' between their meals, and which throws a curious light upon the social customs of the day. The entry 'For my drynkynge before dener and after' is almost as regular as the dinner itself.

Then again there may be something here for the philologist, who may light upon some archaic form of word and phrase worth his attention. Some of the words here occurring are probably local; at any rate, I have not been able to

---

[1] In a warrant of Queen Elizabeth to Lord Burghley (a facsimile of which is given in Wright's 'Queen Elizabeth and her Times') the name is spelt 'Burleigh,' and a line is drawn through it, and 'Burghley' written over in his own handwriting.

find them in any of the old glossaries to which I have had
access. Some measures of land and kinds of tenure, some
forms of legal process in the Court Leet, seem peculiar to
the place, and are not to be found in the ordinary law dic-
tionaries or books of reference. As specimens of the English
language at different dates, and of the purest dialect of
English, according to Fuller, some of these papers will be
found interesting, and, at any rate, it will hardly be doubted
that all such specimens of the popular language and phrase-
ology of a former day ought to be carefully preserved.[1] We
read, for instance, in the depositions (Nos. XVIII. and
XXIII.) how the old bedesman of St. David's at Kingsthorpe thinks that through the action of the conies 'the
grasse and corne that groweth there is greatly hyndered and
apeyred.' John a Latham, the obnoxious keeper, we are
told, 'manassheth and threepeth against the said inhabitants.'
The man who had received a shrewd blow from the keeper
'never lyked after,' and so on. We also find a number of
curious obsolete words, as 'Lomes,' 'Ledes,' 'Cate,' 'Stow-
delfs,' 'Tollfat,' 'Hodhornys,' 'Lowshard,' etc.

Among local words, I suppose, must be placed the word
'cotisal,' or as it appears in the Court Rolls under the forms
'cotecellus,' 'codecellus,' 'cotestetellus,' 'cotsetulus,' 'cor-
sadellus.' It would seem to have indicated some measure
of area (perhaps with a building on it), as we find mention
of a cotisal and a half. For instance, in the Survey of the
Manor made temp. Jac. II. the holding of Robt Pickmer is

---

[1] The late Canon James (*Quarterly Review*) says : 'The provincial
dialects hitherto published have been chiefly curious from their rude
spelling, the broadness of their brogue, their eccentric and abnormal
forms ; but in the midland district not only have we old Saxon words
rather than provincial vulgarisms, but we stand on the native ground of
Shakespeare and Dryden. The worth, then, of the "Northamptonshire
Glossary" is above its abstract philological interest. While it deals with
English in its best and purest forms, it elucidates by actual example, far
safer than the guesses of commentators, some of the most knotty passages
and most obscure allusions of our great authors.'

described, and in the margin 'coi^r voc' le cotecel et dim,'
i.e., 'commonly called the cotisal and a half,' and it appears
in this case to have consisted of the house and grounds of
one acre in extent. We find also a quarter-cotisal mentioned.

It may possibly be a form of cotsethla, but that word is
stated to denote the building or mansion house. Cowell
gives an extract from a chartulary, in which 'cotsethlus
terræ' is mentioned, also from the Malmsbury chartulary,
'Dedi Deo et ecclesie—unam cotsetle cum pertinentiis.'

The word 'quarteron,' 'quarterona,' occurs constantly as
a measure of grassland exclusively, and corresponds to the
roda of arable, each meaning a quarter of an acre of grass
and arable respectively. In the list of Copyhold Claims
(No. XL.) we find 'Johannes Wryght clamat . . . pratum
in coibus pratis iii rod',' and in the margin 'coiter voc' quarterons,' *i.e.*, roods, commonly called quarterons. The quarteron, then, is the same as the quarentena, rood, and furlong, to which last it exactly corresponds in derivation and
meaning, being the fourlong or fourthlong, or fourth part of
an acre.

The form 'quarentena,' from 'quarante,' referring to the
forty square perches of which it was composed, never occurs
in these documents. It precisely corresponds to 'furlong'
if we adopt the common derivation from 'fortylong.' Thus
we have the two words quarentena and quarterona, of different derivations, which are both equivalent to the word furlong, and, curiously enough, the word furlong is capable of
two possible derivations, corresponding to these words;
thus :

furlong = $\begin{cases} \text{fortylong, quarentena, quarante.} \\ \text{fourlong or fourthlong, quarterona, quarta pars.} \end{cases}$

but I think the last is clearly to be preferred.

The derivation from furrowlong is adopted by Skeat,
who explains (after Spelman), 'as long as a furrow, as a

field,' which is a little indefinite. The 'long' in furlong
has probably nothing to do with length, but is merely a ter-
mination like 'ing,' in farthing, ferling, whence ferling-dele,
fardin-dele, or farthingdele, meaning the fourth portion (of
acre), the same as furlong. The word furlong is never used
in these papers as a measure of length.

Another curious local word is the name Semilong,[1] which
has exercised the ingenuity of local antiquaries to explain
its origin. It is however obviously nothing else than the
corrupted form of a word or combination of words of very
common occurrence in these papers, viz.: 'South mylne
wonge,' *i.e.*, the meadow of the South Mill. The word Semilong indicates the tract of ground, in the south extremity of
the parish, extending from Kingsthorpe hollow to the bound-
ary of the parish of St. Andrew's as far as the mill, which
was formerly called the South Mill, now, I believe, St.
Andrew's Mill, and bounded on the west by the river. South
Mill wonge would naturally in rapid speaking become Sum-
milong, and then some puzzled etymologist may have refined
it into Semilong, with the vain suggestion of a classical derivation.

Then again the curious provisions in the old wills, some
of which are given at length in the Court Rolls, are of use
to indicate the religious foundations at the parish church,
which seem to have comprised shrines of the Blessed Virgin
and of St. Katharine, and perhaps several others, the church
itself being dedicated in honour of St. John the Baptist.
Land is bequeathed (*roda luminaria*) for the sustentation of
the lights before the altars.

[1] The late Mr. E. F. Law drew my attention to a correspondence
which appeared in the *Northampton Mercury* some years ago with reference to the origin of the word Semilong. The majority of the guesses
were worthless enough, but one writer, Jas. Cattel, suggested the true
derivation, quoting a deed of the date 1708, where a piece of land is described as lying 'in a furlong called South Mill wong, *alias* the Semilong, next to the meere on one side,' etc. The writer does not seem to
have had much confidence in the testimony of this solitary deed, but the
evidence in these papers amply confirms his suggestion.

The Churchwardens' Accounts are only two in number; one (1565) is interesting as referring to the repairs of the 'Stepull;' the other witnesses to the practice of 'whytyng' the church, which in these days is so offensive to architectural purists. The 'pore scolar' and 'pore singing man' are relieved out of the funds; a 'roop' is provided for the 'Sancte' bell, and other bells are referred to, but of course an earlier set than the present, the oldest bell in the present peal bearing the date 1622.

I hope at some future time to supplement the present volume by another, giving some account of the Church and the Parish Registers, and thus to prepare material ready to the hand of any one who may hereafter undertake to write a history of the parish.

My thanks are due to Mr. Sims, of the British Museum, who made the extension of the French manuscript, and also those extracts from the Court Rolls which are given *in extenso*. In the rest I have thought it better to preserve the original contractions, which will present little difficulty, even to unpractised readers, for whose use, however, a few brief notes are appended.

KINGSTHORPIANA.

THE COMMON SEAL.

THE engraving on the title-page represents the common seal of the Royal Manor of Kingsthorpe. It is made of latten, and is of rather rude workmanship.

The device is a crowned head, surrounded by the inscription, "Sigillum Commune de Kyngesthorpe," and on each side is a fleur de lys, and what is perhaps intended for a branch of planta genista.

The King represented is, probably, Richard II. The peculiar form of the beard with two points is characteristic, and appears in his monument at Westminster. The fleur de lys would indicate that the seal was made after the King's second marriage, in 1396, with Isabella of France.

Richard's first wife, Anne of Bohemia, was, we know, in possession of the manor, and it may be assumed that Isabella held it likewise; and in that case, the introduction of the fleur de lys into the Kingsthorpe seal would be very natural.

I

CALENDAR OF DOCUMENTS NOW EXISTING IN THE CHURCH-CHEST OF KINGSTHORPE.

1. Copy of Grant of Free Warren to Ralph Bassett de Drayton, 34 Edw. III.

    [On paper, damaged, but nearly all legible.]

2. Award by authority of Joan (of Navarre), widow of Hen. IV., respecting rights of fishery in dispute between the Inhabitants of Kingsthorpe and the Prior of St. Andrew's.

    [Written in French on parchment, much injured by damp, and in parts illegible. There are still four seals attached; one with coat-of-arms, another with rebus of name.]

3. Grant of Fee Farm to the Inhabitants of Kingsthorpe.

    [This parchment is so much injured that the date cannot be deciphered, but it appears to be of the time of Edw. IV.]

4. Court Rolls, abstracts of Court Rolls, views of frank pledge, etc., for the following years :

24, 28, 31, 33, 34, 36, 38, 39, 40,		
41, 44, 47, 48, 51	- - -	Edw. III.
1, 2, 9, 10—12, 18, 20, 21	- -	Rich. II.
1—12 -	- - - -	Hen. IV.
26, 36, 38	- - - -	Hen. VI.
6, 7 -	- - - -	Edw. IV.
15—17, 20 -	- - -	Hen. VII.
2, 3, 8, 16—22, 24, 27—29 -	-	Hen. VIII.
1—7 Edw. V., 1 Mary, 1—4 Philip and Mary, in		
paper book.		
12, 13, 32	- - - -	Elisabeth.
1, 2, 4 -	- - - -	Jas. I.

[These rolls are injured by damp, and many almost obliterated.]

5. An Indenture, witnessing that Clement Bacon, Bailiff of Kyngesthorpe, Stephen Sheppard, and John Hobnestye, Constables, and the Commonalty of the said Towne, have demised to William Braunfeld, of Kyngesthorpe, miller, 4 watermills (described), with fisheries, etc., for 10 years, at a rent of 7 marks. Certain conditions and usual warranty follow. Dated at Kyngesthorpe, 12 June, ao. 35 Hen. VI.

6. A General Pardon from Edw. IV. to the tenants and men of the Towne of Kyngesthorpe, by whatever names they might be known, for all transgressions and offences committed before the 4th day of November, ao. 1 of his reign. An enumeration of various transgressions follows. Dated 8 Feb., ao. 2.

7. Customs of the Manor of Kingsthorpe "made in the custumarys within the Towne of Kyngesthorp, renewed . . day of June, the year of the reigne of King Richard the Third, after the conquest the first."

[Parchment roll in fair preservation.]

8. An Indenture, witnessing that Clement Broke, Bailiff of Kyngesthorpe, John Bakon, junr., and John Molle, Constables, and the whole Community of the said Towne, have demised to Henry Wallys of the same, miller, 2 watermills (described) for 21 years at an annual rent of 53s. 4d. Certain conditions and usual warranty follow. Dated 6 Apr., ao. 2 Hen. VII.

9. Draft of Will by one —— Shepherd, probably in the time of Henry VIII. or earlier.

[On paper, in very bad condition.]

10. Letters Patent of King Hen. VIII., reciting previous letters of Hen. VI., Ed. IV., and Hen. VII., and confirming to the men and tenants of the Town of Kyngesthorpe, otherwise called Thorp, in co. North-

ampton, the farm of the said Town, with all its members and appurtenances, from the feast of St. Michael in the 8th year of his reign, to the end of 40 years, at an annual rent of 50 pounds, the said rent having been reduced by the sum of 10 pounds on account of the poverty of the said tenants and the decay of the Town. Dated at Westminster, Dec. 20, ao. 11 of his reign. Endorsed "the Graunte of King Hen. VIII. of the Ferme of Kyngesthorpe."

11. Lease of the North or Farre Mill to John Hopkyns and Margaret his wife.

12. Complaint and petition of the Inhabitants of Kyngesthorpe to Hen. VIII. in reference to the preservation of Game, and the oppressive conduct of one Latham, the under-keeper at Moulton Park.

[This paper seems to have been the rough draft of the petition actually sent. It is mutilated all down one side, but the purport can be readily made out.]

13. A Writing, by which certain Inhabitants and Tenants (named) of Thorpe, alias Kyngesthorpe, in co. Northⁿ., appoint John Hopkyns, Peter Diconson, Thos. Reve, and Simon Baker as their attornies to proceed against one Henry Maye, under-keeper of the Park of Moulton, for the recovery of certain arable and pasture lands in Kyngesthorpe, the fee farm of which had been recently confirmed to them by the King. Dated 12 Oct., ao. 15 H. VIII. Endorsed "A Warrant of Attorney from the Towne of Kyngesthorpe to some of the same Towne."

14. Answer of Hen. Maye to the bill of complaint. Hopkyns, Bailiff of Kyngesthorpe.

[Paper in very mutilated condition.]

15. Indenture, by which Peter Dyconson (Bailiff) of the Township and Liberty of Kyngesthorpe, Richard

Broke, and John Chese, constables of the same, and the whole community, demise to Agnes Hayward, widow, and Ambrose Walker, and Margaret, his wife, all of Northⁿ., 3 watermills (described), for a term of 21 years, at a yearly rent of 8 marks. The conditions and usual warranty follow. Dated on the feast of the Annunciation, ao. 20 Hen. VIII.

16. Indenture, by which Richard Else, Bailiff of the Town of Kyngesthorpe, John Hopkyns, and Robt. Coke, Churchwardens, Rich^d. Broke and Clement Shepperde, constables of the same, and all the Inhabitants and Tenants, demise to Thomas Morgan of Kyngesthorpe, gent, a close, etc., in Walbekke, in the parish of Kyngesthorpe, to hold for a term of 21 years, at an annual rent of 44s. Usual warranty. Dated, 20 Nov., ao. 26 Hen. VIII.

17. An Agreement between Rich^d. Pickmer, Bailiff, William Sheppard, and John Plomer, Constables, and the Commonalty of Kyngesthorpe of the one part, and Gilbert Johnson, of Northⁿ., on the other; by which said Gilbert makes over to the said Rich^d. Pickmer, etc., his house in Bearward Street, Northⁿ., in pledge for the due performance of the conditions of a lease of the Nether Mill to the said Gilbert from the said Rich^d. Pickmer, etc. Made 17 Feb., 30 Hen. VIII.

18. Depositions of Witnesses respecting the keeping of conies in Kingsthorpe and Moulton, with the following headings :

    1. "Examinations taken at the Town of Northⁿ. the xxvi. day of April, in the xxxiii. yere of the reigne of our Sovereign Lord Kyng Henry the Eight, by Sir Edward Montagu, Knyght, and Sir Thomas Tresham, Knyght, by virtue of a Commission to them dyrected for the part of the Inhabit-

ants and of the Town of Boughton and Pysford *against Thomas Latham.*

19 leaves in form of book, much damaged.

2. "Examinations," as above, *on the part of Thomas Latham.*

19 pages in a book.

3. A third similar Examination against Latham.

19. Ordinances and Statutes made by the consent of all the Inhabitants of the Towne of Kingesthorpe, in the time of Robert Coke, Baily there, *anno primo* Edw. VI.

[A revision and enlargement of the code in No. 7, on parchment, injured, and ink faded.]

20. Indenture by which Rich^d. Broke, of Kyngesthorpe, Baily, and Jeffrey Collys, and Thomas Canam, Constables, and the commonalty of the same place, demise to John Sylbell, of North^n., baker, a watermill under the Towne of Kyngesthorpe (described) for forty years, at an annual rent of £4 3*s.* 4*d.* Usual conditions and warrants follow. Dated, 1 July, ao. 37 Hen. VIII.

21. A Journal of the daily expenditure of certain persons, viz., Robt. Coke, Rob. Dykynson, and Rich^d. Broke, who were sent up to London by the Town of Kyngesthorpe, to carry through the "Hundreth" business in the Court of Star Chamber.

[This is on paper, in a very ragged state, but nearly all legible.]

22. "Receipt of Richd Broke, of Kingsthorpe, in the xxxviii^th. yere of the raigne of o^r. most drede Sofferayne Lorde Kinge Henry the Eight, to the use of the Inhabitants of the same Towne," together with his disbursements.

23. Depositions on the part of Sir Thomas Tresham, Knight, taken at Ketering, in the Countie of Northampton, the xi. day of Aug., in the second yeare of our Soverayne Lord Kyng Edward the Sixt, before us Sir Edw. Montague, Knyght, Chyeff Justice of our Soverayne Lord the Kyng of his Com̄ Please, Edward Griffin, Esquyer, the Kyng's Majestie's Solycitor-General commissioned of our said Soverayne Lord the Kyng, by virtue of his highnes' commission to us, directed touchyng a matter dependyng in varyance between the freeholders and the inhabitants of the Township of Kyngsthorpe, Boughton, and Pysford, in the said Countie of Northampton, of the one partie, plaintyffes, and the said Sir Thomas Tresham, Kap^r. of the Kyng's Majestie's parke of Moulton, in the said Countie, and Thomas Latham, under-kap^r. of the same parke, defendants."

Depositions, as above, taken on the 30th day of April, in the 3rd yere of the reigne of Ed. VI., at Geddington, in the Countie of North^n., before the same.

24. List of Questions to be put to witnesses in a suit respecting the keeping of conies in Kyngesthorpe and Moulton, temp. Hen. VIII.

[Long paper roll, much injured.]

25. Abstract of depositions respecting conies.

[Paper roll, one sheet imperfect.]

26. A breviatt of the depositions produced on the parte of the inhabitants of Kyngesthorpe and Bucktone . . . Keepers of Moulton Parke ought to have no warrene of conyes nor hares within . . . . . off Bucktone and Kyngesthorpe.

[Paper roll, mutilated.]

27. Letters Patent of Philip and Mary confirming the grant
of farm previously made by King Henry VIII. (qu.
No. 10), and extending the term from the feast of
St. Michael next ensuing for 40 years. Dat. at Westminster 12 May, an 2, 3 Philip and Mary.

[The lower half of the great seal in white wax remains
attached.]

28. Indenture by which the good and dyscrete men and
tenauntes of Kyngesthorpe, otherwise called Thorpp,
in the county of Northampton, demise to Rob. Cooke
certain watermills as described for a term of 34
years at an annual rent of 50s. 8d. Conditions
and covenant follow. Dated xvi. day of Nov., 3
and 4 yeare of the reigns of Philip and Mary, King
and Queen of England, Spain, France both Cycells,
Jerusalem and Ireland, Defenders of the Faith, Arch-
dukes of Austryche, Dukes of Burgundy, Mellayne,
and Brabant, Counts of Aspurg, Flanders, and Tyroll.

[The common seal of Kingsthorpe attached.]

29. Indenture by which the good and discrete men and
tenauntes of Kyngesthorpe demyse to Jeffraye
Cooke   certain mills in Kyngesthorpe leased to
Thomas Cooke, his brother, by Sir Christopher
Hatton, Knt., by letters dated the 13th Oct., 1589,
and by him willed to the said Jeffraye to hold for
21 years at an annual rent of £4. Usual covenants.
Dated 26 Ap., ao. 35 Elisabeth.

30. Exemplification by Queen Elisabeth at the petition of
Francis Morgan, Esq., of an enrolment of certain
letters patent, dated 5 Ap., ao. 36 of her reign,
granted to the men and tenants of the Town of
Kingsthorpe, confirming the grants made by K.
Hen. VIII., and extending the privileges therein
conceded for a further term of 40 years from the

feast of S. Mich. next ensuing. Dated at Westminster
18 Oct., ao. 41 Elisabeth.

[Fragments of the great seal in white wax remain.]

31. Portion of a deed endorsed "a lease graunted to the men
and tenants of the Town of Kingsthorpe." Owing to
the injury the document has sustained the date is
wanting, but it is probably the "Letters Patent" mentioned in the preceding (No. 30), as dated 5 Ap., ao.
36 Elizabeth.

[Fragments of the great seal in white wax remain.]

32. Complaint of Henry Knolles, keeper of the Park and
Warren of Moulton, co. Northampton, on behalf of
the Queen [Elisabeth], addressed "to the Right
Honorable William Lord Burleigh, Lord Threasourer
of England, Sir Walter Mildmaye, Knt., Chancellor
of the Qu. Majestie's Court of Exchequer, Sir Edward Saunders, Knt., Lord Chief Baron of the same
Courte, and the rest of the Barons there."

[On paper; 9 leaves, much mutilated.]

33. "A True Rental;" being the half-year's rent of Kingsthorpe. Names of Tenants and amounts of payment. No date; but probably temp. Elisabeth.

34. Churchwardens' account headed "The resetts of me,
Robert Cook, one of the Church Wardens in the yere
of our Lord God, 1565, consernyng the stepull and
other matters as hereafter," etc.

35. Churchwardens' account "a bill of the leyings out since
the last account," no date. 16 cent.

36. The Queen's Rent Roll for Kingsthorpe, dated October
the 10th, 1594.

37. List of names with payments, an assessment apparently
for some ecclesiastical purpose—perhaps a Church
rate.

38. Abstracts of the Great Roll of the Pipe, being acquittances to the men and tenants of Kingsthorpe for payment of rent due from the said Town to the Crown, temp. Hen. VII., Hen. VIII., Eliz., Jas. I., Chas. I.

39. Manerii de Kingesthorpe supervisus ibm̄ factus XVI. die aprilis anno 5, Jas. I.

[Upon paper, very much mutilated at the bottom of each page.]

40. Claims of copyhold tenants to lands in Kingsthorpe, without date. 17 cent.

[Ten leaves, rolled, in very dilapidated condition.]

41. An Indenture [much mutilated] by which Mabell Morgan, of Kingesthorpe, co. Northⁿ., widow, covenants for herself and heirs to pay to Francis Barnard, and others, on behalf of the Townsmen of Kingsthorpe, the sum of £4 for the rent of certain watermills there. The conditions follow. Dated 22 Jan., ao. 15 Jas. I.

[Endorsed " Mrs. Mabell Morgan, her deed to the men of Kingesthorpe." A piece of wax without impression remains attached].

42. Indenture dated 9 Charles I., 1633, whereby the Trustees of the Manor grant certain tenements and lands to William Mottershede, in fee simple, being formerly copyhold of the Manor, at a rent of 46 shillings and 4 pence.

43. An Indenture not executed, by which certain Commissioners of the Parliament for the sale of possessions of the Crown make over the Spelhoe Hundred to Mr. F. Cooke.

44. Inquisition into the Charities of Kingsthorpe by Commission under the great seal, 1683.

45. Indenture 4 Q. Anne, 1705, appointing new Trustees of the Manor, and regulating future appointments.

46. Sundry fragments of various dates, including portion of a Royal Grant of the Manor, about the date of Hen. VII. or VIII., being apparently the middle sheet of three, the two others being lost.

[There are also some modern deeds transferring the trust of the Manor Lands to new Trustees at various times.]

I.

[Copy of a grant of Freewarren in all the demesne lands of Moulton, in the county of Northampton, made to Ralph Bassett de Drayton in the 34th year of King Edward III.

It is endorsed 'Recorde out of the Towre,' and is apparently the 'wryghtynge' by Mr. Morgan's man mentioned in No. 21, procured for use in the 'Ster' Chamber in conducting the 'hundreth' matter through that court.

Among the witnesses to the grant we find 'W. Wynton, epo. Cancellario nro,' William of Wykeham, Bishop of Winchester, and subsequently the founder of New College, Oxford, and St. Mary's, Winchester. He had served the King as surveyor of works for many years, and had built for him several important edifices, civil and military, among which were Windsor Castle and Queenborough. He became Warden of Forests, Keeper of the Privy Seal, and at last Chancellor, from which office he was removed in 1371, but was reinstated on the accession of Rich. II. ('Annals of Eng. Hist.' i. 395). The grant is given under the privy seal.

It appears that the Bassett family was one of importance in the county. In a grant by Hen. I., printed in Rymer's federa 'Libertates Canonicis S. Trin. London, concessæ,' the name of 'Rad' Bassett apd Northn,' is found among the witnesses. A Richard Bassett was High Sheriff of Northamptonshire in 1154. In 34 Hen. III. (1250) the King committed his park of Northampton (Moulton Park) to Robt. Bassett, Sheriff of the County. The name Rad' Bassett de Drayton appears in nearly all the lists of Barons summoned to Parliament during the reigns of Edward I., II., III., and Richard II., representing probably three or four generations (vide Dugdale, 'Summonitiones ad Parl.']

. . . . . . rotulo cartarum Regis Edwardi T'tii ao xxxiiii^{to}.

. . . . Sciatis nos de gra nra spali concessisse et hac p'senti carta nra confirmasse dil'to et fideli nro Rado de Bassett de Drayton qd ipse et heredes sui imppm heant libram warennam in ombs dmcis terris suis de Multon in Com Northt

dum tamen tcrc ille nō sint infra metas foreste mē. Ita qd
nullus intret trās illas ad fugand'[1] in eis vel ad aliquid
capiend' qd ad warennā ptineat sine licenc' et voluntate
ipsius Radi vel hered' suor' sup forisfacturā[2] nram decem
librar. Quare volumus et firmit' pcipim' pro nobis et heredibus nris qd pdcts Radus et hered' sui imppm heant libam
warennā in ombs dmcis trís suis ibm dū tamen tre ille nō
sint infra metas foreste mē Ita qd nullus intret trās illas ad
fugand' in eis vel ad aliquid capiend' qd ad warennā p'tineat
sine licencia et voluntate ipsius Radi vel hered' suor' sup'
forisfacturam nram decem librar' ut pdtm est, hiis testibus
ven'abilibus pribus[3] W. Wynton Epo Cancell' nro J. Roffen'
Epo Thesaur' nro Rico Arundell Thoma Warr Ricdo Stafford
Comitibus Guidone Brian Senescallo Hospicii nri et aliis
dat' p' manu Rs apud Westm' xii die Junii p' bre de privato
sigillo.

Concordat cn Record'
per me Edwardu Hales.

[1] To hunt.   [2] Forfeiture, fine.   [3] Præsulibus.

II.

[It would appear that the Manor was frequently granted by the King for the time being to his Queen Consort, who probably retained it for life. Thus we learn from the following document that the Manor was at this time (1 Hen. V. 1413) in the possession of Joan of Navarre, widow of the late King Hen. IV., who also held it as Queen Consort, as appears from the Court Roll, anno 12 Hen. IV.

Richard, the Prior of S. Andrews here referred to, was Richard Napton, mentioned in the Court Roll 12 Hen. IV., *vide* No. 4, p. 26.

'Richard Napton governed S. Andrew's Priory in 1339, after whom we meet with no other till 1452, when John Holder was possessed of it' (Bridges).

There are three seals still attached, one with the device of a flat-fish —probably the seal of Rob. Playce.]

. . . . escritz verront ou orront William Esturmy chivaler chief seneschall des terres notre tres soverayne dame Johanne Royne dengletre, Johan de Tibbaye chaunceller. . . . . Tresorer et Robert Plaice de Çounseill de mesme la Royne, salut'. Cum certayns accordes et appoyntementz se presteront par entre notre dicte dame le Royne dun [parte] [et Richard] Priour de seynt Andrewes de Norhampton dautre part, par endentures entre eux faitz sur certayns grevaunces compleyntz et enjuries faitz et perpetrez par le dit Priour ses commoignes [et serva]untz au dicte Royne et ses tenauntz et lour servauntz de sa ville de Kynggesthorpe et lour servauntz le tenour des queles endentures ensuyst en cestz paroles. Cest endenture faite parentre Johan par la grace de dieu Royne dangletere et de Fraunce et dame Dirlande dune parte et Richard Priour de Seynt

Andrewes de Norhampton dautre parte Tesmoigne lacco . .
. . soubz escritz qe les diverses compleynts ou . . . . mon-
strez par les tenauntz des dicte Royne de son Manoir de
Kyngesthorpe en le Counte de Norhamptone . . . . Royne
Priour ses commoignes et servauntz avaunt ces heur . . . .
avoir de Pescherie en la Ewe qe courge del molyn appelle
Kyngesthorpe mille . . . . illeoqe . . . bateries et autres
diverses trespasses et enjuries sib . . . . Royne come a ses
tenauntz sus ditz et lour servauntz perpetrez et faitz. Ces-
tassovoir que . . . . garderount et . . . . pret envers les
tenauntz du dicte Royne de son Manoir sus dit pur eux et
lour servauntz a lour procurement abettement . . . . le dit
Priour . . graunt per icestz qe il ses comoignes et servauntz
ne pescheront nullement en lewe sus dit sanz monstrer suffi-
ceant matier et evydence a . . . . ques avoir pescherie en
la dicte Ewe. Et outre ce le dit Priour voet et graunt par
icest qil et ses commoignes esterrent a la garde et ordy-
naunce de Mons' William Esturmy chivaler chief Seneschall des terres du dite Royne Jehan de Tibbaye chaunceller, Jehan Everdon' Tresorer et Robert Playce du Con-
seille du dicte Royne de toutz maners pescheries assautes,
debates, trespasses, enjuries grevaunces perpetrez et faitz
devaunt la faisaunce dicestz par le dit Priour et ses commoignes a la dicte Royne ses tenauntz et lour servauntz sus
ditz. Et le dit Priour les ditz ordinances et agarde tiendra
et perfourmera pur luy et ses commoignes en toutz poyntz.
Provisy qe les ditz ordynaunces et agarde soient faite devaunt le mois de Pasqz proscheyn venaunt. Et a toutz les
poyntz articles et accord sus ditz et a chescun deux tenier
et perfourmer per le dit Priour ses commoignes et servauntz
susditz le dit Priour soy oblige per icestz a dicte Royne en
quarant livres desterling' appaiere a mesme la Royne a quele
heure qe il ses commoignes et servauntz ou ascun deux
faillent ou faille de lour parte dascun des articles accord et
poyntmentz avaunt dictes. En tesmoignaunce de quele

chose a lune partie de ceste endenture envers le dit Priour remaignaunt la dicte Royne ad fait mettre son seall et a lautre partie de mesme lendenture envers la dicte Royne remaignaunt le dit Priour ad myz son seall. Don a Westm' le vynt et second Jour de Juyn lan du reigne notre seigneur le Roy Henry quart puis le conquest treszime. Sachez qe nous avaunt dictes William Esturmy, John de Tibbay, John Everdone et Robert Playce le Samady proschein devaunt la moys de Pasques lan du reigne notre seigneur le Roy Henry quynt puys le Conquest primer en la Receit du dicte Royne a Westm' par bone et mure deliberacion et ad . . . de Richard de Nortone, William Skrene, William de Lodyng-ton sergeant du Roy en loy et autres du Counseill du dicte Royne aprez en loy lors illeoqes pre[sents]. . . avons or-deygne [et] ordynons et agardons de notre commune assent . . . . qe touchant le pescherie qe le dit Priour clayme en la dicte Ewe qe un serg . . . . Royne ses tenauntz et lour servauntz et un autre sergeant de loy depar le dit Priour et . . . . nominacion verront la dicte Ewe et ferront fynal determynacion de dicte pescherie per . . . . sils purront eut accorder. Et sils ne purront eut accorder ils ferront report apres le dit moys a Mons' Hugh Huls un des Justices de la banc . . . . ment determiner adjuger et agarder del pescherie susdit sil le voet prendre sur luy et purra ce attendre devaunt la fest de seynt Martin lors prosch . . . . ne voet ou ne purra a dicte agarde atten-dre et le prendre sur luy come devaunt est dit, adonqes les ditz deux sergeantz par les ditz Royne et Priour several-ment nomme . . . . ferront eut lour report a Mons' William Haukford chief Justice de banc de Roy pur fynalment determyner et agarder du dicte pescherie devaunt les . . . . ensuant, et qe le dit Priour mesme le Samady apres la heure de none en lesglise Cathedrall de Seint Paule de Londres soy liera et oblige . . . . obligatorie au dicte Royne en quarrant livres appaier a mesme la Royne a quele heure

qil refuse de ster ou obeyer la garde ou ordynance avaunt
dicte.   Et . . . . tenauntz de Kyngesthorpe pescheront et
occupieront la dicte pescherie come ils ount faitz et usez
devaunt ces heures tanque autrement soit ordeyne come
dessus est dit . . . . en le mesme temps les ditz Priour ses
commoignes tenauntz et servauntz ne pescheront nullement
en la ewe avaunt dicte.   En tesmoignaunce de quele chose
nous avaunt-ditz William [Esturmey], [Johan] de Tibbay,
Johan Ever[don], [et] Robert Playce avons myz noz sealles.
Don en la Receit du dicte Royne a Westm' le Samady proscheyn devaunt le mois de Pasque lan [du reygne] notre
seigneur le roy Henry quynt puis le conquest Prymer.

[Four seals remain attached.]

IV.

[The extracts from the Court Rolls are selected partly for the sake of the allusions to manners and customs of the time, but especially on account of the names of fields and properties incidentally mentioned. Some of these names still remain, but the majority seem to have disappeared. Most of them are comprised in the following list.]

Godefeld
Manuelfield
Wolsterholme, or Worcesterholme
Bokton mere
Slanthorns, or Lanthorns
Genyell
Ffrost
Pykkow, Pykke, or Poke
Lynglies
Swarwell brok, or Swaswell
Gorebrede
Threfdale and Theavedale
Sterwell weye
Kyllyngwell
Port wey furlong
Whithill
Wheteland
Hoselokesende

Sexholme
Buttonfield
Wadenwell
The Styves, Styes, or Styles
Sowrland
Kenesplace
Shutsdam
Pywell hull
Hangyndale
Totyngsthorpe
Hauksplace
Pydale field
Pydale stade
Schirlegedowne
Southmyllwonge
Halywell furlong
Braunfeld
Waynesplace
Ballum docket
Hodell croftys
Blackwell hyll
Swarlbridge way

Galous weye
Myddel furlong
Shottylbridge
Nortcleyelond
Jayes walle
Sidwell wong
Black myle furlong
Hoopyng
Brukfield
Grauntpytte
Warns close
Deadman's irons
Wallbeck
Thystylholme, or Fistylholme
Colkayes
Restow
Pese furlong
Neder furlong
Ober furlong
Heybrome
Smetho

[Other local names will be found in the 'Supervisus,' No. xxxix.]

2—2

EXTRACTS FROM COURT ROLLS.

47 Edw. III.—Robertus Codelyn queritr de Thoma
Gilbert de placito trans plegius[1] de pros', Willelmus Chym-
messon, unde queritr et dicit quod die lune proxima
post [festum Sancti] Nicholai anno regni regis Edwardi
tercii a conquestu xl⁰ vj⁰ apud Kyngesthorpe predictam,
predictus Thomas injuste et contra pacem &c. fregit et di-
lasseravit octo . . . . lance, videlicet de russeto et blanketo
in operando et fullando[2] pannum predictum ad dampnum,
etc.   Et predictus Thomas dicit quod in . . . . et super
hoc ponit se . . qui dicunt quod Thomas Gilbertus non est
culpabilis.   Et predictus Robertus pro falso clamore in
misericordia est[3] xij_d.

41 Edw. III.—Ricardus Harwedone emit unam rodam
terre de Roberto Michel super Oveswog' in Mainwellefeld.
. . . . Et predictus Robertus venit in curiam et inde re-
cepit scisinam ad inveniendum unam ceream ardentem
coram beate Marie in ecclesia de Abyndone.   Datum die
lune proxima post festum Octabas Pasche, a₀. reg. reg. Edwardi tercii a conquestu quinquagesimo primo.

51 Ed. III.—Die maii p͞x͞a post f͞t͞m S͞i Augustini anno
regni reg' Edwardi tertii a conquestu quinquagesimo primo

---

[1] 'Plegius de prosequendo': surety or bail.   'Præpositis nostris et
ballivis prohibemus ne aliquam hominem capiant neque averium suum
quamdiu bonos fidejussores dare voluerint de justicia prosequenda,' &c.
(Test. Philip Reg., quoted by Spelman).

[2] 'Fullando': vide lease of mill, No. v., where a fulling mill is referred to.

[3] 'In misericordia est': i.e., amerced (a merci); the pecuniary
punishment of an offender against the King or other lord in his court ;
such offender is said to be in misericordia.   'There seems to be a dif-
ference between amerciaments and fines.   Fines are certain, and grow
out of some statute, but amerciaments are such as be arbitrarily enforced
by affeerors.' 'Amerciament is properly a penalty assessed by the peers
of the party amerced for an offence done, for the which he putteth
himself on the mercy of the lord' (Cowell), vide Ordinances, 1547.
'That at every Leete called the Great Leete too Feerares to be chosen,
the Bailiff to chose thone and the Thurbarrows another, and they to
assesse all amerciamentes.'

in curiā de Kyngesthorpe venit Johannes de Lapton et dedit Giltō Roce seniori xlviii rod' terr' arabil' in le Godefeld de Kyngesthorpe et unam vergatam p͞ti antiqui p͞rati . . . de Kyngesthorpe habend' et tenend' p͞dto Gilto hered' et assig' in p͞ptm.

R͞eds Harwedone emit unā rodā terr' de Robto Michal super . . . in Manwellfeld.

9 Rich. II.—Thomas de Duffeld, 'rector ecclesie de Kyngesthorp,' gave a place of land to John Kene.

13 Rich. II.—Margareta at Park in bona memoria sua venit in curiam de Kyngesthorpp et dedit Willelmo Holcot post dis' . . . . dimidiam acram terre super Northmylne-forlong juxta le lewe ex parte Australi que extendit a via platea usque ad molendinum, sibi et heredibus et suis assignatis ad inveniendum unam candelam cere ante Sanctum Christoferum coram altare Sancte Katerine[1] in Ecclesia de Kyngesthorpe in eternum, et si contingat quod predictus Willelmus heredes sui vel assignati sui non invenirent illam candelam inde condicio predicta. . . . . Et custodes luminaris Sancte Katerine debent reingredi et aber' dimidiam acram terre ante dictam in . . . . Et prefatum Willelmum heredes sive assignatos totaliter excludere sine fine. Datum die et aᵒ. supradictis.

14 Rich. II.—In dei nomine die martis proxima post festum Sancte Katerine virginis et Martiris anno ab incarnacione domini millesimo ccc. nonagesimo mensis Novembris die videlicet vicesimo nono Nicholaus Cotone alias Goldsmyth sane mentis quamvis infirmitate existens in villa

---

[1] A shrine was dedicated to St. Katharine, probably on account of the connection of the parish with St. Katharine's Hospital by the Tower in London. King Edward II. granted to the hospital the advowson and patronage of the Church of St. Peter, in Northampton, with the chapels of Kingsthorpe and Upton, by charter dated 26 Aug., 1309.

de Kyngesthorpe juxta Northampton Lincoln^s dioc'[1] . . . .
modo et forma sequentibus suum condidit testamentum.
In primis legavit domino Johanni vicario ecclesie parochi-
alis omnium sanctorum de Northampton predicta unum
vetus ordinale. Item legavit domino Johanni Byshop capel-
lano ij*s*. Item legavit Johanni servienti suo unum garne-
ment de suis pannis usualibus. Item legavit seu assignavit
Bartholomeo servienti suo, vij*s*' quos ei debuit. Item dedit
et legavit avicie filie sue unam acram terre arabilis et . . . .
ad seminandum dictam acram super . . . anno, videlicet
tres rodas jacentes in le pesforlong et unam rodam jacen-
tem in le . . . forlong infra parochiam de Kyngesthorp
predicta. Habendum et tenendum dictam acram terre cum
suis pertinenciis eidem avicie ad totam vitam suam de capitalibus [dominis feodi] illius per servicia inde debita et de
jure consueta. Et si contingat dictam aviciam super vivere
Elizabet uxorem dicti . . . . dicta acra terre remaneat dicte
avicie heredibus et assignatis suis in perpetuum Tenendum
de capitalibus . . . . Et si dicta Elizabet supervixerit, dictam Aviciam, tunc post dicessum dicte Avicie predicta acra
terre remaneat . . . Elizabet heredibus et assignatis suis in
perpetuum. Tenendum de capitalibus dominis feodi illius
per servicium inde debitum et de jure [consuetum]. Et
dedit et legavit prefate Elizabethe uxori sue omnia terras
redditus et tenementa sua cum omnibus suis pertinentiis in villa et campis de Kyngesthorp predicta existentibus et alibi ubicunque existentibus. Habendum et
tenendum omnia predicta . . . redditus [et] tenementa
cum suis pertinenciis universis dicte Elizabethe heredibus et assignatis suis in perpetuum, de capitatibus
dominis feodi illius per [servicium inde] debitum et de jure
consuetum. Item legavit dicte Elizabethe duas optimas
partes de vasis suis. Item legavit . . . . partem hujusmodi

---

[1] Northampton was in the Lincoln diocese before the erection of the
See of Peterborough.

vasis Johanni Maggesone et Avicie supra dicte inter eosdem
equaliter dividendum.   Residuum vero omnium bonorum
suorum prius non legatorum legavit Elizabethe uxori sue
ante dicte quam ad istud testamentum fideliter exequen-
dum ordinavit et constituit executricem.

Rich. II. — Alicia Smythe de Kyngesthorpe venit in
plenam Curiam de eadem et dedit Henrico Fulbroke et
Isabelle uxor sue post ejus decessio septem acras terre et
quarteronas pti in Wolsterholme nuper quarteronas Hugonis
Rolfe ad termin vite illor, &c., quarum una roda abuttat in
ptm rectoris dima acra abuttat into Bowkton mere juxta
terram Johannis Broke—alia roda jacet sup' eundem sta-
dium juxt' terr' Georgii Elys ex pte occidentali, una roda
jacet sup' Slanthorns juxta terr' Thome Reve ex pte australi una roda jact in eodem stadio juxta terr' Will' Schep-
pard ex pte australi, una roda jacet into Genyell (?) juxta
terr' Johns Broke ex pte australi una roda jacet super ffrost
inter terram Johs Colle ex—pte, una roda jacet at Wadyns-
well ex pte occidli juxta terr' Johs Pelle una roda sup' Restow[1] juxta terr' luminar' Sancte Marie, una dim' acra jacet
sup' Pykkow juxta terr' Wm. Fote ex pte australi, una roda
jacet sup' Clayllond juxt' terr' Johs Aynscote ex pte austrli,
tres partes rod' jact in Lynglies juxta terr' Johs Grene ex
pte orient' et tres partes rod' jact into Swarwell Brok juxta
terr' Johs Brune ex pte occidli, una roda subter le poke
juxta terr' Johs Aynscote ex pte boreali, una roda et dim'
jact super Swaswell juxt' terr' Johs Brok una roda jac' super
Gorebrede—una roda abuttat into ye Galonmere—dein' acra
jac' super hopys—una roda et dim' jact into Thresdale—
una roda abuttat into Sterwellweye—una roda apud Kyllyngwell—dim' acra jacet prope Portwheyfurlong—una roda
jact super Whithyll, &c.

[1] 'Restoo or Restow Delf,' vide Ordinances of 1483, art. 30, and of
1547, art. 43.

Rich. II.—Elias Pekke emit de Redo Bolson tertiā ptm uni tenementi in Hoselokesende.

Pratum in Sexholme — Buttonfield — Wadenwell — the Styves—unā acr' in Sowrland.

15 Rich. II.—Ad Curiam Anne Regine[1] Anglie apud Kyngesthorpe die Mercri p̄x ante festm Simonis et Jude venit Walfrid de Lucy miles et dedit Alicie Warwyck, Thome Warwyck, et Kateryne uxi ejus, &c., ... anno regis Redi s̄di p̄t cꞵstum xv (1392).

Rich. II. — Henricus Michel clamat v rod' terr' de Thoma Baudeman in terris qū una rod' terr' jacᵗ sup' Shutsdam et ii rod' subt' Pywellhull alia roda super hangyndele una roda apud Totyngsthorp.

Placea in Northende vocat' Kenesplace—una alia placea in eadem villa vocata Haukesplace.

Die maner' p̄x̄ma ante ffest' beate Marie Virginis xx Ricardi Sedi post conqū venit Johēs Bole de Kyngesthorpe in curiā de Kyngesthorp et dedit . . . xvi et unum tenem̄tum in villa de Kyngesthorp situat' nec non tenm̄ p̄dcte Joh's Bole ex parte una et tenementm̄ Joh's Cosin ex pte altera cum curtilag' . . . . videlicet un acr' terr' in Boketonfeld, unam dim' acram recenter in tenura Joh's South alia dim̄ acr' recenter in tenura Radulphi Grene un̄ rod' in Pydalefeld nuper in tenura Willi Draytone, unā rod' et dim' in Pydale stede nuper terr' Joh's Reve un' rod' jac' sup' Schirlegedoune (?) nuper terr' Alicie de Loptone iii acr' terr' in le Milbroke, &c.

---

[1] In 1382 Richard II. married Anne of Bohemia, sister of the Emperor Wenceslaus, who exerted herself to calm the animosities and jealousies which reigned in his court, and thus earned the title of 'The Good Queen Anne.' She died in 1394.

Hen. IV.—Quod Henrūs Coup de North^n legavit in testamento suo tres acras terr' arabil' jac' in campis de Kyngesthorpe super stadio vocat' Sowthmyllewonge.

Quod Nichlaus Day emit de Emota Pekke uxore Redi Fysher de Neuport Paynel portionem, &c., in Wolstersholm.[1]

Quod Johēs Perkyns de domo Sce Trīnitatis,[2] emit, &c.

4 Hen. IV.—Istō Rotulus testatur qd Redus Day de Kyngesthorpe in plena Curia de eadem venit corā multitudine copiosa et dedit Johanni Pekke hæred' et assignat' porcionē unius Crofte in le Ryryzerdes tend' sdm consuet' maner' ville pdcte. Dat ap' Kyngesthorpe die mercurii px pst festm Si Vincentii anno Regis Henrici qrti pst cqstm iiii.

Walterus Delepert emit de Johne Pekke Ballivo ville de Kyngesthorpe dim' acra terr' in stadio vocat Sowthmylnewonge[3] sibi hered' et assig' quæ qdem dim' acra cadit in manus Dmni Regis per defectum redditus, &c.

---

[1] 'Wolstersholm' : this is sometimes spelt Worcestersholm.

[2] The Hospital of St. David or St. Dewes, with which the house of the Holy Trinity was connected, was founded in 1200 by the Prior and Convent of St. Andrew's, who were then impropriators of the tithes of Kingsthorpe. The foundation consisted of a master or procurator, with two chaplains and six novices (*vide* Baker's 'Northn.'). The site and grounds were granted to the Master of the Savoy, 4 & 5 Philip and Mary (*vide* 'Survey of the Manor,' No. 39). The remains of a large arch with two niches may be seen in the wall of the old building now being converted into a dwelling by Lady Robinson, and a few years back the stone framework of the east window of the Holy Trinity Chapel might have been seen in the gable of a cottage near the then-existing toll-bar, but it has now been concealed by another cottage built against it. The object of the foundation was to receive and relieve travellers, poor and sick persons. At St. David's house a large room was provided with three rows of beds. There was also a burial-ground connected with it, and human remains have, I believe, been discovered there in some recent excavations.

[3] 'Sowthmylwonge': *wong*, marsh or lowland (Hallowel); *wong*, a field (Coles). The meadow-land between the nether and south mills, now called Semilong.

Quod Robtus Pine et Isolda uxor ejus emerunt quinque rod' terr' super Halywell ffurlong.

R̄dus Vyse et Petronilla uxor ejus . . . . q̄d vocatur Waynsplace . . . . apud Ballumdocket.

12 Hen. IV.—Et quod Ricardus Naptone, prior Sancti Andree de Northampton et monachi sui et servientes sui piscaverunt in le Shote de le . . . Sowthmylnes subtus Northampton et fecerunt le Were in prejudicium ville de Kyngesthorpe. Et quod Henricus Osberne fecit le Fray super Willelmum Wryte. Et quod Willelmus Page fecit le fray super predictum Willelmum. Et quod Agnes Masone hospitavit contra assisam.

6 Ed. IV.—Ad istam Curiam venit Simon Goldborn et sursum reddidit in manum D̄omi Regis unum dimid̄m qu . . . coscetuli ad usum et proficium Emme uxoris dcti Simonis, &c.

Ad istam Curiam tota com̄itas ville p̄cte ded̄ert et tradi dert Wilhelmo Broke et Rob' Andrew unum vacuum . . . jacent' ad fines coscetulorum p̄dti Wilhelm et Rob' qui abuttant super le hodell croftys hn̄d et reclusand'—locum in ppriis closuris et dent pro fine vi galones sincis (?).

Hen. VII.—Ad istam Cur' venit Philipp Hardyng, Bocher, et petit sesinam . . . vid᷎ duas acr' terr' jac' in campo boreali in le Frost furlong . . . alia acr' apud Boughton merc.

Ad hanc Cur' venit Elizabeth Else vidua et petit seisinam de duab' ac' jac' in Heybron . . . venit Jacobus Latham et petit seisinā de dua' acr' ap' heybron et dim' acr' ap' Blackwelhyll.

. . . Excepto et reservato unum ten̄mtm vocat' Whytehedyshowse . . . et unum clausum vocat Balles close.

Ad hanc Curiã venit R̄icūs Yorke et Ēma uxor ejus filia et hered' J̄ohs Langton . . . . et petunt admitti in unum Cotestetell' et quatuor acr' terr' arabil'.

Agnes Clypson vidua petit seisinam in quatuor acr' et unã rod' terr' arab' unde una acr' jacet apud Swarlbridge-way et du' acr' apud le Galous weye sex rod' . . . in campo vocat Manuelfelde et du' acr' jac' ex parte orientali Myd-delfurlong in le Whetelonde et un' rod' jac' ap' Swarlbrige-hedde.

Ad hanc Cur' venit Margery Ecton et dedit in plena curia R̄co Patman de Northᵃ [bever?] dim' acr' terr' jac in le Styes.

Ad istam Curiã venit Molle et petit seisinã de tribus rodis terr' jac' apud Longland et tribus rod' jac' in shortland in campo boreali que p̄quisivit de Galfrido Rete . . . et super hoc venit J̄ohes filius p̄dti Galfridi et petit cateˡ le p'p' xxs. xxd. et le [bever?] xxd. et non pseq' et J̄ohes Molle p̄et' seisinam inde ut sup'.

Hen. VII.—Itm̄ idem Johēs Molle petit seisinã de tribus rod' terr' jac apud Longlond et tribus rod' terr' in Shortlond quas emit de Galfrido Rete et sup' hoc venit J̄ohes Rete filius p̄dte Galfridi et petit 'a cate' le px hⁱᵃ xxiii iv et p̄dtus Johes Rete non venit neque solvit le cate secdm̄ cons man' ideo Johes Molle habet seisinam.

Ad istam Curiã venit p̄dtus J̄ohēs molle et petit seisinã de duabus acr' terr' empt' de Thoma Broke quar' duar' acr' i acr' apud Southmylwonge et vi rod' jac' apud Shortland in le woodfield et duas quarteron' prat' jac' in le Worcester-mede.

¹ 'Cate, acate, achat': *vide* Ordinances of 1483, art. 18, and 1547, art. 20.
² 'Px. h.' = 'proximus heres.'

Ad istam Curiā venit Robtūs Hondesworth rector ecclē de Kyngesthorpe et petit seisinā de dimō cotecell' et dim' acr' terr', &c.

Robertus Broke petit seisinam de uno tenmto contnt unū cotecell' novem acr' terr' et un' rod' terr' arab' unā quarteron' pti in australi pte in pᵒ dolo et un quarteron' jac' in le mere et un' quarteron' in vᵒ dolo in pte boreali et un quarteron' pti jac in xi dolo in le mere et tertiā ptm dī quarteron' pti jac' in Worcesters holme.

Georgius Else petit seisinam de dim acr' terr' arab' apud Shottylbrigge.

Venit Johēs Molle et petit seisinā de un' acr' terr' apud Southmylwonge de duob' rodis apud Nortcleytelond una acr' jac apud Jayeswalle.

20 Hen. VII.—The word ' cotestecellus ' occurs here, also Shottylbridge, and certain land is described as 'Terra in Stondelvys' and ' In stadio vocat Inglys in Parkfelde.'

Rēdo Hockyn qd fecit affray super servientē Johnīs Browne in mē 4s.

Et dēto Rēdo qd ft affray super quādam muliēr' manent' apud Brykkysworth.

Et Edwardo Hartewelle qd jac' in campo cum arcu et sagitta suspecti'me p' existimac' ad interficiend Willᵐ Roper de cotyna (?).

Il Rico Hockyn qd ft affray super Wᵐ. Roper.

Ed Hartewelle p' tent' sup' pdct Wᵐ. Roper.

Et Willmo Emson qd hospitavit pdctm Hochyn Edwardum Hartewelle et Wᵐ. Roper ut pdct'.

Hen. VIII.—'Excepto uno cotagio in pte boreali vocat' le Almose house.'

In eandum Curiā venit Robtus Stalworthe et filius et heres Johēs Stalworthe et petit admitti ad possessionem et

scisinam de et in quarta parte unius codecelli jacent' in villa
de Kyngesthorpe et septem rodis terr', &c., super quoddam
dolum ibidem vocat' Sidwellwong.

Ed. VI.—Ulterius ordinat̄ est qd uxor[1] Thome Tomlyn-
son recedet a villa et nunquam inhabitabit infra villam post̄
fest̄ annunc' prox' sub pena xiii̯s. iv̯d. Ulterius qd Harosia
Kynge silet recedet et non habitabit in villa ulterius post̄
fest' sanc' Thome apost'.

Querela—Riēdus Broke qur versus Johñm Hurlock de
plēto convent' fracte per iiii boyate straminis voc' Thek et
per coopertur̄a vidz the Thekkynge ejusdem.

3 Ed. VI. —Ad hanc Cūr Rob'tus Diconson sūrs' reddidit in manū Dni Rgis unū mes cont' di' cotesell' voc' le
Betts cū omb̄s pasc' . . . . pastur' cū suis pntiis jac' in villa et
campis de Kyngesthorpe nuper Elizabethe Betts vid' ad
usum Thome Wilson sr de Flower cui D̄ns Rx per Robm
Coke Baily conct seisin̄a hend' sibi hered' et assig3 suis secū
cons', &c., p̄ redd' p̄ salute pdc̄te Elizabeth p̄ term' vite sue
unū conclave in pdc̄to mes et le cle house juxta le . . .
cū libro ingressu et regressu ad pdc̄tm conclave (unto the
backsyde) and cle house cui dedit Dom Rx seisin̄a et admissus est, &c. Itm pdc̄tus Thomas non ponet aliquod
super conclave nec prmittet p̄dt mes esse in decasu p̄
defectu straminis ad nocumentū pdc̄te Elizabeth durante
vita sua.

3 Ed. VI.—Ad hanc Curīa Simon Curt et Alicia uxor
. . . Rich Else defunct' sursum reddidit in manus Regis
. . . Francisci Morgan gen' heredibus et assignatis suis in
perpetuum terram partim unius cotecelli jac' in Kingsthorpe
quondam Brayfelds cui D̄s rex concessit seisinam per redd,'
&c. . . . et tribus proclamt' factis si quis achat peteret

---

[1] *Vid.* Ordinances of 1547, art. 34 ; the myster woman.

vel aliquid diceret in contranā ptem Franciscus Morgan admissus est.

Johannes Astell et Agnes uxor ejus sursum redd' in manum Dni Regis ad usum Thome Curt heredb', &c., unam quart' pte' jac' northwards in le xxvi dole et tribus proclamt' factis Ricardus Broke prox', &c., petit acat.

Johēs Astell et Agnes ux ejus surs redd, &c., ad usū Robti Coke hered' et assig' suis unā quart' pti jac' northward in le second dole et terciā dolā tot' in le more et terciā dota tota in le Northmylholme que quidem due dole cont' ii quarti'r'. Et proclam' factis, &c., Robtus Broke prox' heres petit acat, &c.

Ad hanc Curiā inhitantes et tenent' ville pd' tuno presents sursum redd' Johē Bett duas foreras[1] voc hadlands quar' una jac' in Shortlande in campo boreali et altera jac' juxta viā regiā in Heybrome hend sibi et hered', &c., per redd' viid. ob per annū. Et proclam' fact' pdts Johēs admissus est.

Ad hanc Curiā, &c., Thomas Cannon sursū redd', &c., ad usū Thome Wilson hered' et assignat' dimid' acr' terr' jac' apud Blackmyle furlong int' duas divisas voc' balks. Cui ds Rex concess' seisinā, &c., pr redd, &c. Et proclam' fact' pdts Thomas Wilson admissus est, &c.

Ad hanc Curiā pdts Clemens Talbott sursū redd' in manus dni Regis iii rod' terr' jac' in Hoopyng ad usū Johs Cokks hered, &c. Antony Smythe natus in villa petit Achat sup' Johēm Cokks hoiem franchesiat', &c., ad un' cur' prox' sequent' pdts Antony relaxt suū Achat.

6 Ed. VI.—Ordinatum est per xii qd si aliquis deinceps arat aliquam foreram plus quam debet forf' xiid. unde Ballivo iiiid. ad hoies iiiior qui invenient defectum iiiid. et pixidi pauperum iiiid. et qd ballivus pro tempe assignabit pdct' iiii hoies.

---

[1] 'Forera.' This seems to be the same as *lia* or *lira*, balk or head-land, v. inf. 21.

Itm̄ qd coēs liras voc' balks sint in latitudine iii ped' et plus ubi fuerunt latiores et qd si quis px̄ adjacentium non relinquet tēra in tanta latitudine qd tunc forf' pro quolibet pede deficient' iii*s.* dividend' ut supra in tres partes.

Itm̄ qd quilibet qui falcabit vel repe plus grain vel herbe in verñi p̄te anni quā debet forf' pro quolibet pede iii*s.* dividend ut supra in tres pp̄tes.

6 Ed. VI. — Ad hanc curiam venit Jacob' Kynge et Halvisia uxor ejus sursū redd' in manus Dñi Regis totam illam purp̄ptram[1] et medietatem suam uni' mess' et duas acr' terr' et ii quarteron' p̄ti in Kyngesthorpe nuper Clement Talbott defunct' p̄dte Halbisie ad usum Thome Hyde, &c.

6 Ed. VI. — The xii men be agreed that our foure ale brewers shall bringe in at next corte every one of them a mesure of a gallon, a pottel, a quart, and a pynt, and all of turnmessers of wood next courte, in pene of vi*d.* every one maketh defaute.

Afferat'[2] { Robert Coke.
{ Robert Dyckynson.

7 Ed. VI.—Ordinatum est qd Johēs Estall et Johēs Holby qui sunt impotent'[3] et non valent laborare nō mendicabunt in viis regiis nec sedebunt ad finem ville ea intentione ad mendicandum sed stabunt ultimo fine ville sub pen' xx*d.* et fugient villam infra quartam anni partem.

7 Ed. VI.—Et qd Johēs Shēpd non mendicabit contra formam statuti sub pen' xii*d.* et correctione in statuto limitat'.

---

[1] 'Purprestura est proprie terra alienæ clandestina subtractio ejusdemque vicinæ adscriptio' (Spelm.) : encroachment, whether against the King or a neighbour. Medietas, moiety.

[2] 'Afferat' : the affeerers, v. sup. not. 3.

[3] 'Impotent.' This seems to have been the mode of dealing with men past work. Beggary had to be allowed and regulated.

Et qd le Shephds forf quilibet xii*d.* pro tempore quo permittent oves voluntar' pastre in prato boreali.

Ad hanc Cur' inhabiant' concesserunt Rbto Dykynson et Rcdo Broke pro term' x annor' ad fest' Scti Michel' px futur' unā pcellā aque voc' le middell water redd' pr ann iii*s.* iiii*d.* et facient assignat'.

2, 3 Philip and Mary.—Itm ordinatum est pr xii qd quilibet tenent' hēns les psenepps crescent' in manuell feld sup' terr' suas et les balks destruent les psenepps tam flores quā semina ita qd nullus tenent' habebit aliquas psenepps vel flores vel semina ejusdē herbe sup' terr' suam aliquo anno de incepto die ad vincla S. Petri sub pē quilibet delinquent xl*d.* forisfactur' ad usū ville pro qualibet terra.

Itm qd Johēs Bayly adimplebit fossetum suum apud South mylle wonge juxta molendinum suum infra festū inventionis divine crucis prox sub pen' vi*s.* viii*d.*

Pena posit' est qd Johēs Domport non defodiet lutum deinceps juxta cōem viam per spac' xx ped sub pē xx*s.* p' qualibet vice.

Et qd major pars inquisitionis vid¹ xiii sunt parati ad ponendos lapides voc mere stones sup' hopyng furlong et aliis locis ubi magis expedire viderunt in campis die Jovis in septimana Pentō prox sub pē xii*d.* quilibet delinquent sine causa rationabili.

3, 4 Philip and Mary.—Qd nullus deinceps fodiet in le Hie waye ap' . . . . . ad nocumentu vie sub pe vi*s.* viii*d.*

Itm qd nullus incedet sup' le furlong apud Coll's townes-

end unto the heth sub pe _ii_d. nullus cquitabit sub pū iiii_d._
et nullus fugabit bigat[1] ibm̄ sub pē xii_d._

Ītm̄ qd Georgius madler et null' alius non cariabit les
furres p' noctē neque p' diem nisi p̄p̄as vepres sub pē xl_d._

Ītm̄ qd Alicia Pykard deferet se extr' villā ante fest' nativ'
prox sub pē vi_s._ viii_d._

Ītm̄ qd rector de Kyngesthorpe escur'[2] fac' fossetū suū
voc' mere dyke suffic' ante fest' purificat[s] et quotiens necess'
fu'it postea sub pē v_s._

Ītm̄ qd nullus retallabit panē tantum nisi pistor et servus
suus sub pē v_s._

2, 3 Philip & Mary.—Ītm̄ qd tenentes qui tenent juxta
aliquam liam[3] voc a balk sup' quā liam lapides positi et
ejecti sunt abcariabunt lapides a liis hujusmodi ante festū
purificat' prox sub pen' cujuslibet delinquentis v_s._

3, 4 Ph. Mary.—Ad hanc Cur' venit Franciscū Morgan
serviens sue Regine in p̄pria esson'[4] et petit se admitti ad
unū cotecell' et di' ac tres acras terr' jac' in Kyngesthorpe
—p̄dt cotecell' jac' ex opposit' Rectori ibm̄ et voc' Angevylle
hoᵂse et d̄ct tres acr' jac' divise in campis de Kyngesthorpe
p̄dt vidᵗ in le Northfeld di acr' nuper W. Hedye in le Woodfeld d̄i acr' in Pykks d̄i acr' betwen le Styes apud le parke
yate iii rode apud Blackwellhyll una rodd' in le Brukfeld
apud grauntpytte ii rodd pro quinque libr' solut' p̄ſt' hoīnibus
et tenentibus Regi in auxilium renovationis carte sue feod'
ferme ville de Kyngesthorp p̄dt habend' pſto Francisco et
hered' suis sd̄m consuetud' ville pd̄te cui quidem Francisco

---

[1] 'Fugabit bigatam': drive a waggon.
[2] 'Escuriare': to scour or cleanse. 'Proviso insuper quod quoties
et quando necesse erit et opportunum dicta fosseta nostra mundare
purgare vel escuriare liceat nobis et successoribus nostris totam aquam
dictorum fossetorum convertere,' &c. (Carta Thomæ Episcopi, 4 Ed. IV.,
quoted by Cowell).
[3] 'Lia': 'Charta Johis de Lacy Constab' Cestriæ'......'Confirmavi
Deo et,' etc. '22 acras terre in villa de Allancotes infra lias divisas'
(Spelman, _vide sup._ p. 30).
[4] 'Essonia': excuse for non-appearance, _vide_ Ordinances, p. 38.
The service of the Crown was a valid excuse.

concess' est inde seisina hēnd' sibi et hered' suis s̄dm constd ville p̄dte p̄r redd' iiii*s.* iii*d.* p̄r acr' et admissus est.

1 Jac. I.—. . . . et dicunt qd Thomas Knapp et Humfredus Hopkyns pistores firmar' molendinorum ibidem excessum ceper' tolvetum[1] de granis vicinorum minus juste. fōr² uterque eorund' x*s.*

Dic' et putant qd R̄icus Dikynson Walter Burnet et Thomas Massman existentes tres brassatores cerevisie venalis ibidem illam nimis care infra jurisdictionem hujus lete exposuer' et vendider'.

. . . Ulterius dicunt et putant qd Thomas Wiseman affraiā fecit super Wm. Nutbrounc et traxit sanguin' infra jurisd' hujus lete.

Itm̄ dicunt . . . qd p̄ftus Franc' Morgan ac R̄obtus Sheppard, Thomas Phipps, Ricardus Dikynson, Wm. Billingham, Henricus Weston, Hen. Johnson, etc., fecer' et posuer' sua fumaria et sterquilinia in altis plateis ib̄m ad commune nocumentum . . . et qd p̄ftus Franc' Morgan et Johēs Harris separatim fecer' quandam purpresturā in regia via infra villā ib̄m cum ligno ib̄m posito ad nocument' . . . qd Wilm̄us Broughton posuit silices anglicè brakes in altis plateis ib̄m ad nocum' populi D̄n̄i regis illuc transient'.

. . . qd Franc' Morgan fecit quandam fossam anglice sawpitt super quendam locum voc le grene ad nocum'.

Johēs Peake . . . jurat sup' sacram' suum dicit et putat qd quidam Thomas Ellyott serviens Francisco Morgan Arm' p̄misit oves sub custodia suā facere magna detrimenta tam in segete quam in gramine aliorū ad dampnum non modicum et gravamen.

Jac. I.—Court roll in Latin ; at the end the following entries are made :

Newe orders.

It is now ordered at this Courte by the homage and con-

---

[1] 'Tolvetum' : Tollfat in Ordinances of 1547, art. 61.
[2] Forisfaciet.

sent of the Stewards there that the Townes men shall cause
a cucking-stool to be made before the Feast of All Saints
next ensuing upon payne to forfeit x*s.*

Item.—It is further ordered that Thomas Knapp shall
cause a chymney to be made in a tenement now in occu-
pason of Richard Pitman before the feast day of St. Thomas
the Apostle next ensuing upon payne to forfett xl*s.*

V.

[This indenture, written on parchment, is very much injured by damp, and is in parts illegible. The following extracts are given as containing some words worthy of notice, and also on account of the curious provision that part of the rent should be paid in ale.]

Hec indentura testat' qd Clemens Bacon Ballivus ville de Kyngesthorpe Stephanus Shepperd et Johannes Hobnestyc constabularii ibm ac tota coitas ejusdm ville unanimo eorum consensu et assensu concesserunt tradiderunt et ad firmam dimiserunt Willmo Branfeld de Kyngesthorpe miln^r quatuor molendin' sua aquatica vocat South Mylnes juxta Northampton sub uno tecto simul existencia vidt duo molendina eordum p̄ multura[1] blador' et alia' duo molendina eor' p̄ arte fullonum cū toto apparatu et les goyngeres '[2] cū stagno, aquis, piscar', januis fluctū, pratis, pascuis pastur' et gardinis ex pte orientali stagni p̄dti molendinis p̄dctis spectant'. . . . hend et tenend de p̄fto Ballivo, etc. . . . p̄fato Braunfeld . . . a festo scti Johnis Bapte prox' futur' . . . usque ad finem term' decem ann' . . . reddendo inde annuatim post dctm festū . . . septem marcas bone monete ad quatuor ann' divnes . . . per equales porc'ones et annuatim in temp'e falcationis prator' unam cuvam[3] vel tynam[4] c'rvsie continent'

---

[1] 'Multura'=molitura: the grinding of the corn. Also used for the toll charged by the miller (Cowell).

[2] 'Goyngeres': 'going gear,' *vide* No. XI.

[3] 'Cuva'='keeve,' tub, cask; Fr. *cuvve.*

[4] 'Tyna': cask or vase (Cowell).

vigenti et sex lagenas c'vsie aut duos solidos et duos denar'
in moneta pro eadem c'vsia pro omnib' aliis officiis et de-·
mandis eis molendinis incumbent' et una decima ecclie de
Kyngesthorpe p̄dc̄t' de p̄dc̄tis molendinis annuatim consuet'
. . . et qd p̄ftus Wills Branfeld execut' et assig' sui hēbunt
. . . annuatim herbaguim et vesturam[1] unius holme[2] prati
jacent' inter aquas post primam falcatinem . . . etc., etc.

[1] 'Vestura': the produce, crop.   See 'Supervisus,' No. XXXIX.
[2] 'Holme': the island formed between the river and the mill back-
water.

VII.

[The following document and that numbered XIX. contain the codes of Customs or Ordinances to be observed in the Court Leet. They are interesting as throwing light upon the condition and manners of the people, and presenting a curious specimen of the language of the time. We may notice by comparing the two the change which the lapse of a little over half a century seems to have made.]

Thes ben Customes made yn the Custumarys withyne the Toune of Kyngesthorp renewed . . . day of June the yere of the Regne of Kyng Richard the third after the conquest the first :—

1. Fyrste that the grete courtes called the Letes holden at estern and m'helmasse the dayes that they . . . that the seid courtes be begon at 9 or 10 of the clock at the ferthest in the morrowe,[1] and the persones that have a doo[2] at the seid courtes ben there at the seid tymes duely evy psone uppon [payne] and perrell of amercyment of xii*d*.

2. Also that alle Suters to the seid courtes the on daye of the seid courtes to appere in propre person or ellis

---

[1] 'Morrowe'=morning.
[2] 'A doo'=at do=to do: the infinitive used substantively, as in 'much ado,' a great to-do.

'We'll keep no great ado—a friend or two.'
Romeo and Juliet, iii. 4.

essoigned[1] or [ellis] amercyed, the seconde daye to appere
in propre person or ellis amercyed yf he were essoigned at
the laste, and that alle the essoigned and amercyed so forfette
turne to the avayle of the seid toune as amercyment of the
seid courtes have don aforntyme withoute any pardone of
heme to be hadde withoute resonable mater.

3. Also yf any psone yn pleyne courte tyme beyng
Styward[2] or Bailly rebuke, revyle, or disobey in rightwisnes,
or oute of courte doing hys office, to forfette to the seid
toune the pey of xl*d*.

4. Also yf any psone at any tyme the constables, ffre-
borows or other officers sworne, rebuke, revyle, or disobey
yn doing ther office truely, to forfette to the seid toune as
oftetymes as they so don the peyne of vi*d*.

5. Also that alle thoo psones that brewen to selle that
they cesse of brewyng except ii, iii, or ellis iiii at the moste
in the wek of suche as hathe ledes[1] and other lomes[2] of ther
awne and assigned be the bailly of the seid toune for tyme
beyng uppon the peyne (vi*d*.).

6. Also that no psone wytnne the seid toune harborough
no strange psones after a nyght or day in ther place, but
then to bryng hem to the Bailly of the seid toune or con-

---

[1] 'Essoigned': 'amercyed.' Essoin = excuse. 'It signifieth in the
common law the allegation of an excuse from him that is summoned to
appear and answer to an action real, or to perform suit to a Court Baron
upon just cause of absence. The causes that serve to essoine are chiefly
under five heads, whereof the first is "ultra mare," the second "de terra
sancta," the third "de malo veniendi," which is also called "essoine,"
the fourth "de malo lecti," and the fifth "de servitio regis" (Cowell).
"Amercyed": *vide* note p. 20.

[2] 'Styward.' This would seem to be more accurate than the present
spelling, if the derivation generally accepted is correct ; viz., Sty-ward,
the keeper of the domestic animals. Verstegan, however, derives it
from Stedeward, the keeper of the place or homestead. It is curious
that two such names as Stewart and Howard should be derived from
the keeping of pigs—Styward and Hogward.

[3] 'Ledes': probably a local word for vats or tubs.

[4] 'Lome': 'It seems to be some sort of vessel in Hollinshed's
'History of England," i. 194' (Halliwell).

stables, and they to demene heme as they seme beste uppon the peyn as any psone and as oftyn as any psone aboveseid may be take with defaute to lese and to forfette to the same toune xii*d*.

7. Also at evy courte, that ys to say, ii grete letes at the seid courtes, to chese two ferers[1] to afere the seid courte anon after hit ys holden as ryghte wyll, etc.

8. Also that non of alle the seid toun of Kyngesthorp resceyve ne holde noo tenntes in her tenement yf they ben cōpleyned uppon be resonable and sufficiant men of the seid toune, yn the pleyne courte aforne the Styward and Bailly, to avoyde be a quarter after the seid tenntes yf they be not of gode name and fame, uppon peyne to lese to the seid toune xl*d*.

9. Also alle tho psones that dwellyn and holde housolds yn the same toune that were not born therynne to pay yerely to the seid toune iiii*d*. for ther heds yn to the tyme they bye yt oute of the seid toune, etc.

10. Also that no psone kepe ne holde moo horse then for evy x acr of eyrabell londe in his tenure i horse, as olde custume hath ben aforne tyme, uppon the peyne of xii*d*.

11. Also that alle thoo psones that holde and have any mares and foles wyᵗnne the seid towne of Kyngesthorpe, that they devoyde and utter hem oute of the boundes of the seid towne be twyx this and holy [Trinity] in Maye next comyng, yn peyne of forfeture of the seid catell, mares, and foles : cause this that . . . staunce of the seid toun holden horse and ther pastures and comyns ben right streyte, and so yt ys grete hyndraunce to the seid holders of horse, because they may tye noo horse in the seid comyn and pasture for the seid mares and foles, and also grete hynderers and

---

[1] 'Ferers,' or afeerers : from old French *affeurer taxare*, persons appointed upon oath at the Court Leets to set the fines upon such as have committed faults arbitrarily punishable (*in misericordia*) which have no express penalty appointed (Cowell), *vide* note p. 20.

harmdoers yn corne medowes, leseures, and pastures of the seid towne of Kingsthorpe. xl*d*.

12. Also alle thoo that have neght in the seid towne, and have no fre medowe of her awne as for 1 beste, to pay noo money, and for evy hed over to pay yerely iii*d*.

13. Also a man may be essoigned ii tymes, and at the iii*de* courte appere in plee of londe or of dette, etc., vi*d*.; and yf he come not ynne the iiii*th* courte day in the same anon to be condempned.

14. Also yf any psone knowlege any dette aforne the bailly yn courte or be syde at any mannes sute, yt ys lefull to the seid bailly yn alle haste resonable to make leve[1] of the seid dette, uppon peyne of vi*d*.

15. Also all thoo londes and tenements that any man withyn the seid towne bye and purchas or bequevyth, yt ys lefull to them in her last dayes by vertu of her testament the seid londes and tenements to whome that hem lyke, gyve, selle, and bequeth to his case, etc.

16. Also yt shal not be lefull to noo childe of mankynde or womankynde for to selle any londe or tenement unto that tyme that they of the age of xv yere fully.

17. Also yf any psone sell any londes and tenements to any other psone withynne the seid towne or with oute, that the seid seller of the seid londes and tenements shalle yelde hem up in to the Kynges honde unto the behove of the byer, after custome and man', and there to abyde ix dayes; and yf any psone kynne to the seid seller withyn the iiii*th* degree come withyn the seid ix dayes and aske a cate,[2] yt shalbe delyved hym thus to paye the money that the forseid byer shulde paye, havyng suche day of payment as the seid seller and byer hav they yn the pleyne courte yn ppre psones aforne the Styward and Bailly sworne to knowledge

---

[1] 'Leve,' *i.e.*, levy.

[2] 'Cate': acate, achat (Fr. *acheter*), purchase; from low Latin, *ac-captare*. Compare cater, caterer. For instances of the exercise of this right of pre-emption *vide* Court Rolls, 3 Ed. VI.

the trouth. And yif noo cate of noon suche psone withynne the seid iiii[th] degree, withynne the seid ix dayes, be asked, that then the seid byer come and have lyve of season, after custome and man'. And yf the seid byer come not, the seid londes and tenementis abyde other thre courte dayes in the Kynges honde, that then the seid londes and tentes be the Bailly of the seid towne be seised yn the Kynges hondes, unto avayle and behove of the seid towne for evemore. And yf there be any born men[1] or ffranches men of the towne wyl have the bargayn after the lyvie, the to resceyve yt a fore a foreyn purchasour. Also the same bargyn shallbe kepte hole.

18. Also yf any psone withynne the boundes of the same towne drawe to any psone yn vyolence, swerd, dagger, or knyfe, or any other weapon, to forfette to the seid toun at any tyme that suche defaute ys founde xii*d.* ; and yf they smyte with the same and drawe any blode, to lese to the same towne xx*d.*

19. Also yf any man chaunge any londe or tenement, and any bote be hadde unto the sume of ii*d.* and above, so after the quantyte as yt ys above to paye seeson.

20. Also that all comyn brewers that brewe for to selle, that yn tyme of wynter, ffrome mhelmesse to estern, after the our of ix yn the nyght, harborough nor resceyve noo psone to sell nor gyffe noo vetayle suche as they usyn, nor suffre hem withynne the dores, and yn som[r] seson ffrome the tyme of esterne yn to the tyme of mhelmesse after the oure of x at nyght uppon peyne of ponysshement of bothe ptyes as oftyn as yt may be knowen, iiii*d.*, and that no house of suspecion holde noo comyn brewhouse uppon the peyne of vi*d.*

21. Also yf any catell of any mannes be distressed for rente, dette, or trespasse, or any other thyng resonable and

---

[1] 'Born men,' or 'ffranches men': *vide* Court Rolls, 3 Ed. VI., Clement Talbott's land.

lefull, and putte yt yn pounde, that yf any man take hem
oute woute license of them that so enpked them as oftyn as
yt maye be founde that they so don to lese to the seid
towne (xii*d.*) xl*d.*

22. Also that noo man make noo hye wey, use nor
hawnte over any londes, medowes, lesures, ne pastures, but
suche as have ben usyd of olde tyme oute of mynde, uppon
the peyne of vi*d.*

23. Also yf any man brewe for the avayle[1] of the Churche,
that all other brewers cesse for the tyme uppon lefulle
warnyng tyll that be outred, uppon the peyne of xii*d.*

24. Also yf any psone sell any tenement, londe, or mede
wytnne the seid towne or felde of Kyngesthorpe, and gyff
noo knowlege therof to the bailly beyng for the tyme, be
the next courte day, to lese for evy hole tenement iii*s.* iiii*d.*,
and so forthe to the leste parte therof, after the same rate
of the quantite.

---

[1] 'Avayle of the Church.' It appears to have been customary to raise
the money for the support of the Church services by this most question-
able method. Stubbs, in his 'Anatomie of Abuses,' quoted in Brand's
'Antiquities,' says : 'In certain townes against Xmas and Easter, Whit-
sondaye, or some other tyme, the churchwardens of every parishe, with
the consent of the whole parishe, provide half a score or twenty quarters
of mault, whereof some they buy of the churche stocke, and some is
given them of the parishioners themselves, every one conferring some-
what according to his abilitie, which mault being made into very strong
ale or bere, is set for sale either in the churche or some other place
assigned to that purpose. Then, when this is set abroche, well is he
that can get the soonest to it and spend the most at it, etc. That money
they say is to repaire their churches and chappels with, to buy books for
service, cuppes for the celebration of the sacrament, surplesses for Sir
John, and such other necessaries.'
In the churchwarden's accounts at Bishop Stortford, 1489, the following items appear :

Profit of the Hokkyng Ale	15*s.* 0*d.*
From two drinkings called May Ales	£4 6*s.* 8*d.*
Of the profit of the play	20*s.*
Of the issue of a drinking made in the church here on Sunday after the day of the aforesaid play	26*s.* 7*d.*

(Glascock's 'Records of St. Michael's, Bishop Stortford.')

25. Also for ēvy quarteron of mede on the southe syde so solde, the bailly noo knowlege hevyng be the next courte day, the seller to forfette to the seid towne xii*d*., and so forthe to the leest parte after the q̄ntyte of the seller.

26. Also any psone yͭ sellyth a q̄uteron mede uppon the northsyde, the bailly noo knowlege havyng be the next court day, the seller to forfette to the towne x*d*., and so forthe to the lest pte after the q̄ntite of the seller.

27. Also any psone that sellyth an acre of londe, the bailly noo knowlege havyng of hym by the next courte daye to forfette and lese to the seid towne iiii*d*., and so forthe to the lest pte after the q̄ntyte.

28. Also yf any psone sell any tenement, lond, or mede wyͭn the seid towne or withoute to any other psone that than the seid seller shall yelde up hem yn to the Kynges honde to the behove of the seller withyn courte dayes after yt ys solde, or ellys to lese and forfette yt to the seid towne.

29. Also yf any man repe or mowe any lond thoroughly or the bailly and the comynte ben agreed to forfette and lese to the seid towne vi*d*. ; and yf he begynne uppon mo londes than on won, to forfette and lese to the towne xii*d*.

30. Also yf any man digge yn restowe[1] delff on the white erthe denyg the wey, to lese to yᵉ towne xii*d*.

31. Also yf any man denye the Kynges hye wey with stone or tymber over a quarter, except he be a belder, he shall lese to the seid towne of Kyngesthorpe vi*d*.

[On the back appear some traces of other ordinances, but almost entirely obliterated. The two following can be made out :]

32. Also that no man kepe nor holde no moo but for ēyy

---

[1] 'Restowe delff': in the later ordinances 'Restoo delf.' The word Stowdelf occurs apparently for stone quarry.

acre ii shepe, uppon peyne to lese to the seid towne of Kyngesthorpe for evy shepe ob'.

33. Also ordeyned that the Bailly from tyme to tyme shall chose and electe oon of the xii men, and the Steward an other, for the comynalte of the towne, ffor evy officer as Bailly, Steward, and other officers, and this election at altymes to be hadd, made, and yeven[1] in the cort house accustomed, upon peyne att any tyme doying the con-trarye xl*d*.

---

[1] 'Yeven,' from *yeve*, to give, appears to be an old form retained in this peculiar meaning when the form 'give,' 'given,' had come into ordinary use = given, datum, dated, *vide* Ordinances (1547), art. 52.

IX.

[This is apparently the draft of a will, and is valuable on account of the number of local names it contains. It has no date, but is of the time of Hen. VII. or VIII. On account of the loss of the first lines, it is uncertain what chapel is referred to as containing the testator's tomb. Every other local reference is to Kingsthorpe, but the mention of the houses of Dominicans and Franciscans 'ibid' seems to point to Northampton.]

[Beginning imperfect.]

. . . pd͞cte capelle pro tumulo meo ib͞m . . . item lego ad sustentacionem luminis . . . item lego ad sustentacionem domus ffratrum pr͞dcator ibid iiii*d.* Item lego ad sustentacionem domus ffrat͞m myno͞r ibid . . . item lego Roberto Shepherd filio meo unam ollam eneam unam parapsidem[1] electrinam[2] . . . ii sawcers electrina . . . unum coopertorium voc a coverlet et unum par linthiar.[3] Item lego Alicie filie mee unam ollam eneam unam patellam eneam ii parapsides electrinas ii sawcers electrin' ii dish electrin' unam matteras unum coopertorium unum par linthiarum unum manutergium diapere, etc. Item lego ad sustentacionem luminis animarum omnium fidelium defunctorum meam dimidiam acram terre arabil' jacent' apud pesefurlong hend͞m pro dicta sustentacione in pp͞etuum. Item lego ad susten-

[1] 'Parapsidem': dish.
[2] 'Electrinam': electrum, a mixture of gold and silver. Cups made of it were supposed to detect poison.
[3] Sheets, towels,

tacionem cantarie p'rtnentis predicte capelle beate Marie virginis in ecclesia sup'dcta unam rodam et dim terr' arabil' jacent' . . . nederfurlong in heybrome juxta terram Clementis Broke habend' ad sustentaconem pdctm in pptuum. Ulteriusque do et lego Isode uxori mee totum tenementum meum cum omnibus suis prtntiis in quo modo maneo ac decem acr' terr' arabil' et duas quarteron prat' jac' in campis et pratis de Kyngesthorpe prdct' quarum quidem terrar' prdct' iii rode jacent ex parte boreali de le Milbroke i rod jac' in stadio vocat' le ffrost dimid' acr' jac' apud Smetho, dimid' acr' jac' apud Boughton mere dim' acr' jacent' apud finem borealem pdcte ville de Kyngesthorpe juxta terram Ricardi Shepherd . . . acr' jac' apud Gilberts furres i rod jac' apud Parsonstownesende subter viam vocat' Milnway i acr' jac' apud Parkfield extendent' ad le Heth i rod' jac' apud Shortlandes i rod jac' apud le Delves dim' acr' jact apud ffystellholme dim' acr' apud Manuellfeld . . . extend^{ns} juxta culturam vocat' Longlande, dim' acr' jac' apud Gepdale iii rod' jac' apud Netherfurlong in Heybrome i rod' et dim' apud Heybrome in dict' le Netherfurlong juxta les hadon Johannis Rede i rod' et dim' jac' pr' domũ Ste Trinitatis iii rod' jac' apud Blackwellhill dim' acr' jac' apud Oberfurlong in Haybrome juxta terras Thome Sm— ii quarteron prat' jac' ex parte boreali ville ibm hend' et tenend' totum pdct' tene^{ta} et omnes decem acras terre arabil' et duas quarteron' prat' cum omnibus ear pertintiis ut pdct Isode uxi mee ad tm vite sue de capitalibus dominis feodi ill' pr servicia inde debit' et de jure consueta ita quod immediate' post discessum pdcte Isode uxoris mee omnia et singula pdct' tenement' 10 acre arabilis duæ quarteron' prati cum omnibus earum ptnciis pfto Roberto filio meo hered' et assignat' suis rem'[1] in pptuum tenend' de capital' dominis, etc. Quod si contingat pdctm Robertum filium meum obire et pdct' Isode uxore mea sup'vivente volo tunc qd omnia et singula pdct' ten' decem acre terre arabil' et due quarteron'

---

[1] Remanere.

prat' cum omnibus earum p̄tnciis Alicie filie mee hered' et
assign' suis rem in pptuum tenend' de capital' dms feodi p'
servicia inde debit' et de jure consuet'.   Quod si contingat
tam p̄dct' Robertum filium meum quam d̄ct Aliciam filiam
meam obire et dict' Isode uxore mea eis supervivente volo
tunc quod eadem Isode uxor mea in vita sua caussabit
omnia pmissa p . . . . decessum vendant[r] et pecunie inde
percepte pro salute animar nostrar omnium amicoru nostror
ac omnium defunctorum in donis benedict[s] et elemosinis
caritativis distribuant[r].   Ac insuper do et lego Alicie filie
mee iiii acr' terr' arabil' et unam quarteron' prat[s] quarum
quidem terras p̄dctar . . . apud Boughton Mere i rod' jac'
inter les Styes dim' acr' jac' juxta les pyttes prope . . .
Childe, dim' acr' jac' apud T . . . versus domum Se Trinitatis iii rod' jac' apud Heybrome i rod' extendent' vie voc
. . . . et una quarteron' prat' jac' ex parte australi ville
p̄dcte hend' et tenend' p̄dct' terr' arabil' et quarteron' prat'
cum omnibus earu ptciis ut p̄dct' est p̄fte Alicie filie mee
hered' et assign' suis rem in pptuum quandocunque sit in
plena etate videlicet de anno xiiii et usque eundem annum
quod p̄ficia d̄ct iiii acr' terr' arabil' et quarteron' prat' . . .
p̄dcte Isode, uxori mee reddentur et disponentur si ex divina
gracia tam diu vix'it.   Item do et lego Ricardo Shepherd
consanguineo meo dim' acr' terr' arabil' jac' apud pesefurlong hend' et tenend' hereds et assign' suis in pptuum
tenend' de capital' domis feodi pr servicia inde debita et re
jure consueta.

X

[The following is a specimen of the Royal Grants made to the inhabitants. According to Baker ('History of Northamptonshire') the constitution of the manor of Kingsthorpe was peculiar, 'the inhabitants themselves being permitted to hold their town at farm by lease from the Crown. It was probably first demised to them by King John, for in 8 Hen. II. (1223) the sheriff was commanded to give the men of Kyngesthorpe full seisin of Spelho hundred as parcel of that manor, and held with it in the reign of King John. In 20 Hen. VI. the King demised the manor of Kingsthorpe, *alias* Thorpe, to his tenants there for forty years, rendering £50 yearly. In 4 Hen. VII. the men of Kingsthorpe paid a fine for confirmation of divers charters, and in the following year the King confirmed the lease of his predecessor, lowering the rent from £60 to £50 on account of their great poverty. The manor continued to be held by successive leases till 14 Jas. I., when it was granted in fee to Thomas Hollis, Francis Morgan & Co., feoffees in trust for the other freeholders, at a yearly rent of £40, which rent was purchased by Lord Chief Justice Rainsford in 1674 of the trustees for the sale of fee farm rents, and is now vested in Miss Wrighte. The feoffees, when reduced in number, are filled up by the nomination of the survivors. The Enclosure Commissioners allotted 14 a. 2 r. 14 p. to the feoffees, which is called the Town Land.']

Henricus Dei gratia rex Anglie et Francie et dominus Hibernie omnibus quos p'sentes lie p'vennt saltm Inspeximus lias patentes dni Henrici nup regis Angl' septimi post conquestum prius np fcts in hec verba Henricus Dei gratia rex Angl' et Francie et dns Hibernie omnibus ad quos psntes tie pvennt saltm. Inspeximus lias patentes dni E. nup' regis Angl' quarti post conquestum fcts in hec verba Edwardus dei grā rex Angl' et Francie et dns Hibernie omnibus ad quos psentes lie pvnnt saltm Sciatis qd ex

4

humili supplicatoē homm̄ et tenentm n̄rom ville n̄re de
Kingesthorp alias nuncupat' Thorp in C̄om Northt accepim'
qualit' Henricus nup' rex Angl' sextus de quo nup' tenentes
ville pdcte villam illam tenuerunt ad firmam pro sexaginta
libris p' annū tunc considerans qd villa pdcta tunc in decasum maxime recidebat et ruinam qd ad valorem sexaginta
ibrar p' annū qumvis de tenentibs foret occupata se non
extendebat sicut p' quandam supplicatoēm inde fctm et in
canceller' ipius nuper regis retornatam plene liquet de grā
sua spcli concesserit pfatis nup' tenentibs et eorum successoribus tenentibs ejusdem ville qd ipi herent et tenerent
dtam villam cum omnibs membris et ptns eidem ptinen' in
die obitus Johanne nuper regine Anglie usque ad tmn̄m
quadraginta annor ex tunc px sequen' reddend' inde eidem
nup' regi et hered' suis annuatim quinquaginta libras dumtaxat p' omnbs oneribus et pficiis que eidem nup' regi hered'
et successoribs suis aut alicui alie p'sone p' jus Dni debend'
fieri possent seu solvend' dcto t'mno durante prout in liis
patentibus ipius nuper regis plenius continetᴿ.   Acetiam
cum nos p' lias nras patentis quar dat' est septimo die Julii
anno regni n̄ri septimo de grā n̄rā spcli concessimus carissime
consorti n̄re Elizabethe regine Anglie inter alia quadraginta
libras p' annū de firma de Kingesthorp alias Thorp in c̄om
Northt pcipiend' a festo Pasche anno regni n̄ri septimo
durante vita ipius consortis p' manus hoīm tenentm seu
Ballivorum ejusdem ville et successor' suor' aut Vic' dcti
c̄om Northt aut aliorum receptorum ejusdem ferme p' tempore existen' ad tmnos Pasche et Si Michls p' equales por-
coes prout in eisdem lris patentibs n̄ris inde confectis
plenius continetᴿ qualiter etiam nunc tenentes ville pdcte ad
tantam paupertatem villaq' illa de tenentibus desolationem
hiis diebus devenerunt qd si tenentes pdct dctm firmam
sexaginta librar' ex nunc singulis annis p'rsolverent finalis
distruccio et desolatio ville illius infra die consequeretr.
Nos premissa considerantes non modicam paup'tatem te-

nentm nrom et decasum ville pdcte compacientes de grã
urã speli concessimus et p'p'sentes concedms eisdem hoibus et
tenentibus nris ville illius et eorum successoribus tenentibus
ejusdem ville qd ipi heant et teneant de nobis dctm villam
cum omnbs membris et ptns quibuscunq et dcte ville
ptnen' a festo Pasche anno regni nri quartodecimo usque
ad tmnm quadraginta annor extunc px' sequen' reddend' inde annuatim quinquaginta libras dumtaxat
videl't quadraginta libras inde annuatim p'fat' consorti
nre durante vita sua pdct' in plenam et annualem solucoem
p'missorum quadraginta librar' annuar' ut pdctm est ei con-
cessar' ac decem libras inde residuas nobis et successoribs
nris annuatim durante dcto trmno quadraginta annorum
pdctor' pro omnbs onibs et fermis que nobis et heredbs ac
successoribs nris aut alicui alie psone p' jus nri debend'
fieri possent seu solvend' dcto trmno quadraginta annorum
durante et qd nec ipi nec heredes nec successores sui a
dcto festo Pasche p' non solucone alicujus melioris firme
que nobis fore posset solvend' infra dctm tmnm onentr et
impetantr sed tm pdcta firma quadraginta librar' p' ann' ut
pdct est solvend'. Et insuper de grã nra pdta ac ex dcta
scientia et mero motu nro p'donam' remittim' et relaxam'
pfatis hoibus et tenentibs hered' et successoribs suis tenentibs
dcte ville de Kingesthorp alias Thorp dctas decem libras
parcellas de dcta firma sexaginta librar' p' annum et qd ipi
tenentes heredes et successores sui tenentes ejusdem ville
de dctis decem libris parcella de dicta firma sexaginta librar'
p' annũ erga nos et heredes nostros durante dcto trmno
quadraginta annor' penitus exon'entr et quiet' existent aliquo
actu statuto sive ordinacoe in contrm fact' non obstante in
cujus rei testimoniũ has lias nras fieri fecimus patentes teste
me ipo apud Westm' primo die Junii anno regni nri quinto
decimo nos autem lias pdctas ac omnia et singula in eisdem
contenta rata hentes et grata ea p' nob' et hered' nris
quantum in nob' est acceptam' et approbam' ac diltis nob'

nunc hoibs et tenentibs ville pdcte et eorū successoribs
tenore ps'entiū ratificam' et confirmamus p'ut liē pdcte
ro'nabilit' testantᵣ in cujus rei testimonium has lias nras fieri
fecimu' patentes teste me ipo apud Westm' vicesimo tercio
Octobr' anno regni nri quinto. Nos autem lias pdctas ac
omnia et singula in eisdem contenta rata hentes et grata ea
p' nobis et hered' nris quantū in nob' est acceptam' et approbam' ac diltis nobis nunc hoibs et tenentibs ville nre pdcte
et eorū successoribs tenore psentiū ratificamus et confirmam'
p'ut liē pdcte ro'nabilit' testantᵣ. Et ulterius ex humili sup-
plicatioe nunc hoium et tenentm pdctor' ville nre pdcte ac
pmissa considerantes necnon nimie paup'tati et indigencie
tenentm nror' pdctor' et decasum ville pdcte pie compacientes de gra nra pdcta ac ex certa scientia et mero motu
nostris concessim' et per p'sentes concedim' eisdem nunc
hoibs et tenentibs nris ville nre pdcte et eorū successoribs
tenentibs ejusdem ville qd ipi heredes et eorū successores
tenentes ville pdcte hcant et teneant de nob' et hered' nris
dctam villam cum omnbs membris et ptin quibucunq'
eidem ville ptinen a festo Sti Michis Archi anno regni nri
octavo usque ad finem et tmnm quadraginta annor' reddend'
inde nob' et hered' nris annuatim quinquaginta libras p'
omnimod' onbs et firmis que nob' et hered' ac successoribs
nris aut alicui alie psone p' jus suū debend' fieri possent seu
solvend' et qd nec ipi nec heredes nec successores sui p'
non solucom majoris firme que nob' vel hered' aut successoribs nris fore posset solvend' onentᵣ seu impetantᵣ sed in
pdcta firma quinquaginta librar' p' annū tantum ut pdctm
est solvend'. Et insuper de gra nra pdcta ac ex certa
sciencia et mero motu nris p'donam' remittim' et relaxam'
pfatis hoibs et tenentibs ac successoribs suis tenentibs dcte
ville de Kingsthorp alias Thorp dctas decem libras p'cellas
de dcta firma sexaginta librar' p' annū necnon omnia arre-
ragia ejusdem firme a pdcto festo Sti Mchlis Archi anno
regni nri octavo quovismodo reddend' seu solvend' et qd

ipī heredes et successores sui hōies tenentes ejusdem ville
tam de dctis decem libris p'cell' de dcta firma sexaginta
librar' p' annū qū de arreragiis pdctis erga nos et heredes
nros penitus exonentᵣ et quiet' existent aliquo actu statuto
sive ordinacone vel restrictoē in contrar' fact' non obstante.
In cujus rei testimonium has lias nras fieri fecimus patentes
leste me īpo apud Westm' vicesimo die Decembr' anno
regni nri undecimo.

[Endorsed.]

Irrotlat' in memor' Sccii de anno undecimo Regis Henrici octavi inter Recorda de primo Sti Hillarii rotlo ex pte
rememoratoris Thes'.

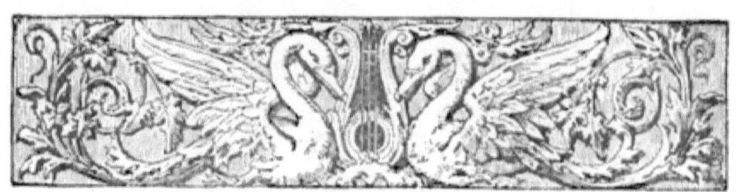

XI.

[There were three watermills in ancient Kingsthorpe, thus mentioned in 'Domesday': 'Ibi iii molini de xliii solidis et iiii denariis.' They were described as the North or Farre Mill (being furthest from the village), the Nether Mill, in the village, and the South Mill, adjoining Northampton. They still exist, and the last is now usually called St. Andrew's Mill. On the alienation of the manor they all came into the possession of the Morgan family of Kingsthorpe, and so to the Robinsons, by whom they were sold within the last few years to different purchasers.]

This indenture made the xxviii^th daye of Aprill, in the xii^th yere of the regne of Kyng Henry the eight, betwen Simon Bakon, baylly of Kyngesthorp in the countee of North^n., William Wryght and Thomas Carte, constabulls of the same Toune, and all the hole cominaltie of the seid towne of Kyngesthorp, on the oon ptie, and John Hopkyns, of the same towne, miller, and Margarett his wife, on the other ptie, Witnesseth that the seid bailly, constabulls, and comnaltie of on assent and consent, hathe graunted, betaken, and to ferme sett unto the seyd John Hopkyns and Margarett his wife, and to eyther of theym, the mille of Kyngesthorp aforsaid called the north mill or farre mill of Kyngesthorp, with alman^r, medowes, holmes, lesues, pastures, willowes, waters, dikes, and all other comodites and pfitts to the seyd mille appteynyng, or in eny wise belongyng, to have and to holde all the foresaid mille, and all other the pmisses, with their apptennces, unto the seyd John Hopkyns and Margarett his wife, and oon such psone as the

seyd John or Margarett shalle name or assigne ffrome the
ffest of thannunciacōn of oure Lady the virgin last past
before the date of these psents unto thende and tᵣme ot
xviii yeres then next ensuyng, and fully to be complete and
ended, yeldyng and paying therfore yerely duryng the seyd
tᵣme unto the seyd baylly, constabulls, comnaltie, and theire
successors or assignes ffyfty shillings viii*d.* of laufull money
of England at too times or ffests of the yere; that is to sey,
at the ffestes of Seynt Mighell tharchangel and the Annun-
ciacōn of oure Lady the Virgyn by even porcōns. And yf
it happen the seyd rent of l*s.* viii*d.* by yere or eny pcell
theroff, to be behynde unpaid after eny ffeste of the ffests
aforeseyd be the space of oon month, if it be askyd then it
shall be laufull unto the seyd baylly, constabulls, comnaltie,
or their successours, or eny of theym, to entre into the seyd
mille, all other the pmisses, with their apptnnces, and evy
pcell of the same, and distreyne, and the distresse so founde
and taken laufully, to lede, dryve, chace, bere, and cary
awey, and withold, retayne, and kepe unto suche tyme as
the seyd rent, together with arreragis of the same, yf eny be
to theym truly and fully contented and paid. And in case
the seyd rent or eny pte therof fortune to be behynde in pte or
all unpaid after eny ffeste of the ffests aboveseyd by the
space of a quarter of oon yere, and noo sufficient distresse
of and upon the pmisses may be hadde ne founde for the
seyd rent doo beyng behynde, that then it shalbe laufull
unto the seyd baylly, constabulls, cominaltie, and theire
successours, and eny of theym, to reentre into the foreseyd
mille and all other the pmisses, with theire apptnnces, and
the same to have ageyne and peasiblie enoy as in theire
former astate, this indenture in eny wise to the contrary not
withstandyng. And the seyd John Hopkyns and Margarett
his wyfe covennten and graunten by theyse psents to the
seyd bayly, constabulls, and comnaltie, that they, the seyd
John Hopkyns and Margarett his wife, and their oon as-

signey shalle yerely during the seid t^rme of theire owne $\overline{ppre}$
costs and charges bere and make alman^r rep$\bar{a}$c$\bar{o}$ns, what-
soevr they be, belongyng to the seyd mille, and all other the
pmisses, with theire apptnnces, as well above the grownde
as all other goyng gere and water worke under the grownde,
and kepyng of the lowshards[1] of the bank of the ryver and
mille dame. And soo at thend of the seyd t^rme all the
seyd mille and other the pmisses, with theire apptnnces,
wele and sufficiently repaired at thend of the seyd terme,
the seyd John and Margarett and theire oon assigney, or
oon of them, shall leve by the ovsight of iiii indifferent men
of Kyngesthorp aforsaid, then there dwellyng. Also the
seyd John Hopkyns and Margarett his wife covennten and
graunten by these psents unto the seyd bayly, constabulls,
and comnaltie of the seyd towne, that they, the seyd John
Hopkyns and Margarett his wife, and their oon assigney, at
theire ppre costs and charges, shalle yerely during the seyd
t^rme discharge the seyd towneshipp ayenst the pson of
Kyngesthorp and his successors of alman^r tithes herafter to
be due and payble yerely during the seyd t^rme out of the
seyd mille and all other the pmisses, with theire apptnnces,
and also yerely paye the mede money of their seyd costs
and charges, and also make the planke at the mille dore to
goo on the medowe, provided alwey that the seyd John
Hopkyns and Margarett his wife, nor theire assigney, nor
non other psone or psones for theym, shalle at noo tyme
herafter duryng the seyd t^rme felle by the grownde nor
plukke up noo man^r tree or trees belongyng to the said
mille and other the pmisses, or eny pte of the same, nor
make noo unlaufull loppe nor toppe by these psents. In
witnesse wherof to the oon pte of these indentures with the
seyd John Hopkyns and Margarett his wife remaynyng, the
said baylly, constabulls, and comnaltie hath sett their comon

---

[1] 'Kepyng of the lowshards,' *vide* No. XV., note.

seale of Kyngesthorp aforesaid, and to the other pte of these indentures with the seyd baylly and constabulls and comnaltie remayning, the seyd John Hopkyns and Margarett his wife hathe sett theire seales the daye and yere abovescid.

XII.

[The curious document which follows is one of those referring to the dispute about conies which seems to have exercised the minds of the men of Kingsthorpe for many years. The claim of free warren in this and neighbouring parishes was probably undisputed for some centuries, but about the time of Hen. VII. and VIII. the grievance arising from it had reached a point which aroused active resistance.

The petition sets forth the views of the inhabitants, and assuming the statements to be true, they certainly make out a hard case. The claim probably was legal, but had by force of circumstances become a hardship, and doubtless had to be modified, though there is nothing in these papers to show what was the issue of the agitation. This document is evidently only the original draft interlined and corrected. The paper is injured all down one side, but the missing words can be easily supplied, and are inserted in brackets.]

In most lamentable man^r sheweth and compleyneth . . . your orators and humble pore subjects, tenents, and inhabitants of Kingsthorpe, in the county of Northmpton, that wheres yor [said petitioners] and predecessors have holden the said Towne and all man^r [of . . . and] pastures lying within the ffeldes and pyshe of the same Towne of your Hyghnes and of your most noble p'genitors in fee ferme tyme . . . . they and their auncestors and p'decessors have yerely, until the xxth yere of the ryghte noble Kynge Henry the VI., yelded and payed unto y^r said p'decessor . . . the yere whyche said ryghte noble Kynge Henry VI., considering the pov^{r}tie and necessytie of his said tenents of Kyngsthorpe and the great [decrease] of the Towne, and howe that evy acre of lande in the ffeldes of Kyngesthorpe [was] than charged w^t the yerely rent of vi*d*., whyche was more than [they were] worthe, upon great and mature dlyberacion and advyse, by his gracious [grant], bearynge date at Westm the xvii day of Apryll, in the xx^th yere of his reigne, among other thynges did graunt unto the tenents [of the said] Towne of Kyngesthorpe, then beynge auncestors and p'decessors [of y^r orators], and to their heyres and successors, that they, their heyres, [etc., should have] and holde of his Hyghnes and of his heyres and successors the said [Towne], with all the members and apptenences, whatsoever they wer, to the same [Town belonging], from the day of the death of Johan, the late quene of England, for the time of xl yeres than next ensewyng, yelldyng therefore [to the said Kynge and his] successors deuryng the said tyme ffyftie pounds for all man^r of [rent] whyche to the same, his heyres or successors, or to any other psone, [by right ought to] be made or payed; and after the end of the said xl yeres your [most noble] p'genitor Kyng Edward the fourthe, uppon lyke consyderacions, dyd by his letters patents, bearynge date at Westm the ffyrst daye of June in the xv yere of his noble reigne, give and graunt unto the tenants and inhabitants of the said Towne of [Kyngesthorpe], then beyng p'decessors and auncestors of your beseechers, that they [their heyres and successors] shuld have and holde of his hyghnes and of his heyres and successors the Towne of Kyngesthorpe, with all the members and apptenences, whatsoever they were, to the same Towne belonging, from the ffeaste of Esture in the xiii yere of his noble reigne unto [the term of] other xl yeres than next ensewing, yelldyng therefore yerely to his hyghnes [his heyres and] successors deurynge the said time, ffyftie pounds for all man' of charges which to the same, his heyres or successors, or any other persone, by right shuld be made or payed, after the whyche end of xl yeres y^r Majte royall ... letters patent, bearynge date at Westm the xx^th day of

Decembre, in the [eighth] yere[1] of y^r Majte noble reigne, dyd gyve and graunt unto the said tenants of the said Towne of Kyngesthorpe then beyng that they, their heyres and [successors], shuld have and holde of y^r hyghnes and y^r heyres and successors [the said Towne], w^t all the members and apptenances, whatsoever they were, to the same [Towne] appertayning, from the ffeast of Seynt Mychaell the Archangel, in the viii yere [of y^r] most noble reigne, unto the end and term of xl yeres than [ensewing], yelldyng therefore yerely to your said hyghnes, your heyres and successors . . . Towne ffyftie pounds for all man' of charges and fermes whyche to your hyghnes or successors, or to any other psone, by your ryght ought to be [made or payed].

So it is, moste excellent soverayne Lord, that one Thomas Latham, underkeeper of the parke of Moulton in your said county of Northampton, adjoyning to the ffelde of Kyngesthorpe aforesaid, by the color of the custody of the said parke as well of [his own] power, as by the myght berynge and mayntenance of his ffriends, w^toute . . . color or consyderacion doyth daily norysshe and longtyme hath norysshed conyes as well in suche prells of errable ground w^tn the said ffeldes wherefore your said orators do p'ticularly paye yerely unto y^r said hyghnes [for every] acre v*d*., as also on the other lees and pastures lyinge w^tn the said ffeldes, [which] y^r said orators and their auncestors have alwayes kept and yett do kepe [for the] pasturage of their horses, neete, and shepe, for their lyveing and sustenance, [and which are] environed and compassed about with the corn ffelds of the said Towne, [and by] the occasyon of the great number of conyes, so in the pmysses wrongfully norysshed, the beasts, cattell, and shepe of your said orators do daily [pine] and be starved for lacke of meate, and their corne growynge in the said fields [is] yerely etyn, spoyled, and dystroyed in the quantitie of thre hundreth acres, for the

---

[1] *Vide* Royal Grant, No. X.

whyche ground your orators paye yerely to your Grace v*d*.
an acre, [and there is] no profytt of the same, whyche is to
their yerely loss and damage ... and above to their utter
undoyng and impovyshment, and doyth w^t [power] and
myght continue the same, and manasshethe and threapeth
so y^r said orators [that they] dare not for jeapdye of their
lyfe put away any of the said conyes ne make [any] resistance in the same onless they shuld gyve occasyon to have
your graces peace [broken] and stand in danger of their lyfe,
and so the said Latham hath yerely with power and myght
noryshed, brought up, and kylled yerely out of the said
ffelds, by the space of this vii yerys past, about the nombre
of two thousand, whyche comyth no pfytt ne gayn to your
gracious maieste by no man' [of means], notwithstandyng
that y^r said orators, y^r Grace's tenants, are greatly dampni-
fied and hurt by the same; yet furthermore, moste dread
soverayne Lord, the said Latham, [not] thus beyng contentyd, but of his further crueltie, injuriousness, and froward
mind usually beatythe and woundythe the shephds and
herdmen, y^r subjects, whyche do kepe the shepe or beasts
of y^r said orators upon the said ffelds of Kyngesthorpe, and
kylleth their doggs, beyng tyed in at their gyrdells, and
menasshethe and threateneth the said shpds of y^r orators
in such manr and forme that they dare not well kepe any
shepe or beasts in any such place whereas the said
Latham doyth of his myght and power norysh any conyes
in the ffelds of Kyngesthorpe aforesaid, whyche yerely paye
their rents truely to your Grace for the same, and all to
oppresse and trede under the fete y^r said poor tenants to
make them to [do after his] wyll and pleasure, so that if
quick redresse be not shortly hadd for [these things], your
said pore tenants and orators are lyke shortly to be utterly
undon and impoverished for ever, in tender consideracyon
whereof the premisses ... it may please y^r most excellent
majste of y^r accustomed justice ... to graunt y^r writ of

subpene to be dyrectyd to the said Thomas Latham commanding him by the same to appere before y^r moste honable Courte of ster[1] chambre at Westm' at a certyn daye and under a gret payn, ther to make answer unto the pmisses, and that y^r said orators may be [allowed] and authorysed by y^r moste noble grace from henceforthe to destroye and kyll the said conyes, accordyng to ryght and conscyence, and that the said Latham be compellyd to make recompence unto y^r said orators for their several [losses] and damages susteyned in that behalf, and to abyde such further order concernyng the pmisses as by y^r most noble grace shalbe thought to stand in ryght and conscuence.

[1] This court was established 3 Hen. VII. in violation of Magna Charta, but Henry only reduced to a system what former kings had done irregularly and occasionally, the King's Council having from time immemorial dealt with both civil and criminal causes, unfettered by the rules of law. The court was to be composed of the Lord Chancellor, the Lord Treasurer, the Keeper of the Privy Seal, a Bishop, a Lord of the Council, and the two Chief Justices; their power embraced the punishment of murders, robberies, perjuries, and 'unsureties of all men living,' in as full manner as if the offenders had been 'convict after the due order of the law' ('Annals of English History,' ii. 119).

XIII.

[The men of Kingsthorpe seem to have been very much in earnest on the coney question. The following document proves them to have been stronger in zeal and determination than in grammar and spelling.]

All true Cristen people to whome this present writyng shal come, rede here or see. We, John Hopkyns, husbondman, Peter Diconson, yoman [with forty-two other names], inhitannts and tennts of o^r sovaigne lord the kyng of hys town of Thorp, otherwyse called Kyngesthorp, in the countie of Northt^n, senden gretyng in o^r Lord God evlastyng. fforasmoche and where as nowe of late tyme certeyne discencōns, discords, variannces, and debats hathe ben and yet is dependyng betwenè us the foreseid kynge's tennts and oon Henry Maye, underkep^r of the kyng's prke called Moulton Prke, next Kyngesthorp afforseid, of, for, and upon the very trewe title, right, and possession of certeyne arrable lands, pasture, w^t thapptennces and with al other man^r of pfights in Kyngesthorp afforseid, wiche evmore hathe leyne, and of very trewe right hathe longed to the seid tennts of Kyngesthorp, and prcell of the ffee ferme of the seid town, wiche wase and hathe byn a great helpe, pfight, and socour to us afternamed tennts and our predecessours in mayntennce of o^r seid ffee fferme, accordyng unto divse grunts of divse kyngs to us therof grunted, wiche dothe pleynly expresse and shewe that we, the forseid tennts, owght to have the seid ffee fferme w^t all man^r com-

odities and p̄fights therunto belongyng, and specially, as it
dothe appere by the kyng oᵣ sovaigne Lord's moste honorable grunts to us lately grunted, not-wᵗ-standyng where as
the right honorable Sir Nicholas Vaux, knyght, late Lord
Vaux, decessed, ruler and master, kepᵣ of the forseid p̄rke,
of his myghty power and auctoritie by force kepte and with-
held from us afforenamed and oᵣ predecessours, tennts of
Kyngesthorp afforseid, the forseid arrable lands, felds, and
pastures, and occupied the same as waren grownds, and
wold not suffre oᵣ p̄decessours to enyoy the same accordyng
to the seid graunt, but wᵗheld the same by strong power
and might unto suche tyme as oᵣ seid p̄decessours were
fayne to make sute unto the kyng's grace that ded is ffadre
unto oᵣ sovaigne lord the kyng, who[se] soul J̄hu p̄rdon, by
fforce, wherof at that tyme it wase fynally concluded and
detmyned by the kyng's moste honorable counsaile then
beyng that the forseid then tennts of Kyngesthorp, oᵣ p̄de-
cessours, shuld enyoy the seid lands now in variannce as their
owne as p̄rcell of the ffee fferme to theym and their successours for ev, accordyng to their grunt.　Notwᵗstandyng
aftward thurghe entreatie and desier of the forseid Lord
Vaux, and for and by cause the seid Lord Vaux shuld be
goode and lovyng to oᵣ forseid p̄decessours and to al the
town afforsaid for the sum of 13s. 4d. stling yerely, to be
paied towards the p̄fight off Kyngesthorp afforseid, for a
knowlege that the forseid lands wase theires, the seid then
tennts were contented that the seid Lord Vaux and his de-
puties shuld have the occupacōn of the forseid land and
grownds now in traves[1] from yere to yere at the pleasures
of oᵣ seid p̄decessours, and for no longer tyme, wiche wase
and hath byn a great hyndernnce of al dwellars and tennts
there, and yet is, and nowe where as we thabovenamed
kyngs tennts immediatly after the decesse of the forseid
Lord Vaux in savyng the right and title of the forseid town

[1] In dispute.

entred peasiblie upon the pmisses as prcell of or ffee fferme
and accordyng to the kyng's grunts to us therof grunted.
Albeit the forseid Henry Maye, now underkepr of the seid
prke of Moulton, by force and strong mayntennce hathe
wtstand oure possession, and of pure malice and mayntennce
hathe indicted al us affornamed, the kyng's tennts, of riott,
and untrewly forswere hym that his evydence wase true, and
so by force dothe wthold the seid lands from us contrary to
al good right and consience, to or utter undoyng, except
shorte remydie there for maie be had and founde. Knowe
al men therfore by these presents, us the affornamed al the
kyng's tennts of oon assent and consent to have ordeyned,
made, assigned, and constituted, and by these presents do
ordeyn, make, assign, and lawfully constitute or right trustie
and well belovyd neighbours John Hopkyns, Peter Diconson,
Thomas Reve, and Simon Bacon, or ffaithful, laufull, and
trew attoneys, pctours joyntly and sevally to folowe, psecute,
pcede, implede, deffend, and spede ayenst the fforseid
Henry Maye and al other for him or in his name what so
ever ther be by wey of peticon, compleynt, or other wyse, as
well afore or sovaigne lord the kyng and his moste honorable
counsaile as in eny other court or courts, spuall or tempall,
wt in this the kyng's royalme, afore eny juges or justices, of
and for recorde of al the forseid lands nowe beyng in traves,
gyffyng and gruntyng to or seid attorneys and pctos or full
auctoritie and power and comandement to maynteyne and
folowe in or name and sted ayenst the seid Henry Maye and
al others, and to make sute as is afforeseid, consnyng the
pmises, and furthermore, if nede shal requyre, to make, constitute, and retain in the names, and for us divse attorneys,
counselos, and pctors to the further mayntennce of the sute
in this be halfe to be had and doon, and furthermore, if nede
that requyre, to make by vtue herof divse instruments, as
many as shalbe thought necessarie, to be had for the ful
spede of or seid matters and causes, and also fynally to folow,

psecute, conclude, and detme of and in al the pmisses after
form of law as best shalbe thought and devyse to be had,
doon, and made, as thoughe wee thabovenamed inhitnnts
were there in o^r owen ppr prsonys present. In wittnesse
wherof to this o^r present writyng we have sett o^r sealles, and
for a more faithffull wittnesse, suertye, and knowlege of the
pmisses to be trewe, we have hereunto set the comon seal of
Kyngesthorp afforseid, dated the xii daie of October the
yere of the reigne of o^r forseid sovaigne lord the kyng, by
the grace of God of England and France kyng, deffendor of
the faithe, and Lord of Irland[1] after the conquest the fif-
teeneth.

[1] The word eighth has been omitted here.

XV.

This Indenture, made in the ffest of the Anunciacon of
oure Ladye, in the xx yere of the reign of kyng Herry the 8th
of Englond and of France, kyng, defender of the feythe,
and lord of Irelond, [between] Peter Dyconson [balyffe], of
the townshyppe and lybtres of Kyngesthorpe, in the countie
of Northton, Richard Brouke and John Chese, constables,
of the same townshyppe, and all the hole commynalty therof,
onne ptie, and Agnes Hayward, of the town of Northᵗ,
wedowe, and Ambrose Walker, of the same town of Northᵗ,
and Margarett his wyff, on the other ptie, witnessethe that
the said Peter Diconson, the constables and commynalty
afforseid, by one hole assent, concent, and agrement, have
graunted, dymysed, betaken, and to fferme letton, and by
these psents, graunten, dymysen, betaken, and to fferme
letton, all thow ther three water mills, wᵗ the apptennes and
all the apparell therunto belongyng, callyd the south mills
of Kyngesthorpe afforseid, late in the tenure and occupacon
of onne Willm Pntice of Northampton afforseid, whiche
seid three mills bene corne mills, and also almanʳ of apparell,
houses, damms, closurs, holms, medows, lesurs, and pasters,
willows, watʳs, diches, plytts, and comodytyes to all and evy
of the seid mills apprtenyng or belongyng, and also the
south mill holm[1] wᵗ the apprtennes, to have and to holde

---

[1] 'Holm' = the island formed between the river and the mill back-
water.

all the fforsaid three mills and other the p̄misses, w^t all and
synguler ther apprtenncs, as it is above said, unto the said
Agnes Hayward, Ambrose Walker and Margarett his wyffe,
and to one other p̄sone ther laufull and sufficyent assigney,
and to evy of theym ffrome the daye of the makynge herof
unto the end and trme of 21 yers then next onsuwyng, and
fully to be complette and ended, yeldyng and payinge ther-
for yerely duryng the said terme unto the said balyffe, counstables, and commynaltie, ther successours or assigns, eight
mark stlyng, that is to saye, for the seid mills onely and for
the seid south mill holme yerely vis. viiid. stlyng, ffor the
yerely rent of the waters iiis. viid. stlyng, and for the wold
cye yerely xiid. at towe times in the yere usuall, that is to
saye, the ffest of Seynt Michell tharchanngell and the Anun-
cyacon of our Ladye, by evyn porcons, and if it ffortune the
seid rents or any p̄rcell therof to be behynd unpayd in p̄rte
or in all by the space of one moneth next after any of the
seid ffests at the whiche it ought to be paid, and not paid if
it be laufully askyd, then it schall be laufull for the seid
balyfe, counstables, and ther successours and assigns to put
in to evy of the seid three mills and other the p̄mysses, w^t
ther apptenncs, and distreyn, and the distresse so ther hadde,
found, and taken laufully, to leede, dryve, carry, and chase
aweye, and theym to w^thold and kepe unto such tyme the
seid rent or rents and the rrerages therof, if any be to theym,
be trulye contentyd and paid, and if it ffortune the seid
rent or rents or any p̄cell therof to be behynd unpaid in
prte or in all by the space of towe moneths, after any of the
seid ffests at the which it ought to be paid, if it be laufully
askyd, then it shall be leefull to the seid balyffe, counstables,
ther successors and assignes, to reenter into all the seid
three mills and other the p̄mysses, w^t all and singler ther
apptenncs and evy p̄rcell therof, and theym to enyoye and
have ayayn as in ther first estate this indenture in [any]
wyse notwithstandyng, provided alwaye duryng the seid

leasse that the seid Agnes Hayward, Ambrose Walker and
Margarett, and their one assigney as is afforseid, shall not
let nor set to fferme any of the seid three mills or any other
of the pmysses to any prsone or prsones beyng spuall. The
seid Agnes, Ambrose, and Margarett covennten and graunten
to and with the seid balyffe and counstables, that theye and
ther assigney schall and sufficyently duryng the seid terme
of xxi yeres repare, susteyn, maynteyn, and kepe uppe or
cause to be repared, maynteyned, and kept uppe all and
singler the seid iii mills, w^t ther appurtnncs, as well in dep-
ness, higthe, lengthe, and bredythe as in all other man^r of
repcons and apparrell of mill warke, houses, ston walls, ston
tymber warkmanschipp, kepyng lawschards[1] and schoryng
of diches to evy of the seid mills and other the pmysses belongyng at ther costs and charges, and so all these seid iii
mills at the end of the seid terme they well and sufficyently
reparyd shall leve by the ovsyght of six indefferent men of
Kyngesthorpe afforseid, and ov that the seid Agnes Hayward
Ambrose Walker, Margarett, and ther one assigney shall
yerely duryng the seid terme discharge all the afforseid
townshipp mills and other the pmysses of and for almanr
of tythe duwe from the date herof, or to be duwe to
the prsone of Kyngesthorpe afforseid, or to any other prson
or prsones, and of and for all other manr of charge belongyng to the kyng, if any fall, ensuwyng out of the seid mills
and other the pmysses att ther' own costs and charges ;
ffurthermore, the said Agnes, Ambrose, and Margarett, and

---

[1] 'Lawshard,' sometimes written 'lowshard and 'laushard.' In
No. XI. we find 'kepyng the lowshard of the banks of the river.' Aker-
man's 'Wiltshire Glossary' has the word 'linchard,' meaning a pre-
cipitous slip of land on a hillside left untouched by the plough—from
A.S. *hline*, a bank. Keeping the lowshard or laushard of the banks,
which seems to have been the ordinary duty of the miller, may have
been keeping the river bank in proper form by cutting back the rushes
and other vegetation obstructing the watercourse. 'Shard' means
something shredded off ; we find further on in this indenture 'shreddyng
of the trees,' *i.e.*, topping them. Or, perhaps, lowshard may be only
another form of lowshot, which is in use here for overshot.

their assigney shall yerely duryng the seid terme at all tymes
gryndc or cause to be ground alman^r of grayn and corne that
to any of the said mills shall be brought by any inhabitant or
inhabitants of Kyngesthorpe aforesaid, and to serve theym
and evy of theym at the fyrst comyng unto the seid mills
before any straunger[1] as sone the bene or benys shall be
emptye, and also the said Agnes, Ambrose, and Margarett,
and ther assigney duryng the seid terme shall yerely paye
or cause to be paid towards the mowyng of the south mill
holmes ii*s.* ii*d.* stlyng, provided alwaye by the presents that
it shallbe lefull to the seid Agnes, Ambrose, and Margarett,
and ther assigney, yche of theym yerely duryng the seid
trme to have, receyve, and take to ther use and uses almaner
of laufull loppe and schreddyng of trees belongyng to the
same mills and other the pmysses, w^t ther apptnnces, wt out
any impechement of waste, plukynge uppe, fellyng, or destroying of trees wt out license of the Balyffe of Kyngesthorpe aforeseid. In witnesse wheroff to the one pte of
these indentures remaynyng with the seid Agnes, &c., or
one of them, the said Balyffe, counstables, and comnalty of
Kyngesthorpe aforeseid have sett their comyn seall of the
townshipp, and to the other pte remaynyng with the said
Balyffe, constables, &c., and their successors, the said Agnes,
Ambrose, &c., have sette ther sealls the daye and yere
aboveseid. Provided alwaye that the said Agnes, Ambrose,
&c., shall yerely paye duryng the seid trme for Walbek
brouke unto the seid Balyfe, &c., viii*d.* stlyng, pvided alwaye
that the seid Agnes, Ambrose &c. shall yerely have and
occupye during the terme aforeseid the south milne holme
from such tyme as the fyrst croppe be clerely off of the
grounde unto the fest of the purificacon of our Lady then
next ensewyng.

---

[1] This priority of having their corn ground was secured to the inhabitants by the Ordinances (1547), art. 64.

XVIII.—Part I.

Examinacions taken at the Town of North[n] the xxvi day of Aprill, in the xxxiii[d] yere of our Soverayne Lord Kyng Henry the eight, by Sir Edward Montagu, Knyght, and Sir Thomas Tresham, Knyght, by virtue of a commyssion to them dyrected for the parte of the Inhabitants of the Towne of Boughton and Pysford against Thomas Latham.

Henry Tanner, of Boughton, in the Countie of North[n], husbondman, born in Cokefeld, in the Countie of Sussex, tenant and servant to my Lord Vaux, of the age of 57 yeres, sworne and examined, deposeth and saith upon his othe in man[r] and forme folowing, that is to say, that he hath dwelt in Buckton, in the said Countie of North[n], these 40 yeres past and above, and by all that tyme he nev[r] knowe ne harde that Anne, late Countess of Warwick, or any other psone or psones beyng owners of the man[r] of Moulton, ne any keap[r] of the park of Moulton, ever claymed to be warreners or ever had or claymed to have any franke or free waren wit[n] the feldes of Buckton and of Pysford.

And he saith further upon his oathe that above 40 yeres now past one Thomas Aylmer, being Bayliffe then of Buckton aforesaid, and servant unto Sir Thomas Greene, Knight, with whom this depnent at that tyme dwelled, kept in hys owne house at Buckton aforesaid as well greyehoundes, ferretts, purse netts, and other yngines for the kyllyng of conyes, and that at that tyme he did accustomably kyll conyes in the said feldes of Buckton and Pysford, both wit his long bow, his dogge, ferretts, and pursenetts, w'out lett or intrupcion of any pson or psones. And he saith further that the said Thomas Aylmer wold nevr rydde betwene Northn and Buckton but that he wold have his crossbowe hangyng at his sadle bowe wt hym, to the intent to kyll conyes by the waye. Itm, the said deponent knoweth not howe and after what manr the furst brede and encrease of conyes began witn the said feldes of Buckton and Pysford, and further saith that he knoweth not whether the furst borowes and clappers[1] for conyes were made by the hande of man or by onely dyggyng and labours of conyes, and howe many yeres past the furst borow or clapper began this deponent knoweth not. And further this deponent saith that he hymself all hys lyfe tyme hath kyllyd conyes there wt his bowe and dogge without denyall of any keapr there or of any other pson or psones untill now wtn these ii yeres last past the said Thomas Latham did forbydde hym to kyll any conyes there; and ffurther this deponent saith that the tennts and inhtants of Buckton and Pysford have ever frely at their owne pleasure hunted and kyllyd conyes w'out lett or intrupcion of any keapr there. And saith further that the late Lord Vaux was owner of the Lordship of Buckton and Pysford at the same tyme that he was keapr of the said park of Molton. And further he deposeth the said Latham hath nourysshed and mayntened many clappers of conyes wtn the churche yarde of Buckton aforesaid, insomuche that the great number of conyes wtn the same have dygged up many mennys bones in the same churche yarde, that it is dangerous for men to go in it for breaking of their necks. And further what number of conyes the said Latham, defendaunt, hath yerely kyllyd out

---

[1] From French *clapier*, a hutch ; a coneyhole or clapar (Palsgrave). A clapper for conies, *i.e.*, a heap of stones or earth, with boughes or such like, whereunto they may retire themselves, &c. (Minshen).

of the said feldes by the space of vii yeres this deponent knoweth not. And further this deponent saith that grasse ground lying in the feldes of Buckton and Pysford, turned up by the conyes whiche the said Latham there nourysshed, amounteth to the number of ii^c (200) acres, and further a great part of their corn destroyed by the said conyes, but of what value the corne is of this deponent knoweth not. And further this deponent saith that their charge to make redy one acre of grounde to be sowne w^t rye or barley, and to sowe the same w^t rye or barley, amounteth to *vs.* at the lest. And further he saith upon his othe that there lyth xxx acres of tyllage land this yere laye for fere lest it shuld be destroyed w^t conyes, and what number of acres hath lyen laye¹ these vii yeres past he knoweth not. And further this deponent saith that the great number of conyes hath so overronne and underdigged their feldes and devoured and spoyled their comon, whereupon their bests and cattel shuld lyve, by means whereof the bests and cattel of the Inhabts of Buckton ben almost sterved and redy to dye for hunger. And further this deponent saith that the said Latham hath kylled their herde dogges whose names hereafter followeth : Thomas Mylle, Willm Cane, Thomas Wilbe ; and also did sore beate and wounde one Symon West of Boughton, aforesaid, w^t his dagger, to the great pell of the said Symon lyff. And further examined howe he knoweth the same, saith that he was psent at the same tyme when the said West was so hurt by the said Latham ; and further this examinate saith that the said Latham hath forbydden the Inhabts of the said Towne of Bouckton to use their long bowes in their feldes, and hath taken bowes away from dyverse yong men that hath byn shotyng in the feldes there. And moreover this examinate saith that the said Latham and his folk byn of suche a stobberne and froward mynde against all men that walke in the said feldes of Bouckton w^t dogges, that about

---

¹ 'Lye laye,' *i.e.*, untilled ; layland = fallow (Cowell).

iii yeres past one John Wyntr, s̄v̄nt to the said Latham, made assaute of one Marten Williams, s̄v̄nt to mastr Humfrey, of Boughton aforesaid, bycause he was wont to walke in the felds of Boughton wt doggs, and there slewe the said Williams.

[Then follows John Crow's evidence, almost identical with the preceding ; in the latter part he says :]

And that there is so great a nomber of conyes in the said feldes that they have turned up and made borowe at the lest iiᶜ [200] acres of grasse grounde, and that there is in the said feldes yerely by the said conyes eten and spoyled iiiixx [fourscore] acres of tyllage londs, wherby oftetymes they have not corne to sowe their londs agayne. And also they [were] compelled, fore feare lest they shuld losse all aswell their corne sowne as their labor, to lett a hundred acres of land lye leye, to the uttr undoyng of the poure Inhitannts of the same Townes. And saith further that the Churche yarde of Boughton aforesaid is so dygged wt the conyes whiche the said Latham hath there norysshed, that a man can go skantly in a corner of yt but he shall fynde it full of dead mennes bones, a thing most pytyous to be seen, and that the said Latham will not suffer this examinate nor hys chyldren to use shottyng wt their long bowes on his grounde.

[Willm Wilbe, of Bouckton, says :]

'That the nombr of conyes that have byn nourysshed in the said feldes have yerely eaten and destroyed by the space of vii yeres c [100] acres of sowne lond, whiche hath amounted every acre to xs., which now [is] clerely lost ; and further this examinate sayth that they be compelled, for care lest conyes shuld destroye it, to lett at the lest xx acres of land to lye leye whiche was sowne wtn these iii yeres. And further this examinate saith that the said Thomas

Latham aboute vi yeres nowe past did sore beate and wound one Symon West w^t a wood knife to the pell of his lyfe bycause his dogg did ronne at conyes in Kyngesthorpe feld ; and further examined howe he knoweth this to be true, deposeth and saith that immediately after the said West [was] wounded, this deponent cam to the said West's house to Kyngesthorpe, and there kept hym by the space of foure dayes, fearyng that all that tyme he wold have died. And further this examinate saith that one John Wynter, svnt to the said Latham, dyd kyll one Martyn Williams, svnt to Maistr Humfrey, of Boughton, thre yeres past, but for what cause he knoweth not, and more cannot depose.'

[John Miller, of Sprotton, husbondman and freeholder, repeats nearly the same evidence :]

' He hath known all the keap^{rs} of Molton park that hath byn these xl yeres, yet he never knewe any of theym to kyll any conyes out of the said parke, and further saith that he hath seene in his tyme suche a lytell number of conyes w^tn the said feldes, that his neighbours could not kyll w^t their ferretts skantly one conye in a houre there ; but howe these conyes furst came into the said feldes this examinate knoweth not.'

[Edmond Wryght, of Pysford, in the course of his evidence :]

' Saith further that he hath yerely sustained these vii yeres past suche losse, by reason that the conyes abydyng in their felds hath spoyled his corne, that he is almost uttirly undon sines he came to the Towne, and saith further that in harvest nowe ii yeres past he sent his srvts into the felds w^t his dogge to dryve swyne oute of his corne, w^t whom ii of Latham srvts did mete, and not only kylled his dogge, but also beate his srvts very sore. And saith further that one the morrowe next folowing Latham hymselfe came w^t iiii other men to this examinate, unto the feldes where he had a nother dogge lying by his carte in the felde, and there forthe w^t kylled his other dogge w^t a woodknife.'

[Richard Carvell, of Harlston :]

The great nomber of conyes nourisshed by the said Latham have so underminded the Churchyarde of Bouckton aforesaid, that it wold abhorre any Crystiane manys harte in the world to se it. And also the said Latham, not myndyng to have the said conyes destroyed w^tn the said churchyarde, will not suffer any dogges to rome w^tn the said churchyarde, but will kyll them. And also this examinate saith that the fourthe pte at the lest of the corne and grasse of the said Townes is spoyled and destroyed by the said great nomber of conyes remaining in their feldes, over and beside the destruction of their comon, so that it is an great starvyng and famysshyng of their bests, to the utter undoyng of the said Inhabtnts, this beside the losse of their corne.

[William Starmer, of Harlston :]

And there byn norrysshed in Buckton church yarde many conyes, by means whereof they byn many dead mennes bounes dyggyd up and gnawen w^t conyes. And the inhabitants being able goo to the said churche evry holyday to hygh masse and dyverse tymes in the week days. And the said Thomas Latham hath had yerely this vii yeres as he supposeth iv or v thousand cople of conyes w^tn the felds of Bouckton and Pysford; and he knoweth that one Wynter, servant to Thomas Latham, cam to one Robt Porter, beyng shephard to this examinate, havyng a dogge in hys strynge at his gyrdell, and cott the dogges throte, and divers tymes bett the same Porter, so that he wold no longer kepe shepe in the folde of Pysford; and also he kylled the nettsherd dogge called John Mondyn, and bett one Thomas Warde and broke his hedde.

(Signed) Edward Montagu, Thomas Tresham.

Part II.

Examinacions taken at the Towne of North_n the xxvi day of April, in the xxxiii' yere of the reigne of our Soveraine Lord Kyng Henry the viiith, before Sir Edward Montague, Knyght, Sir Thomas Tresham, Knyght, and Richard Catesby, Esquyer, by virtue of the Kyng's Comission to theym dyrected for the pte of Thomas Latham, keap^r of the Parke of Molton.

Richard Scott, of the Towne of Northampton, of the age of lxxiii yeres, born at Norton Davyd, otherwyse called Bromsnorton, in the countie of North^t, where he dwelt unto suche tyme as he came unto the age of xii yeres or therabouts, and from thence he went to Boughton, where he dwelt from the tyme that he was of the age of xii yeres until he came to the age of xxiii yeres, and from that tyme to the day of the taking of these deposityons he hath dwelt in the said Towne of Northampton . . . . all the said tyme he dwelt in Boughton aforesaid after that he was svnt to John Colls, Esquyer, by the space of x yeres next ensuyng his departyng from Boughton, sworne and examyned, deposeth and saith that one Watkyn Chundeler, beying svnt to Kyng Richard the iii^d, was keap_r of Molton pke, in the said countie of North^{ton}, all the tyme of his reigne, and had warren of conyes and other bests and fowles of waren aswell in the felds of Kyngesthorp, Boughton, and Pysford as in the said Molton Parke and felds of Northampton ; also he saith that the conyes in Kyngsthorp felds had moste comonly their . . . and resort in and upon the north fylde of the said Towne. . . . Also he saith that one Nicholas Asshcton, gent

beyng under keap^r to Sir James Harryngton, knyght, of the said
pke, James a Latham, yoman, and William Harryngton, yoman,
underkeap^{rs} to the said Sir James of the said waren and conyes
wtin the said felds of Kyngsthorp, &c., from the beginning
of the reigne of Kyng Henry the vii untyll Blackheyth feld,[1]
which the said deponent supposd was above the space of
xiv or xv yeres, had the keapyng of the said waren, toke the
pfits of the conyes w^{t}in all the said felds of Kyngesthorp, &c.,
wtout lett or intrupcion of any pson or psones ; and
further the said deponent . . . sayd William Harryngton
. . . . Sir John Chese beyng chauntry prest of Boughton,
at the dore of hys chauntry for huntyng in the said waren.
And over that the said deponent saith that to his jugement
the nomb^r of conyes w^{t}in the said felds of Kyngesthorp,
Boughton, and Pysford is rather encreased then mynyshed,
but not to any suche nomb^r that the corne and grasse grow-
yng in the same felds is clerely destroyed and spoyled. . . .
. . . . . . there are not the thride part the nomber that
were there in the tyme of the said Sir James Harryngton.
And imedyatly after the said Backhethfeld the said Sir
James Harryngton was put from the office of the said Pke
and waren, and then the same office was gyven to Sir
Nicholas Vaux, and he was Mast^r Keap^r of the said Pke
and waren . . . his life, which was by the estymacion
[of the said deponent the] space of xxviii yeres . . .
H. Maye, gent, was his underkeap^r of the said pke and
waren, and had the keapyng and pfetts of the conyes w^{t}in
the said felds of Kyngsthorp, &c., duryng the said tyme of
xxviii yeres or therabouts, savyng at one tyme aboute
xxi yeres past the inhabytaunts of the said towneship of
Kyngsthorp complayned to the kyng's moost honorable
counsaill that the said keap^r and warener had increased the

---

[1] Blackheathfield, A.D. 1497. Parliament had granted a subsidy for
the war in Scotland ; but the people of Cornwall resisted the tax and
marched upon London, but were defeated at Blackheath June 22, and
their leaders executed.

nomber of the conyes witn the felds of Kyngsthorp aforesaid
so greatly, that their corne and grasse in the same felds of
Kyngsthorp was utt^rly destroyed and spoyled, and when they
could not upon their said complaynt gain redresse and
remedy, that then the said inhabitaunts did put in tyllage
and ayre w_t ploughs the same ground where the conyes had
made their clappers and had their moost resorte ; and after
the death of the said Sir Nicholas Vaux . . . son Lord
Harryngton had . . . beyng his underkeap^r by the space
of iii or iiii years; and the same Richard Humphrey had
Wagstaff under him to walk and keape the said warens, and
duryng the said tyme of iii or iiii yeres the said Richard Humfrey and his underkeap^r had the keapyng of the said waren,
and toke the pfetts of the conyes in a peysable man^r, as
any other prsone or prsones dyd at tyme w^tin the remem-
braunce of the said deponent.

John Relson, of Kyngsthorp . . . of the age of lxxi years
or therabouts . . . in the said townes of Boughton and
Kyngsthorp by the space of lv yeres last past, and now he
is a bedesman in Seynt Devys in Kyngsthorp aforesaid,
sworne and examyned, deposeth and saith that he did know
James Latham, Nicholas Aysheton, and William Harryngton,
underkeps to Sir James Harryngton, knyght, whiche Sir
James had by the kyng's gyft the keapyng of the said parke,
and his said underkeap^rs had the keapyng of the conyes
w^tin the said felds of Kyngsthorpe, &c., and toke the pfetts
of the same conyes by the space of xiiii or xv yeres, but
whether they had any waren w^tin the said felds of Kyngsthorp, &c., or not, he knoweth not, and furthermore, the
said deponent saith that the nomb^r of conyes is increased in
the felds of Kyngsthorp in dyverse places, wherby the grasse
and corne that groweth yerely there is greatly hyndred and
apeyred,[1] but he saith that he hath known many moo conyes

[1] 'Apeyred': injured, impaired; apeyringis = losses in Wyck-
liffe's New Testament, quoted in Halliwel, ' But whiche thyngs weren
to me wynningys, I have deemed these apeyryngis for Crist' (Phil. iii. 7).

w^tin the said felds in a certeyn place called Blackwell Hill
than are at this present day of his deposition.

Richard Abbey, of the towne of North^n, of the age of
lxii yeres . . . saith that one Sir James Harryngton,
Knyght, at the begynnynge of the reigne of Kyng Henry
VIIth, was maist^r keap^r of Moulton pke, and in that tyme
one Thomas Abbey, father to the said Richard, another
called John Lawforde, of the seid towne of Northamp^n,
bocher, went oute of North^n towne in a dark nyght w^t a
lantern and a candell lyght in the same unto the warren
betwene the felds of the said towne of North^n and Kyngsthorpe feld, intending to stele conyes w^t a ferrett and purse-
nette, and then the underkeap^r of the said pke for that
tyme beyng mette w^t them, and they told him they went to
seek for a bullock that was broken from them, and they
inquired if the said keap^r had sene any, and he said nay,
and dyd bydde them goe on theyr weys to loke if they could
fynde hym, and after they were depted from hym they had
that that they dyd come for.

Part III.

Examinacion taken at North^n the xxvi daye of Aprill
anno reg. H. VIII. xxxiii, before Sir Edward Montagu and
Sir Thomas Tresham, for the parte of the Inhabitants of
the towne of Bockton and Pysford by virtue of the said
comission to the said Sir Edward and Sir Thomas directed.

Robert Crow of Harlestone, of the age of lx yeres, sworne
and examyned, deposeth and saythe . . . that he never
knewe that any psones beyng Lords of Molton at any tyme
claymed or had any frewarren w^tn the townes or feldes of
Bockton or Pysford . . . he knoweth one Thomas Aylmer,
beyng bayliff of Bockton, and divers others of the tenants
of Bockton, kepe greyhoundes, ferretts, hounds, and nettes,
and hunted daylie and kylled both hayres and conyes to

the wall of Molton pke, wᵗout any manʳ of denyall by any
keapʳ there, which he knoweth to be true, for that this
examinate hath gon and hunted hymself among theym
many tymes, and never denyed until the tyme of one
Latham, beyng underkeapʳ to Sir Nicolas Vaux, late Lord
Vaux, decessed, beyng the Lord of Bockton and Pysford,
and keapʳ of Molton Pke, and they suffered the conyes to
increase for the Lord's plesure, whiche then were few in
number to those that be nowe there. The tenants myght
then take their plesure for the same conyes, so that they
wuld then do small hurte, and now the churchyarde of
Buckton is so full of concy earthes and conyes, and ther be
bones of dede psones dygged up wᵗ conyes in the same
churche yarde whiche would fylle a scutle. And the inhabitants of Buckton beyng able, do go evy holyday to the
said churche to hear masse and service on week dayes also,
and this examt sayth further that the conyes whyche the
said Thomas Latham hath yerely taken in Buckton and
Pysford feld hath byn worthe yerely to hym and hys master
xiii*li.* vi*s.* viii*d.* at the least, and there is destroyed wᵗ the
great number of conyes in grasse grounde and corne
grounde above c. acres, by means whereof their cattill byn
lost and pynyd for lack of mete, and if there were no conyes,
the inhabitants of Buckton and Pysford would sowe yerely
fourty quarters of corne more than they now doo or dare
sowe for feare of destruction wᵗ conyes, for there lyeth
above lxxx acres of grounde leye and unsown for fear of
the conyes wᵗn the said two felds of Buckton and Pysford
. . . and the rent, sowyng, arying, foldynge, and sedynge
of an acre of rey wyll cost the tenant therof fyve shillings
and above, and an acre of barley iii*s.* iv*d.*, and he thynketh
upon hys othe that there be xx acres of rey and barley
destroyed in Buckton and Pysford wᵗ conyes, and he saith
further that Thomas Latham, now keapʳ, dyd beat and kyll
one Martyn Williams, svnt to Richard Humfrey, in Buckton

6

feld, because the same Williams chalenged the said Latham
for breaking of hedges of Mr. Humfrey, and hath beaten
one Simon West upon the hedde and in the necke that he
never lyked after,[1] and also the same Latham shott at a
great masty of the said Richard Humfrey standyng in Mr.
Humfrey's dore, and shote hym thorowe, and also kylled a
shepperd's dogge of one Canne, a shepperd, beyng in the
churche yarde, and bett divers childern, shepherds, and
svnts in suche sorte that they durst not kepe a dogge
in the felde, and so toke from one Pallady a bowe and
arrowes, and from dyvers others, and wold not suffre any of
the inhabitants of Buckton ne Pysford to shotte in the
comn felds wᵗ ther long bowe, but toke away the same and
put the owners of the same in danger of ther lyves if they
sayd any thing.

[Next follows the evidence of Richard Wade to nearly
the same effect. Amongst other things he says :]

' An acre of lande sown in reye stondeth the tenant in
sowing vii shillings at the lest, and there ley in Buckton
felde above thirty acres, whiche the tenants dare not sowe
for feare of destruction wᵗ the conyes.'

[Speaking of Latham, he says :]

' He will not suffre any shepperd to have a dogge at hys
gyrdell in the feld.'

[Part of Richard Wade's evidence is as follows :]

'That he knewe Sir James Harryngton, who had the
keaping of Molton pke above fiftie yeares synes, at whiche

---

[1] To lyke = to be in flourishing condition. Comp. Ps. xcii. 13,
'They shall be fat and well liking;' Dan. i. 10, 'Why should he see
your faces worse liking?'

tyme he hard hys ffather saye that there was but four conyes in Buckton and Pysford feld, and that the fyrst conyes that were brought in those feldes were brought by one Master Greene, Lord of Buckton, who dygged a clapper for theym in Pysford felde, and he never knewe any keapr pretende to have any fre warren,' etc., etc.

XIX.

Ordinances and Statutes made by the consent of all the inhabitants of the Towne of Kyngesthorpe in the tyme of Robert Coke, Bayly there, anno primo Edwardi sexti (1547).

1. Fyrst, the great Corttes called the Leetes, holden at Easterne and Mychelmas the dayes that the said Corttes and Leetes shall be holden, shallbe kept and begone at ix or x of the clocke in the fore nowne, and that every person or persones whiche to yt are sommoned to appere at the said courttes shallbe their at evy tyme or tymes, upon lawfull warnynge, upon payne of every one makyng de-faute, x*d*.

2. Item, that all suters to the said courttes that be warned lawfully shall the one day of the said courte to appere in ppre person, or elles assyned, or elles amerced xii*d*., the seconde day to appere in ppre person, or elles to be amerced xii*d*.

3. Item, if any customery tenant or suter or other person do revyle, rebuke, or dysobey the Baily or the Steward at any other tyme, for any matter concernyng their office, that then they to forfait to the said offycers iii*s*. iv*d*.

4. Item, if any costomery tenant or suter at any tyme do rebuke, revyle, or dysobey the constables, thurbarowes, ale-tasters, haywarde, or other officers sworne in doyinge

their offyce, to forfayt to the said offecers as often as they so do vi*d*.

5. Item, that they [who brewe beer] to sell within the Towne but too, three, or elles foure at the most in every week . . . or other brewynge vesselles of their owne, and assyned by the Bayliffe of the . . . uppon payne of every one makynge defaute vi*s*. viii*d*., the one halfe . . . or halfe to the use of the Towne.

6. Item, that there shall . . . in any ale wyth out the Towne to sell agayne wythin the Towne, with out license of the Bayliffe, uppon the payne of every one making defaute xii*d*.

7. Item, that no p̄sone shall withe in the said Towne harber or lodge any strawnge persones more then one night and one day in their howses, but they gyve the Bayliffe knowledge, upon every one makynge defaute iii*s*. iv*d*.

8. Item, that at every Leete, called the great Leete, too ffeerares to be chosen, the Bayliff to chose thone and the thurbarros an other, and they to assesse all amerciamentes that be putt in to their handes before the said Leete be adiorned, in payne of every on makynge defaute xii*d*.

9. Item, that every p̄sone that is found fauty by the xii men and worthy to avoyde the Towne shall avoyde the Towne by the day appoynted them to avoyde, uppon payne off every one makyng defaute v*s*. vi*d*.

10. Item, all thos p̄sones that dwell and kepe householdes in the same Towne, that were not ther borne, shall pay yerly to the said Towne iiii*d*. for their hedd unto the tyme they do by it out of the Bayliffe in the presens of the Courte.

11. Itm, that no p̄sones shall kepe and holde mo horses then for every x acres of errable land in his tenure one horse, as the olde custome before hathe beene, uppon payne for every moneth for every horse more then aforesaid lymyted x*d*.

12. Item, that no psones shall kepe any mare or mares withe in the libertes of the said Towne, except they kepe them in their owne severall closses, uppon payne of every one makynge defaute iii*s*. iv*d*.

13. Itm, all they that have neyt above a yere olde and have not free medowe of their owne, that ys to say, for every nette a quarten, and if they have mo, for every beast xii*d*., and that no man shall geeste¹ more cattell but his owne, except they hyer them, being mylchk beastes, uppon payne of every beast iii*s*. iv*d*.

14. Itm, the Bayliff to have the one halfe of the mylchk beastes' money and the Towne to have thother halfe.

15. Itm, that a free man, defendant, shall be assyned too tymes after he be warned, and the third courte shall appere in a plee of land or of dell, or elles to be amerced xii*d*., and if he come in at the fourthe courte day, that then he forthe withe to be condempned.

16. Itm, if any psone do knowledge any dett before the Bayliff on the Courte or besyde the Courte at any other tyme, at the sute of any persone or persones, that then it shall be lawfull for the said Bayliff, in all hast resonable, to make, leve, and dystrene for the said dett upon the goodes and cattelles of the said dettor or dettors, uppon the payne of iii*s*. iv*d*. of hym that resystethe the dystresse and the levynge of the said dett.

17. Itm, if the Bayliff do not mynyster justice in exe-cutynge his office consernynge the said compleyntes, as often as he is found fauty therin to forfayt to all other offecers withe in the said Towne vi*s*. viii*d*., and the halfe to use of the Towne and thother halfe to the said offeceres.

18. All thos lands that any man do purchase with in the said Towne, or that any man hathe by testament of other,

¹ 'Geeste.' The verb is not to be found in the glossaries. It means to place cattle to feed in the common pastures. 'Gisting' and 'agist-ment' are met with.

yt shallbe lawfull to them in their last dayes by vertu of their testament or elles by surrenders, accordynge to the olde awncient custome, to give, sell, or bequethe the same at lyberty.

19. Itm, yt shall not be lawfull to any childe of male or of female for to sell any landes or tenements unto the tyme the man childe be of the age of xxi yeres and the woman childe of xvi yeres.

20. Itm, if any psone sell any landes or tenements to any other psone withe in the said Towne or withe out, that the said seller of the said landes or tenements shall yelde thym upp in to the Bayliff's handes ix dayes before the courte unto the behoffe of the byer, and if any psone kyn to the seller withe in the fourth degree come withe in the said ix dayes, and aske a cate,[1] yt shallbe delyvered them the next courte day, to pay the monye that the byer shulde paye withe in ix dayes after the Court, or elles to lyes his cate or tytle, and havynge suche day of payment as the said seller and byer was agreed of, and the seller in the pleyne Courte in ppre persone, before the Bayliff and Steward, shallbe sworne to knowledge the truthe of the said bargaynes, and if their be any men borne withe in the Towne or franches man of the Town, will have the bargayne after the byures withe in the fourth degree have refused they to receive it before a straunge purchaser, and the same bargayne shall be kept hole and well to them as to the byures abovesaid in all maner of poyntes.

21. Itm, if ther be no cate of no psone withe in the said fourthe degree, nor no borne men nor franchesmen withe in the said ix dayes be asked, that then the said byer shall have lyvery off seison accordynge to the custome and maner in playne and full Courte.

22. Itm, if ther be any man of full age withe in the realme, and out of prison, or woman sole unmarid, that

---

[1] 'Cate,' *vide* Ordinances (1483), art. 17, and note.

ought to have any landes or tenementes by inheritance or
by will or by any maner of purchase, that they shall come
in to be admyted as heires or other wase to procede to
their possession withe in three Courte dayes next folowinge
after that they have any right to any suche landes or
tenements, or elles the Bayliffe shall seysse all such landes
and tenements in the Kynge's handes to the use of the
Towne for evermore.

23. Itm, that every heire, or such as have landes by will
or testament, shall paye for their sesianynge vi*s.*

24. Itm, that every purchaser shall pay for a cotsedill
sesianynge vii*s.*, and so after the rate to the leste parte.

25. Itm, for every quarton of medow south warde for the
sesianynge, v*s.*

26. Itm, for every acre of the furlonge that shottes uppon
walbekke close, the whiche furlonge ys called domynycall
Land, shall paye yerely to the kynge for every acre vi*d.*,
and for sesianynge of every acre of the same furlonge xii*d.*

27. Itm, the sesianynge of every acre that is purchased
in all other places, vii*d.* the acre.

28. Itm, for every quarton northe warde for the sesianynge, xl*d.*

29. Itm, if any psone withe in the boundes of the said
Towne draw at any psone in violence sword, dager, or
knyfe, or any other wepon, to fforffaytt to the said Towne at
every tyme that suche default is made xx*d.*, and if they
smyte withe the same and drawe blowde, to leys to the said
Towne xl*d.*

· 30. Itm, if any man do chaunge any landes or tenements,
gevynge botte to the sum of ii*s.* or about, so after the quan-
tyty as ys above said, to pay for sesionynge after costome
and maner.

31. Itm, that all common brewers that brewithe to sell
that in tyme of wynter, from Mychelmas to Candlemas,
thei shall not suffer no mane's servantes to be in their

howses after ix of the clock in the nyght, and in somer season from candlemas . . . hower of x of the clocke in the nyght uppon payn of penysshement . . .

32. Itm, that no suspect psones shall kepe no . . . Bayliffe or his assygnes, uppon pane for every . . . said Towne vs.

33. Itm, if any mane's cattell be distressyd for rent, dett, or trespass, or any other resonable thynge, and it in pound, that if any psone take it out withe out license of hym that so do impounde the said cattell, that then thei to forfayt to the said Town xl*d.*

34. Itm, that no man nor woman shall take into their hows or howses any myster[1] woman beyng with childe, ther to be dlyvered, wtout the lycence of the Bayly and her neyghboures, upon the payne of vis*h.* viii*d.* to the Bayly and vis. viii*d.* to the Towne as often as they so doe.

35. Itm, that evy parson that puttyth his matt^r to a Jure or unto arbitrament shall stand to suche ende as the Jure or arbitrars shall make, without further trobyll, uppon payne of xxs.

36. Itm, that no man shall make any highe waye, use or haunt on any other man's land, medowes, lesows, or pastures but suche as have ben of olde tyme accustomed out of mynde upon payne of xii*d.*

37. Itm, if any parson do brewe ale for the avayle of the churche, that all other brewers shall cesse for the tyme

---

[1] 'Myster woman,' *i.e.*, pauper; from *mistere*, a trade; *ministerium.* Hence mystery used in the sense of a trade, as in the phrase 'art and mystery'—a word, however, which has no connection with the word mystery (*mysterium*), and ought rather to be spelt 'mistery.' From the necessity of work and service probably arose the sense of want. Thus Chaucer's 'Romaunt of the Rose':

'That he of meat hath no mistere.'

In James V.'s answer to Henry VIII.'s letter counselling him to secularize the monasteries, he says, 'I thank God I am able to live well enough on what I have, and I have friends that will not see me mister.' —'Life of Sir Ralph Sadler.'

untill the churche ale be utteryd havyng lawfull warnynge upon payne of every pson doying the contrary xl*d.*

38. Itm, if any pson or psons as sell any tenement, land, medow, or pasture wn the Towne and feld of Kyngesthorpe, and do give no knowleage therof unto the Baily for the tyme beyng by the next court day after suche sale made, to lese for every hooll tenement vi*s.*, and so fourthe to the lest parte therof after that rate.

39. Itm, that if any parson do sell any medowe on the Towne syde of Kyngesthorpe, and do geve the sayd Baylye no knowleage therof by the next court, the seller to forfayte unto the said Towne for every quarter'n ii*s.*, and so fourthe after the same rate to the least part therof.

40. Itm, in lyke maner for every quartron medowe sold on the northe syde w*t*out knowleage gevyn to sayd Bayly as is aforesaid, the seller to forfayte to the Towne xx*d.*, and so fourthe after the same rate to the least part.

41. Itm, likewise for the sale of every acre of land the seller to forfayte to the Towne xii*d.*, and so fourthe after the same rate to the least part.

42. Itm, if any pson do denye the Kynge's highewaye w*t* stone or wood or any other thynge above one quarter of a yere except he be in buylding, he shall lose to the said Towne of Kyngesthorpe xii*d.*

43. Itm, if any pson do digge in Restoo Delfe on the whole herth, denying the highe waye, to lose to the said Towne for every lood xii*d.*

44. Itm, that noe person or psones of this Towne shall cary no furrys[1] but there owne excepte Restowe Delff, uppon payne of every one making defaute xii*d.*

45. Itm, that noe parson shall suffre no kyte, busserd, pye, nor flesshe crowe to brede and ther yonge to fly away from the grounde, uppon payne of losyng xii*d.*, and the said

---

[1] *Vide* Court Roll, p. 33. 'Qd Georgius Madler non cariabit les furres. . . nisi proprias vepres.'

xii*d.* so forfayted shallbe gethered Whitson weeke by the
Baylye, and the money theerof to goe to the mendynge of
the hye wayes.

46. Itm, that the six Thurbarrowes shall present the
trespasses unto the Baylye, and they to have of every trespasser ii*d.*, and they to present the defautes so founde by
the last hoole day in Whitson weeke, upon payne on every
Thurbarrowe doyng not his duty to forfaytt xii*d.* to the mendynge of the said hye wayes.

47. Itm, that every fermer of the mylles shall geve the
Thurbarrowes every half yere vi*d.*, or elles a brekfast worthe
vi*d.*

48. Itm, the Baylie shall have all the affore said
paynes, excepte those that be appoynted to the churche,
towne, or hye wayes, or other officers, or any other wayes
appoynted.

49. Itm, that the ale Tasters shall have for every bruynge,
or for every weeke of a Tnnr, a quart of ale when they come
to their howses and a peny to their kepe.

50. Itm, that no parson or parsones kepe no beere goinge
assawte, uppon payne of every on makynge defaute xv*d.* as
often as thei so do.

51. Itm, that no man nor woman kepe nor holde no mo
shepe but for every acre too shepe, uppon payne to lese to
the said Towne of Kyngesthorpe for every shepe ii*d.*

52. It is ordeyned that the Baily allwayes shall elect and
chose of the xii men one that hath been Baylye and borne
office in the Towne, and the benchers then to chose and
elect a nother for the comynelty of the same Towne for
every offecere as Bayly and other officers. This electyon is
at all tymes to be had, made, and *sorted* (?) yeven[1] in the
court house accustomed, that ys to say, the Sunday next
after the chesyng of the Meyre of Northampton, uppon

---

[1] 'Sorted yeven,' *vide* Ordinances (1483), art. 33. The meaning of
'sorted' is not very clear; possibly this may be an ancient legal formula.

payn at every tyme doyinge the contrary the Bayly to lese and forfaytt to the said Towne xxs.

53. Itm, that no parson nor parsones shall sue nor make no maner of sute of pley of londe, det, or action temprall [out of the courte] without licence of the Baily and Constable of the same Towne for the tyme beyng, uppon payne of xxs. of every trespasser so offendynge to be leved for the Towne for ever more.

54. Itm, that no parson nor parsones shall ley no londes nor tenements to morgage above iii yeres, uppon payne of forfaytynge of all such londes and tenementes to the use of the Towne for ever more.

55. Itm, that no man of no out Towne shall not digge nor dame nor fyshe in the broke called Walbeck broke, from Swarbrong hedd to Walbecke, uppon payne of every one makynge defaute iiis. ivd.

56. Itm, that no howse holdere shall not fet nor send for fier in a wispe to ther neyghbour's howse, uppon payne of every howse holdere makynge defaute xiid. as often as thei so doe.

57. Itm, that there shall no inhabiter wasshe no clothes at the comen welles before daylight, and further that thei shall laye no clothes nor wrynge no clothes withe in the damynge or headds of the said welles, uppon payne of every one makynge defaute xiid.

58. Itm, that there shall no man spyrituall nor tempall inhabytinge withe in the Towne hunte nor with fferettes nor nettes withe in the liberty of the same Towne, except he or thei have licence of the Baily or the Constables for the tyme beynge, uppon payne of makynge defaute vs., and forfaytting . . . nettes so founde of huntynge.

59. . . . licence to ferryt, and if they dygge any grounde . . . from the grounde, uppon payne.

60. Itm, that no [brewer that brewethe] to sell shall grynde their malt at any querne, uppon the payne for every strike so grounde xiid. to the Baylee.

61. Itm, that all thos psoncs that have quernes shall suffer noe body to grynde theirat above a Tolfatt,[1] uppon payn for every Tolfatt more then their owne at any tyme so doynge iiid.

62. Itm, that the millers shall make a sufficient planke to goe over at all tymes, uppon payne of every one makynge defaute xxs.

63. Itm, all inhabiters shall grynde at the Towne myllnes, uppon payn of anyone makynge defaute vis. viiid.

64. Itm, that the inhabyters shall have their corne grounde before a stranger, uppon payne of forfaytyng vis. viiid.

65. Itm, that the Mylners shall make suffycient meale and mett, uppon payne of losynge vis. viiid.

66. Itm, that the Courtes called the Leetes shall be holden and kept withe in a fortenyt after Michellmasse, and lyke wise after Easterne, uppon payne of losynge to the Churche xxs.

67. Itm, that the Baylie from hense fourthe shall have the pofyttes of the sesonynge beynge under the value of xiiis. iiiid.

68. Itm, that if the sesonynge be above a marke, the Baylie shall have but halfe the marke and halfe the ovplus, and . . .

69. Itm, that all wavys and strays from hense forthe shalbe delyvered to the Baylie by the Thurbarrowes, and the price of the stray namyd, and to brande them with the comon brande, and the Baylye so to have them in his kepynge withe in the libertyes, after ancyent and olde custome of this realme.

70. Itm, that every of the sixe thurbarrowes shall alwayes

---

[1] 'Tolfat :' some measure of capacity ; probably from toll, or from the miiler's fee. Tolhop is a toll-dish by which they take toll for corn sold in market overt (Cowell). Tolcorn is corn taken for toll at grinding in the mill.

do their duty as often as he or thei shalbe called, uppon payne of every one makynge defaute xii*d.*

71. Itm, that their shalbe no mo olde shepe in a flocke but xiiii score, and for every shepe that is above as often as they be so tryed by stayne men alymyted to lose for every shepe *ob'* to the affore said men.

7ᴣ. Itm, their shalbe iii folde makes in a flocke at the lest, uppon payne of every monethe iii*s.* iiii*d.*

73. Itm, that the Thurbarrowes shall not from hence forthe take any soynynge mony of any freeholder at Easterne Leet, uppon payne of xii*d.* for every i*d.* so taken.

74. Itm, the Baylye shall alwayes at Easterne Leete gyve the thurbarrowes ii*d.* ffor the somonynge of the Leete.

75. Itm, that no man or woman of the Towne shall at any tyme lodge any sturdy begger, uppon payne of every one makynge defaute iii*s.* iiii*d.* to the Towne and iii*s.* iiii*d.* to the Baylye.

76. Itm, that no parsone shall by any stuffe of any such begger except they make the Bayly prevy to the same, uppon payn of losynge iii*s.* iiii*d.* to the Towne and iii*s.* iiii*d.* to the Baylye.

77. Itm, that every man that ought to clense the comon gutters, that is to say, Bette's gutter, Page's gutter, Ambrosie's gutter, Dyconsis' gutter, Cowke's gutter, that every of the gutters may be clensed so that the water may passe at all tymes, uppon payne of every one makynge defaute xii*d.*

78. Itm, that the chosynge of the kynge and quene for the May gaymes shalbe chosin uppon Eastern day after Evynsonge, and he or she that do refuse the election shall forfaytt vi*s.* viii*d.*, and the Baylye to distresse immediately for the same, and for to have the one halfe for his labor and the other halfe to the Churche.

79. Itm, that the pson or his depute shall at all tymes scowre the more dytche as often as need shall require, that

is to say, the Baylye shall geve the p̄son or his depute warnynge, and after warnynge be geven that it be done w̄ in
xii dayes after, in payn of iii*s.* iiii*d.*, that is to say, to . . .
his owne water that comes from the p̄sonnage to the
stile in the corner of the more that turnes agayne to the
ryver.

XXI.

[The inhabitants seem to have deputed three of their number to go up to London and obtain the necessary legal assistance in bringing their case before the courts of law ; and probably they had their good reasons for conducting it in the 'Ster chamber,' which had been established about sixty years before by Henry VII. The names of these commissioners frequently occur in the records, and they were no doubt prominent men in the 'Toune.' Mr. Morgan, the counsel whom they engaged, was most likely connected with the Morgans of Kingsthorpe, who were established there about this time. Rob. Coke was 'Baily' in 1547, in which year, as we gather from internal evidence, the present journey was taken.

The expenses of these persons seem to have been defrayed by the sale of goods of some kind, possibly the property of the church. The mention of wax, silver and gold plate, etc., seems to point to this. Unfortunately there is no record left of the furniture, vestments, plate, etc., belonging to the church, and nothing to show what became of them, unless the present document refers to their disposal.]

THYS be the passels that Robert Coke, Robert Dykkynson, and Richard Broke have lyde out for the towne as here after follo.

Sondaye.	It. at stony stratford, ye daye of October, for shoying of Robert Dykkynson hors	v*d.*
	It. same daye for our supper there	vi*d.*
	and for our horse myte the same nyght there	xi*d.*
Mondaye.	It. for our dynner and horse myte at Donstabill	xi*d.*
	ye same daye at Synte Albons for o^r supper	ix*d.*

Ye same daye at night for horse meyte   xii*d*.

Ye same daye at Lond' for ii pare of

    shoes   .   .   .   . xviii*d*.

Tuesdaye.   It. at Barnyt for o^r brakfaste and hors

    meyt   .   .   .   . viii*d*.

    Ye same daye at Lond' for o^r dynner .   vi*d*.

    Ye same daye for our supper there   .   vi*d*.

Wydnesdaye.   It. for our iii dinners   .   .   ix*d*.

    It. pay'd the same daye to Richard

    Broke for hys expysses to Lond.   . xviii*d*.

    It. the same daye to Master Morgan,

    menepaye Reteyned hem for our

    counsell   .   .   .   . iii*s*.iv*d*.

    It. the same daye for our supper   .   ix*d*.

Thorsdaye.   It. for our dinner   .   .   .   ix*d*.

    It. the same daye for o^r supper   .   ix*d*.

    It. the same daye before dinner and

    after supper   .   .   .   iii*d*.

    It. the same daye for a payre of shoes

    for Richard Broke   .   .   ix*d*.

Ffridaye.   It. for o^r dyner   .   .   .   ix*d*.

    It. the same daye Master Morgan for

    hys ffe at the bar in the Ster chamber[1] iii*s*.iv*d*.

    It. the same daye to Mr. Tauornd (?)

    for hys fee in the same offys   .   xx*d*.

    It. the same daye to the Kynges' At-

    turnay servants for rewards   .   xx*d*.

    It. the same daye for our drynke before

    diner and after[2]   .   .   .   iii*d*.

---

[1] 'Ster Chamber': *vide* note to No. XII.

[2] This custom of drinking between meals was probably universal, and was known, I think, as the bever. There is a passage in Samuel Ward's 'Sermon on the Life of Faith' (1630): ' Why should not thy soul have her due drinks, breakfasts, meals, undermeals, bevers, and aftermeals, as well as thy body?' where the word 'bevers' seems to

Satterday.	It. for o^{r} dener and sopper . .	xviii*d.*
	Itm. for o^{r} drynkynge before dener and after	iii*d.*
Sundaye.	Itm. for o^{r} dener and sopper . .	xviii*d.*
	It. for o^{r} drynkynge before and after .	iii*d.*
Mondaye.	It. for o^{r} dener and sopyer . .	xviii*d.*
	It. for o^{r} drynkynge at the tavern and o^{r} freynds	vi*d.*
Tewysdaye.	It. for o^{r} dener and sopper . .	xviii*d.*
	It. before dener and sop. . .	iii*d.*
Wedenysday.	It. Mr. Morgan for his fee in the Excheckar	iii*s.*iv*d.*
	It. Master Browne for hys feys in the same Courte . . .	iii*s.*iv*d.*
	It. for o^{r} dener and sopper . .	xviii*d.*
	It. for o^{r} drynkynge before dener and after	iii*d.*
Thorsdaye.	It. for o^{r} diner and sopper . .	xviii*d.*
	It. for o^{r} drynkyng before diner and after	iii*d.*
Ffrydaye.	It. for o^{r} ferrying to Wystminster and hom	iv*d.*
	It. for o^{r} diner . . .	ix*d.*
	It. for o^{r} drynkynge before diner .	ii*d.*
	It. at ye taffern and o^{r} drynkynge at night	vi*d.*
	It. ye same daye to sergant Morgan for hys counsel in makyng of o^{r} pleye .	iii*s.*iv*d.*
Sattordaye.	It. for o^{r} ferrying and o^{r} counsel to Westminster and hom ageyne to Lond'	vii*d.*
	It. ye same daye diner and supp^{r} .	xviii*d.*

---

refer to this practice. The custom may perhaps still survive in the eleven o'clock beer and the afternoon beer of the workmen in some places.

It. yᵉ same daye Master Morgan's man
for wryghting[1] of the copye of yᵉ
towre . . . . iiis.ivd.

It. for oʳ drynkynge before diner and
after . . . . ivd.

Sundaye.   It. my dener and sopper . . vid.

It. befor dener and after . . iid.

Mondaye.   It. paid out for solyn off my shoys and
for yᵉ makyng clene of all oʳ botts . vid.

Yᵉ same daye for my dener and super vid.

Yᵉ same daye for my drynkynge before
dener and after . . . iid.

Towysdaye.   It. for my dener and sopper . . vid.

It. for my drynkynge . . iid.

Wedonysday.   It. for my dener and sopʳ. . . vid.

It. to Mr. Morgan for hys fee . xxd.

It. for other charge . . . iid.

Thursday.   It. for my dener and my drynkynge . viid.

It. yᵉ same daye for my horse and
Richd. Brooke and Rob. Dykonson's
horse, meyt yᵗ we did have whe . . .
come home . . xis. viiid.

It. laid out yᵉ same daye for my horse
mytt for iiii days . . . xvid.

yᵉ same daye for oure (hodhornys) (?)[2] iiid.

It. yᵉ same daye for wesyng of my
shurte . . . . id.

It. yᵉ same daye for rewards to yᵉ
servants . . . . ivd.

---

[1] This refers to the copy of the grant of freewarren, No. I. in this collection.

[2] 'Hodhornys': this is a difficult word, about which one is left to conjecture. It has been suggested that it means 'ordinaries,' but that will hardly suit the context. Could it be connected with 'hodiorns,' or 'hodierns' = 'journals,' whatever that might mean? 'Adiorn' stands for adjourn in the Ordinances.

Frydaye.	My dener at y^s styll [worth] . .	iv*d*.
	It. in the morning for my drynkynge and a boytt to Westminstre and home	ii*d*.
	It. the same daye to Mr. Morgan's clerk for wryting off a byll .	ii*d*.
	The same daye for my drynkynge at after none and at nyght . .	ii*d*.
Satterday.	It. for my dener and sopp^r . .	viii*d*.
	It. for my drynkynge same daye .	ii*d*.
	It. the same daye to Mr. Eden for our pte of the decreys . .	v*s*.
Sunday.	It. for Harye Tanner and me for oure dener and oure sopper, Thystyll-worth[1]	xvi*d*.
	It. ye same daye for a wherrye bott to Shene	xvi*d*.
	Itm. the same daye for a pottyll of seke y^t I be stowyd of my lord prector's servant . . .	vi*d*.
	Itm. the same daye before dener and after supper . . .	iii*d*.
Munday.	Itm. for o^r dener at Thystyllworth and one of mye Lord's servants .	xii*d*.
	Itm. for o^r ferrying over to Shene twyse and again to Hystyllworth .	ii*d*.
	It. for o^r drynkynge in the mornyng .	ii*d*.
	Itm. the same day for o^r drynkynge at our loging at Hamsmyth . .	iii*d*.
Teuysday. All Hallow day.	Itm. to Mast^r Morganys mane and for copying of boyth decreys . .	xx*d*.

---

[1] 'Thystyllworth.' In Domesday the name is 'Gestelworde;' in subsequent ancient records uniformly 'Istelworth,' afterwards occasionally 'Istleworth.' About Queen Elizabeth's time in conversation and sometimes in records it was 'Thistleworth.' The name Isleworth is quite modern (Lysons).

	Itm. for my dener and my sopper .	viid.
	Itm. for charges before dener and after	iiid.
Wedneysday.	Itm. for my dener and my sopper .	viiid.
	Itm. before diner and after . .	iid.
Thursdaye.	Itm. for my dener and sopper .	viiid.
	The same daye for a boytt to the Wycht Hawle to the Temple for Mr. Syssyll[1] and me . .	iid.
	Itm. the same day for my drynkynge before dener and after . .	iid.
	Itm. the same day to Mr. Taverner for his feys	xxd.
	The same daye for pyr tronke hose and a paire of shoys . . .	xiiid.
	The same day to Rychard Brook for hys charge from home to Lond' .	xxiid.
	Itm. to the same Rychard for shawying of his horse at Dunstable . .	vid.
Ffrydaye.	Itm. for our dener . . .	viiid.
	Itm. for our drynkynge before and after supper	ivd.
Satterday.	Itm. for our dener and sopper .	xvid.
	Itm. for drynkynge before diner and after	iiid.
	Itm. the same day for a boyt to the Courte	iid.

---

[1] 'Mr. Syssyll': Wm. Cecil, afterwards Lord Burghley. His father was Master of the Robes to Hen. VIII. He was educated at St. John's, Cambridge, and afterwards entered at Gray's Inn. The King conferred upon him the reversion of the office of custos brevium in the Common Pleas in 1541, which fell into his possession in 1546. In 1547 the Lord Protector Somerset appointed him his Master of Requests. In 1548 he was appointed Secretary of State, and was the first person chosen of the Privy Council under Elizabeth, and from that time to his death he may be said to have directed the affairs of England. In a pedigree in Lord Burghley's hand (given in facsimile in Wright's 'Queen Elizabeth and her Times') the name is written in the first places 'Sitsilt,' afterwards 'Sicell,' and again 'Cyceld.'

Itm. the same day to Mast^r Morgan for
making off a byll and other payings vi*s*.viii*d*.

Itm. the same day for rewards to Mr.
Morgany's men   .   .   .   xii*d*.

Sunday.   Itm. for our dener and sopper   .   xvi*d*.

The same day for our drynkynges   .   iv*d*.

The same day for the solyng of my
shoys   .   .   .   .   v*d*.

Itm. the same day for x days horsemeytt and two days Harye Tanarys
horsemeytt .   .   .   .   v*s*.

Munday.   Itm. for our dener and sop   .   .   xvi*d*.

Itm. before dener and after   .   .   iii*d*.

Tewysdaye.   Itm. for our dener and sopper   .   xvi*d*.

Itm. paid Mr. Broke for hys . . . yng
in y^r Exchequr   .   .   .   xx*d*.

The same day for our drynkyn before
dener and after   .   .   .   iii*d*.

Wedonesday.   Itm. for our dener and sopper   .   xvi*d*.

Itm. before dener and att ye taverne .   ii*d*.

Itm. the same day for a brakefast at
Westmynster for husse and Mast^r
Brown and Mast^r Smyth   .   .   xii*d*.

Itm. the same day to Mr. Syssyll for
hys payns to my lord Ptector for
the report for oure matt^r .   .   xx*s*.

Itm. to Mast^r Smyth for the report off
our hundreth matt^r to my lord Cheyf
Baron   .   .   .   .   v*s*.

The same day to Sir Clement Smyth
for the dyscharging of our hundreth
tyll a tyme .   .   .   vi*s*. viii*d*.

Itm. the same day to Mr. Browne for
helpeyn husse to fynyshe oure matt^r iii*s*.iv*d*.

Itm. the same day to Mr. Morgan for
   the copye . . . forth of the Towre .   xx*s.*
The same day before diner and after
   supper   .   .   .   .   iv*d.*
same day for a boytt to Westmynster .   ii*d.*

Thursday.   Itm. for viii days horsemeytt, v*d.* the
      day, sum   .   .   .   . iii*s.*iv*d.*
      Itm. for rewards in o^r Hyn   .   .   iv*d.*
      Itm. for o^r brakefaste at Lond^n   .   iv*d.*
      Itm. the same at Barnytt for our dener
      and Thomas Buttras and our horse-
      mett   .   .   .   .   xv*d.*
      Itm. the same daye att nyght at Dun-
      stable for a sopper and a botyl of
      secke and a faggot .   .   .   xiii*d.*

Ffryday.   Itm. att Dunstable for our horsemeytt
      at nyght   .   .   .   .   ix*d.*
      Itm. the same day att Stony Stretford
      for a diner and horsemeytt   .   xv*d.*
      Itm. hyer off my horse from Hyegatte
      to Stretford   .   .   .   xii*d.*
      Itm. . . . Northampton in expenses . . .   iv*d.*

    *   *   *   *   *

      Sm^a totalis, ix*li.* iv*s.* vi*d.*

    *   *   *   *   *

      Itm. lyde owt for a pap^r boke for the
      towne   .   .   .   .   iv*d.*
      Itm. payd for the towne gronds to the
      king's rynt   .   .   vi*s.*viii*d.*
      Itm. payd to John Horloke for the
      towne hole for part of hys wynter-
      ryng   .   .   .   .   iv*d.*
      Itm. He must have iii*s.* more and the
      herd ii*d.* for dryffynge of hem to
      Horlock.

Itm. payd to John Hopkyns xiii*d.* that
the Church owt hym for hys account.

Sm̄ ix*li.* xvii*s.* vii*d.*

It. I paid to Rychard broke xxii*d.*

Debett, v*li.* xiii*s.* iiii*d.*(?)

[On another page the following :]

It. Reseyved of the Towne as hereafter folls. :

It. for iorn, brasse, latȳ, and wyxe	.	.		xl*s.*
It. for wyght plat	.	.	.	.	viii*li.* viii*s.*
It. for gylt plat	.	.	.	.	v*li.* v*s.*

Sum, xv*li.* xiii*s.*

XXII.

[Richard Broke and Robert Coke were two of the three commissioners sent to London on the 'Hundreth' business.

The Duke of Somerset is here called Protector, so that the date is after Henry VIII.'s death.]

Money receyvyd by Rycharde Broke, of Kyngesthorpe, in the xxxviii yere of the Rayne of o^r most drede Soverayne, Lorde Kynge Henry the eight, to the use of the Inhabitants of the said Towne.

Itm. That was taxyd of the lott grasse there .	xl*s*.
Im. receyvyd of Henry Pagdale for the rent of Walbecke Closse . . .	xx*s*.
Itm. from Francis Morgan for another halfe yere's rent of said closse . .	xxii*s*.
Itm. of Master Wm. Morgan for the Towne corne	xxix*s*.
Summa recepta . .	v*li*. xi*s*.

Unde payd to my Lorde p̄rtr for the hole yere	iii*li*. xiii*s*. iv*d*.
Itm. payde to Mr. Butler for that he laid out for us in ffees	xx*s*.
Itm. that the toune shyppe owt me at my last accompte made the xii daye of Aprille .	xviii*s*. xd.
The sum layd out .	v*li*. xii*s*. ii*d*.

So the Towneshippe owth to the said Richard Broke xiiii*d*., the which they have payd, and so they be even x die December anno sup' scripto.

[There is a note at the side :]
Itm. that Robert Coke, Bayley, layd out x*d*. for the towne the same day to pay the said R. Broke.

XXIII.—Part I.

Depositions on the part of Sir Thomas Tresham, knyght, taken at Keteryng, in the countie of North^n, the xi daye of Aug^t, in the 2^d yere of our soverayne lord kyng Edward the sixt, before us, Sir Edward Montagu, knyght, Chyeff Justice of our sayd soverayne lord the kyng of his Com Please, Edward Gryffin, Esquyer, the kyng's majestie's Solycytor-general, commissioned of our sayd soverayne Lord the Kyng, by virtu of his highness commyssion to us dyrected, touch-yng a matt^r dependyng in varyance betweene the freeholders and the inhabitants of the township of Kyngsthorp, Bough-ton, and Pysford, in the sayd countie of North^n, of the one partie playntiffes, and the sayd Sir Thomas Tresham, keap^r of the Kyng's majestie's parke of Molton, in the said countie of North^n, and Thomas Latham, underkeap^r of the same parke, on the other part defendants as hereafter ensueth.

Robert Wyllyams, of Molton, in the countie of North^n, tenant to the Ladye Elizabeth Grane [Grene]? . . . deposeth that the great lodge of the park of Molton ys w^{t}in the paryshe of Kyngesthorp, and ys prcell of the manor of Kyngesthorp, and that the keap^r there dwellyng dothe paye his offryng to the pyshe churche of Kyngesthorp, and that all psones dying out of the same great lodge be buryed wi^{t}n the same pryshe churche of Kyngesthorp, and that the same keap^r

fyndyth the hallowed loffe[1] when hit chaunsyth to hys torne
to fynde the same, and he hath known thys so used thys
fyftye yere. . . . the sayd deponent sayth that there is certyn
wast grounde lying wi'n the feld of North", were unto the
gallowes there, upon whyche grow certeyn furzes, but how
many acres the sayd wast conteyneth this deponent knoweth
not . . . sayth that he hath knowne that the kyng our soverayne lord that nowe ys and hys mooste noble pgenytors
kyng Henry VII. and kyng Henry VIII. have had and used
to have waren of conyes and for all other beasts and fowls
of waren wi'n the felds of North", Abyngton, Kyngesthorp,
Boughton, Pysford, and Lytle Byllyng, next adjoynyng to
the sayd park, by the space of liii yeres last paste.

. . . above xxiv yeres past the inhabitants of the townshyp of Kyngesthorp did plough up a hole clapper of conyes
lying upon the flat beneath the foxholes, lying next the place
called Whyte Hills, and that the Lord Vaux did indyte the
sayd inhabitants of ryot to the nomber of xxx psones for the
ploughing up the same in a a ryotous manner.

. . . and that the townshypps of Pysford, Abyngton,
Boughton, and divers other towns wi'n the sayd countie of
North", to the number of vi score, do and tyme out of mynd
have usyd to paye their rent yerely towards the mendyng,
upholdyng, and repayryng of the sayd walls of the sayd
park.

Another witness states that he lived . . . 'at Lychborough
about xxx yeres . . . was constable there, and that the
same townshyp of Lychborough did then paye yerely iiii*d*.
towards the makyng, mendyng, and repayryng of the walls
of the sayd park . . . that one Gregory Cosbye about 8 or
9 yeres past was indyted at a cessyons holden at North" for
huntyng of the hare in the feld of Pysford beyng wi'n the
waren belongyng unto the park of Molton.'

---

[1] From this it would seem that bread and wine for the service of the
church was provided by certain inhabitants in turn.

Wyllyam Tymes, servt to my ladye Parr . . . sayth that about 26 yeres past he was svnt to one Henry Maye, then beyng keapʳ, and at the same tyme thys deponent was at the takyng of one Thomas Elmer, then bayliff of Boughton, otherwise Buckton, whyles the same Elmer was ferretyng in the sayd fyld of Boughton, and that this deponent and his companie did then take away the ferrett and pursenetts of the sayd Thomas Elmer, and carryed away the same ferrett and pursenetts to the park lodge. And at another tyme this deponent toke away a ferrett and pursenett from the sonne and svnt of the sayd Thomas Elmer, bycause they did frett in the sayd fyld of Buckton, and that the sayd Henry Maye about 29 years past toke away a brase of greyhounds, that is to say, a dogge and a bytch, from one Braynsford of Northⁿ, then svnt to Mr. Lucye, for huntyng of the hare in Kyngesthorpe in a crteyn place called Wallbeck, and that the same Braynsford was layde in the Stockes in the same great lodge of the said pke. Robert Parkdale, svnt to Thomas Latham about viii yeres past, dyd take one John Landsdale for stelyng of conyes in the nyght tyme, and brought the same John Landsdale to the parke Lodge, and from thence he was had to the castle of Northⁿ, and there quitt by proclamation at the next assisses following. . . . further sayth that hit ys and of old tyme hath byn engraved upon diverse of the stones of the said wall [of Molton park Lodge] how farre every towneshippe sholde repayre, amende, and make the said walls. . . . That the Kyng's Masty that now ys and his noble pgenitors have tyme out of mynde made and usyd to have made holls in the bottom of the walls of the said parke, to thintent the hares and conyes solde issue oute into the felds of Northⁿ, Abyngton, etc.

Part II.

Depositions on the part of Sir Thomas Tresham, &c., &c., as in the last document.

Extracts.

Evidence of Simon Malory. . . .

That the Towne of Giddington doth pay yerely vi pence towards the repayring and mendyng of the wall of the said Parke [of Moulton], saithe that he knew Nicholas Assheton and William Harryngton, keap^rs of the same pke under Sir James Harryngton, Knt., and after them he knewe James Latham, keap^r of the same pke under Sir Nicholas Vaux, Knt., and after hym he knew Thomas Latham, keap^r under the late Lord Parre, and that all the same keap^rs during their tymes dyd use, occupye, and keape the libtie of warren w^tin the said felds of Kyngesthorp, &c., for huntyng and hawkyng, and also have usyd to keape conyes in dyverse places of the same felds. . . . That the said James Latham did oftentymes take the deponent in stellyng and kyllyng of conyes in Pysford feld w^t hys bowe, and dyd oftyn take away the bowe of this deponent, but upon the gentle en-tretye of this deponent the said James Latham did always restore to this deponent his bowe agayn. . . . That he hath redde the names of many Townes engraven upon the stones upon the walls of the said pke, the names wherof he doth not now well remember, the which townes he hard saye then and many tymes sythens that the same townes engraven upon the same stones have payde their yerely rent towards the mendyng of the same walls . . . continually by the space of threscore yeres he hath knowne holes and muses[1] in the bottom of the walls.

John Avery, 'svnt to Edmund Kaysho, of Northampton,'

---

[1] 'Muses': passages for game through a wall or hedge (Halliwel).

amongst other things, deposes . . . that about xiv yeres
past Thomas Latham, keap[r] of the said pke, dyd lett to
ferme to one Francis Avery,[1] last Pryor of the late Pryory of
Seynt Andrewes in North[n], brother to this deponent, one
clapper or berye[2] of conyes lying and beyng w[t]n the felde of
North[n], upon a crteyn place there called North[n] hethe, for
the whych clapper or berye of conyes the said Pryor dyd
paye yerely to the said Thomas Latham vis. viii_d_., the whych
clapper the said Pryor dyd holde and occupye by the space
of two yeres untill the dyssolution of the said Pryory. . . .
Saith that he dyd ferrett in Pysford feld about xxvi yeres
past, and the ferrett this deponent dyd borowe of one John
Shughburgh, of Pysford, and dyd delyv[r] to the said Shugburgh a horse in pledge for the same ferrett, the whyche
ferrett the said Henry Maye dyd take away from this deponent, and also his pursenettes, and dyd lede this deponent
to the park lodge to the intent to have layde hym in the
stockes, but this deponent dyd so gently entrete the said
Maye that he forgave hym that ponyishement for that tyme.
At whyche tyme this deponent could not gett hys ferrett
nor pursenettes of the said Henry Maye, nor could not gett
hys horse ageyne of the said Shugburgh, tyll suche tyme as
one Raufe Standysshe, of Wolvage, in the countie of North[n],
esquier, dyd sende for the said Maye to Wolvage to dyne
w[t] hym, and there the said Mr. Standysshe entted[3] the said
Maye to delyv[r] the ferrett and pursenettes ageyne to this
deponent, at whos request the said Maye delyvered the
ferrett agayne to this deponent, and he had his horse ageyn.
. . . Doth well remember that one underkeap[r] to the said
Henry Maye dyd cut the plough geares of crteyn of the inhabitants of Kyngesthorpe at such tyme as they would have

---

[1] 'Francis Avery': Bridges, 'Hist. North.,' has the following:
'Francis Abree, alias Leicester, who was the last Prior of St. Andrew's,
was, on the dissolution of the Priory, 33 Hen. VIII., made Dean of
the Cathedral Church of Peterborough.'
[2] 'Beryes': a word still in use = burrows.
[3] Entreated.

eyred[1] w'n the hethe of Kyngesthorp, and that none of the
inhabitants of Kyngesthorpe dyd never lett to ferme any
clappers or beryes of conyes to any prson or psones, for
they had no suche authority so to do, as he supposeth.

. . . the said Henry Hayward was ymprysonned by a
crteyn space for hunting and pytchyng of hayes[2] for the
takyng of conyes. And at an other tyme, about fiftie
yeres past, one Camfeld, keap[r] of Molton towne warren, was
ponysshed and chalengyd by the said Simon Malory for
takyng conies with setting his haye.

. . . To the viii interrogatory he saythe that eversythens
he may remember there was cteyn holes made in the bottom
of the said park walls, that the hares and conyes w'n the
said park myght ronne out of the said park into the felds
for relyeff, and that the same conyes and hares were not
hurten nor hunted.

. . . That the townshippes of Walgrave, Crannesley,
Moulton, Orlingbere, Hannington, and dyverse others townshippes, do paye a rent towards the reparations of the wall
of the said pke. . .

One Henry Maye, decessed, dyd lett to ferme to one
Phipps, of North[n], decessed, and after hys death to John
Barnard, Esquier, decessed, two beryes in Northampton
feld, and that the said Phipps and John Barnard dyd paye
yerely to the keapers of the said pke, to the trust of our
soverayne Lord the Kyng, vis. viii*d*.

Baldwyn Willoughby, of Weston, mentions inquiries which
he and others made by commission as to the number of
conies, and says that they . . . 'found not above the number
of five hundred cople of conyes in the same feld of Buckton,
and for the feld of Kyngesthorpe and Pysford there were
dyvers of the inhabitants of the same townes present to the
number of iv or v psones, whyche declared before this exa-

---

[1] 'Eyred': ploughed.

[2] 'Hayes': a hay is a net used for catching hares or rabbits (Halliwell).

minate and others that there was no suche number of conyes in the said felds as was conteyned in the said compleynt, whos saying this examinate and others dyd credytte and believe, and so surveyed not the same two felds of Kynges-thorpe and Pysford. . . . Beyng in Buckton feld, this exa-minate and dyverse other psones perused the conyes' boroughes w^n the same felds, and also the destruction of the corne in the same, at whyche tyme this examinate estemed the number of conyes not fyve hundred cople in the said felds. The corne beyng destroyed in the same felds exceeded not above the value of xxx*sh.* or thereabout, but whether the conyes or shepe destroyed the said corne this examinate cannot depose.

XXXIII.

THE TREW RENTALL, BEING THE HALFE YEARE'S RENT OF KINGSTHORPE.

Taken out of an old booke almost 50 yeares since.*

Imprimis Mr. Ffrancis Morgan, Esqr., for his house and Land . . .	xxs.
Itm. for halfe a cotisall bought of Mr. Frier	vid.
Itm. for Welford Land . . .	xxiid. ob.
Itm. for Mr. Wm. Samwell's Close . .	xiid.
Itm. for Bridsall's House . . .	vid. ob.
Itm. for Camfielde's House and Land .	iis. xid.
Itm. for Chadweeke's House . .	xiid.
Itm. for halfe a cotisall of Betts at Walbeck	vid.
Itm. for Trase's Land . . .	iis. ivd.
Itm. for Mr. Mottershead's House and Close	xiid.
Itm. for Ffloyd's Close att Walbacke .	vid.
Itm. for Ffloyd's House and Land . .	viis. id. ob.
Itm. for Hollis his House . . .	xiid.
Itm. for Clement Dickinson's House .	id. ob.
Itm. for Hugh Edward's House and Land .	iiis. ixd.
Itm. for Hantorne's Spennie . .	xiid.

* The names of F. Morgan, Thomas Knapp and Richd. Dickenson are found in the Court Rolls 2, 3, Phil. and Mary and 1 Jas. I. The list was probably drawn up about the last date.

Itm. for the South Milles . . .	lixs. iid.
Itm. for the nether mills . . .	xliis.
Itm. for the north mills . . .	xxvs.
Itm. for St. Davie's Close at Walbacke	iis.
Itm. for St. Davie's House and Land .	xviiis.
Itm. for Willimsonn's House and Land .	vs. viid. ob.
Itm. for Land belonging to Haddon's House	iis. id.
Itm. Mr. Ffrancis Barnard, Esq. . .	xxvs. xd. ob.
Itm. Mr. Wm. Mottershed . . .	xxivs.
Itm. Mr. Richard Mottershed for his House and Land	iis. ivd.
Itm. for Edwardes his Close . .	xiid.
Itm. for Ludlow's Hous . . .	xiid.
Itm. for Mawbbes his house . .	vid.
Itm. for Reves his house . . .	vid.
Itm. Mr. Abraham Ventris for Jennawaie's farm	xxis. vid.
Itm. for Mr. Lambard's Land .	viiis. viid.
Itm. for the white House . . .	iis. ob.
Itm. Thomas Wiseman for his Land .	ivd. ob.
Itm. Phillip Jeffes for his Land . .	xvid.
Itm. Mistris Cooke for her farme . .	xviiis. vid.
Itm. for Ann Cook's Land . . .	iid. ob.
Itm. for Land bought of Simon Wallis .	is. id.
Itm. Mr. Crow	xixs.
Itm. Barnaby Brookes . . .	ixs. iid.
Itm. Alexander Lucas . . .	xxiiid. ob.
Itm. John Wrighte	ixd.
Itm. Ffrancis Weston . . .	vid.
Itm. Thomas Hollis . . .	iis. ixd.
Itm. Thomas Hantorne . . .	xiiid. ob.
Itm. Izachar Brookes his wife . .	ivs. iid.
Itm. John Webb	vid.
Itm. William Brookes Clarke . .	viiis. viiid.
Itm. John Smith the younger . .	ixd.

Itm. William Harriott	. . .	i*d. ob.*
Itm. John Willsonn	. . .	i*d. ob.*
Itm. Robt. Porter .	. . .	v*id.*
Itm. John Harris .	. . .	iii*d. ob.*
Itm. Robert Bell the elder .	. .	iii*s.* iv*d.*
Itm. for Elmes his house .	. .	xiii*d.*
Itm. Robert Sheppard	. . .	xi*d.*
Itm. Thomas Anson	. . .	xiii*id.*
Itm. Roger Colbye .	. . .	ix*d.*
Itm. Richard Dickinson	. . .	iv*s.*
Itm. Thomas Dickinson	. . .	iii*s.* iv*d.*
Itm. Thomas Knabb [qu. Knapp?]	.	xx*d.*
Itm. Edward Wallis the yonger	. .	vii*s.*
Itm. Matthew Ayer .	. . .	xxii*d.*
Itm. Simon Morris .	. . .	ix*s.*
Itm. Richard Morris	. . .	xxiii*d.*
Itm. Robert Morris	. . .	xxiii*d.*
Itm. Robert Pickmer	. . .	xiv*s.*
Itm. for Alice Cooke's Land	. .	v*id. ob.*
Itm. John Powell .	. . .	xx*d. ob.*
Itm. Robert Jeffes .	. . .	xiii*d. ob.*
Itm. John Dickinson	. . .	vii*id.*
Itm. Thomas Pickmer	. . .	vii*id.*
Itm. William Gardner	. . .	vii*id.*
Itm. Thomas Childe	. . .	iiii*s.* ix*d.*
Itm. Walter Burnell	. . .	iii*s.* i*d.*
Itm. for Land bought	. . .	ii*s.* i*d.*
Itm. for his Close .	. . .	xii*d.*
Itm. Simon Robers .	. . .	iiii*s.* i*d. ob.*
Itm. for Chorley's Land	. . .	xii*d. ob.*
Itm. John Hadden .	. . .	ii*s.*
Richard Brookes .	. . .	v*s.* ix*d.*
Widow Wrighte	. . .	v*id.*
Anthony Smithe .	. . .	iv*s.* v*id.*
Simon Cowper and his mother	. .	xiv*d.*

John Pye	ivs. viiid.
Nickolas Walker	xiis.
John White	vid.
Simon Smithe	iiis. xid.
Richard Larrance	xvid.
Richard Momford	ivs. vd.
ffor Edwards his lande . . .	iis. vid.
ffor Lande bought of Simon Wallis . .	viiid.
Thomas Heyward	vid.
Simon Wallis	xvis. vid.
George Ayer	iiis. xid.
Robert Bell (?) the yonger . . .	ixd.
Edward Wallis the elder . . .	viis. iid.
ffor Westonn's Land . . .	iis. id.
Henry Draper	viid.
James Dabbins	vd. ob.
James Smalley	iiid.
John Glover	id. ob.
Thomas Starmer (?) . . .	vid.
The Bayliffe of the Hundred . .	xxvis. viiid.
Mᵏᵉ Terringham	vs.
The Churchwardens of Abington . .	iis. vid.
Henry Denthon	xiiid.
John Marrill of Brampton . . .	xxid.
George Hillier	vid.
Widdowe Laan	iid. ob.
Mr. Atkines	iid. ob.
Mr. Hatton	iid. ob.
William Cooke	xiid.
Margery Hopkins	ivd.

XXXIV.

I͞hu.*

It. The Resets of me Robert Cook, one of the Churche-
wardens in the yere of oʳ lord god 1565, consernyng the
Stepull and other matters as hereafter, etc.

It. Reseved off Geoffory broke, townesman,
  ffor wood and other resetts . . vii*li.* iiis. x*d.*

It. Reseved of my selfe for the comenes of
  the northe mille holme for xx yeres . v*li.*

It. Reseved of myself for the sesonyng of my
  hows and lande bowthe of Antonye
  Smythe to the towne, as I payd to the
  ballye that ys . . . . xiiis. iv*d.*

       Sum totalis . . . xii*li.* xviis. ii*d.*

It. Rᵈ of Alhalow day of the Townes men . xx*s.*

The leyngs out for the Towne.

It. payd to Wylliã Hall for the derssing of
  owre stepull with hys ernest . . viii*li.* xiis.

It. payd for lyme and sand to him and chyld,
  and for carying of one lowed of stone . xxixs. ii*d.*

* The custom of placing the sacred monogram at the head of the page
was usual at this date, *vide* North's 'Chronicle of S. Martin's, Leicester,'
p. 90. It appears on every page of the Document No. XXI. p. 96 *ante.*

It. in expenses at Northehants and at tymes
    at home   .   .   .   .   .   xxiii*d.*

It. payd to Wybster's wyfe and cowper's wyfe for
    work   .   .   .   .   .   v*s.*

It. payd to Notbrone for hostershels   .   .   ii*d.*

It. payd to Master Tallar for v pere of trasses .   xxiii*d.*

It. payd to the Smythe for jorne worke   . iii*s.*

It. for fyer wood and poll's hors grase .   . x*s.*

It. to Halman, Hadon, Lasye, and Wybster for
    carrying of ladders to the churche and rear-
    ing of them, and for carrying them home . xiiii*d.*

It. payd for carrying of John Spencer and his
    graffe making   .   .   .   .

It. payd for a Sant's beyll roop .   .   .

It. payd to the Smythe for mending of the
    Churche dore lokes   .   .   .

It. payd to Sir Boull for a pore scollar .   .

It. payd for a windo to Master Wells of Thynden
    for the Court House*   ,   .   .   vi*d.*

It. payd to Symon Chyld for fycheyng of yt home iii*d.*

It. payd to Sir Boull for a pore synging man .

It. payd to Marten for hys workmanshyp at the
    Court House   .   .   .   . iii*s* iv*d.*

It. payd to Berchell for hys workmanship at the
    Court House   .   .   .   .   v*d.*

It. payd to Chylde for carrying of morter thather viii*d.*

It. for a pees of wood for the Court House .   ii*d.*

It. payd for a server to Sir Mertyn   .   .   xii*d.*

It. spent at the visitacion   .   .   .   v*d.*

It. payd to Wylsone for makyng clene of the
    bertylment of the Churche   .   .   vi*d.*

It. payd to a pore man at the Churche .   .   xii*d.*

It. payd when the Constables went to Grafton .   vi*d.*

---

* Built by Lady Pritchard for the use of the Manor Court; now the
property of the Thornton family.

It. payd to Barter for ernest for the Churche   xii*d*.
It. payd to Prokter for lime   .   .   .   xii*d*.
It. payd to Symond Smythe for carrying of ii
     loyde of morter and carrying of the lyme
     into the churche .   .   .   .   vii*d*.
It. payd to Clomsone the sawyer for sawing .   iii*d*.
It. spent at Homans when Willyā Dobens the
     smythe and Borchett dressed the bells .   vi*d*.
Itm. payd to the Smythe for yorne and hys
     workmanship .   .   .   .   ii*s*. x*d*.
It. payd to Burchett on hys wages .   .   ii*d*.
It. payd to Prokter for v quarters of lyme .   xiv*d*.
It. payd to Wyghtyng for lx foot of pavear .   vi*s*. viii*d*.
It. payd to the smythe for nails for the bels .   vi*d*.
It. payd to Symond Chyld for ii lode of lyme and
     one lode of ston from Northehampton .   ii*s*.
It. payd to the same Chyld iii loods of ston from
     Harlson .   .   .   .   .   ii*s*. vi*d*.
It. payd to the same Chyld for iii loods of sand
     and morter .   .   .   .   ix*d*.
It. payd to the same Chyld for vi loods of ston
     at hom .   .   .   .   .   v*d*.
It. payd to Thomas Story for tember for the stels   xii*d*.
It. payd to Wyrght the sawer .   .   .   iv*d*.
It. payd to Burchett for hys wages .   .   ii*s*.
It. spent at Holmans at the carrying of the stels   xx*d*.
It. for borde to make the dore for the stels .   vi*d*.
It. for nails for the dore .   .   .   iv*d*.

     This document is endorsed as follows :

D.   The xi daye of November, in the seventh yere of the
m.   raigne of the Quene's Majesty, came yn Robert Cooke
     and Thomas Jeffs, Chwardens, and made ther account,
     and theye ar dyscharged, and the same daye came yn
     Jeffre Browke and Henry Sheppard, and made ther
     cownte, and they are dyscharged.

XXXV.

A bill of the leyings out since the last account.

Item. Paid to John Starmer for lime for the
church . . . . . xviii*s*. vi*d*.
Item. For 9 strike of heare . . . iii*s*.
Item. Paid for laith and nayles . . . i*s*. iv*d*.
Item. Paid to Robert Garner for three weekes'
worke . . . . . xxi*s*.
Item. Paid to Wm. Homes for his worke . xii*s*. vi*d*.
Item. Paid to Leakines for fower dayes' worke . iv*s*.
Item. Paid to Wm. Wright for fower dayes'
worke . . . . . iv*s*. viii*d*.
Item. Paid to Edmund Wallis for 3 dayes' worke iii*s*. iii*d*.
Item. Paid to him for fetching of lime and sand ii*s*. x*d*.
Item. Paid to Banes for glasinge the windowes . xiii*s*.
Item. Paid to Harris for mending the Churche
yate . . . . . iv*d*.
Item. Paid to Garner for leading the lime . vi*d*.
Item. Spent on the workmen at Briges at severall
tymes . . . . . i*s*.
Item. Paid for 5 strike of lime to white the
Churche . . . . . ii*s*. vi*d*.
Item. Paid to Garner for whiting the Churche . xviii*s*. vi*d*.
Item. Spent on the workmen wan they made an
end of their worke . . . vi*d*.

Item. Paid to the Clarke for clenynge the
    Churche at several times   .   .   .   *iis. vid.*

Item. Paid to Symon Rogers for making the
    bars for the windowes and for mendinge
    the Churche yeate hinges   .   .   *is. vid.*

Item. Paid to Goodwife Hantorne for washing
    the Churche linen .   .   .   .   *is.*

Item. Paid to George Epson for bread and wine
    at Midsomer   .   .   .   .   *vis.*

Item. Paid to him for bread and wine at
    Michelmas   .   .   .   .   *vis.*

Som . £6 4s. 5d.

R^d of Mr. Hatton for a grave .   .   .   *vis. viiid.*

Paid to Edward Wallis for leaing (?) downe the
    grave   .   .   .   .   .   *xxd.*

Pade to Peter Whalie for mending the churche
    bible and the prayer-booke   .   .   *vid.*

XXXVI.

The Queen's Rent Roll for Kingsthorpe, dated October the 10th, 1594.

	£	s.	d.
Francis Morgan, Esq. . . .	4	8	3
Harvey Ekins, Esq. . . .		5	
Lile Hackett, Esq. . . .			10½
John Wright		1	1
Richard Pilgrim		1	1
Thomas Haspittall . . .		2	1
William Pipping . . .		2	1
William Bates		1	6
Edward Causbie . . .		1	6
Francis Pery (pays at Michelmas) . .			1½
Mary Wood			4
John Doxie, for Wilson's house . .			10½
also for land of Richard Haspittalls .	1		½
William Atkins	1	0	8¼
Hatton Atkins, for part of Crick's land .		4	7
Thomas Gardner . . .			4
Thomas Easton . . .			2
James Lack . . .			2
Thomas Draper			4
William Pratt			6
John Wakefield . . .			1½
Walter Dickenson . . .			1½

	£	s.	d.
Michael Pratt			6
Thomas Brownknafe . . .			9
William Butling			$1\frac{1}{2}$
Thomas Tebbs			$1\frac{1}{2}$
John Steevenson (for D. Jennowaye's land) .		3	5
also for land of Hatton Atkins .		3	
Francis Ladd, for his house and leys . .			8
for land of Dr. Connants . .		9	
Richard Hollis, for his house and land .		2	4
also land of Dr. Connants . .		8	4
also for land of Rob' Pickmer .		11	6
Jonas White			3
Ffrancis White			3
George Timms, for Wm. Wrights . .			7
William Marret, jr. . . .			2
Elizabeth Atkins, widow . . .		4	
Francis Cooke, gent. . . .	1	17	5
Francis Billingham at the Cock . .		2	3
William Greene, his owne . . .		1	
also for land late Dr. Morgan's .	1	0	11
Judith Weston, pays at Lady day . .			$1\frac{1}{2}$
William Swain			3
William Garrett, pays at mich' . .			6
Richard Gibbons . . .			11
Thomas Townsend . . .		11	10
Richard Tyte, sr., his owne . .		1	$6\frac{1}{2}$
for land of Bridget Jannoway's .			$7\frac{1}{2}$
Richard Billingham . . .			$9\frac{3}{4}$
also for land of Thos. Bradshaw .		1	5
William Greene, his owne . . .		3	4
also for land of Jas. Percival .		4	2
Alexander Knight . . .		10	$7\frac{1}{2}$
Edward Horcombe . . .			4
Thomas Causbie, for Heny Satchell . .		1	$2\frac{1}{2}$

	£	s.	d.
Samuel Cumberpatch			6
Henry Milward .		8	$\frac{1}{2}$
William Stanhurst			4
William Fasan .			4
John Wallson .			4
Elizabeth Wayte			6
John Childe .		2	4
Clement Darlow			9
Samuel Cricke, for his owne		11	1
for land of Jno. Darlow's		9	$11\frac{1}{2}$
William Brookes		2	6
Roger Cumberbach			3
John Wood, for his owne .		3	6
for land of Rob' Wilkins his .		3	4
Thomas Lucy .			6
Mary Cannel, wid.			7
John Billingham, for Hatton Atkins' land		3	9
for Elizabeth Hantorne's house			3
Richard Campe .			3
Daniel Jaquest .		1	8
Sarah Brooker, wid.			6
John Cooch, for Esq. Lant's land		2	1
John Bellingham, his owne		4	$3\frac{1}{2}$
for land of Mr. Morgan's		6	$10\frac{1}{2}$
For the new close		2	6
For land of Mr. Goodays .		4	4
Eor land late of Childe's .			1
Francis Bellingham			11
Richard Tyte, jr. his house			6
for land of Thomas Dentt's .			8
Priscilla Kilsby, wid. .		15	9
for land of Hannah Morris .		1	10
for land of Willm. Morris		1	4
David Selby .			3

	£	s.	d.
William Chapman			3
John Causeby, for Mewes his house and land		3	2
for land of Dr. Connants		4	2
for land of Mr. Goodays		5	
Edward Foster			6
William Morris			4
John Rigby			6
John Fitzhugh, for all the land late of Mr. Peter Cannons		16	8
John Billingham, for S. David's		8	9
for land of Robt. Morris		2	1
Abington land		2	6
Joseph Dobson		2	2
Mrs. Potter's land			2

XXXVII.

List of names with payments; no date, 16—.

	£	s.	d.		s.	d.
Mr. Coock	1	1	4	Thos. Brookes		7
— Thos. Morgan		9	4	Jno. Wood		7
— Job Walker		7	3	Rich. Morris		
— Rich. Gibbings			8	Widow Tite		4
— Wm. Draper			4	Clement Ayres	9	6
— Thos. Hollis		1	7	Robt. Brownknave		4
Widow Cobley			4	Symon Ayre		4
John Fade			4	Rich. Bellingham		4
Widow Smith			3	Jno. Esson		4
The over mill		5	0	Bartoll Dix		4
The nether mill		4	0	Widow Hofford		4
Widow Hantorn			8	Walter Bellingham		4
Wm. Wallis			4	John Thomas Binn-		
Rich. Wells			4	yon		4
St. Miles			4	Thos. Hoyerd		4
Anthony Dyer			4	Casby Brownknave		4
Edw. Boot			4	Dan. Smith		8
Simon Ladd			4	Wm. Hart		4
Wm. Homes			4	Goodman Swene		4
Fr. White			4	Widow Cannid		4
Geo. Morris			4	William Watterfall		4
Jno. Morris			4	Widow Casby		10
Wm. Morris			4	Widow Wallis		4

	s.	d.		s.	d.
Thomas Crase . .		4	Robert Garner .		3
John Mumm .		4	— Offen . . .		6
William Wright .	3	0	— Abrahams . . 6	6	0
Zachary Hantorne .			— Billingham . .		4
John Wilson .			Samuel Wright. .		4
Thomas Child . .	1	8	John Crick . .		4
Jasper Billingham .		4	Rd. of Rich^d. Billing-		
Simon Child . .	2	8	ham . . . 6	6	8
William Marsh .	9	0	Rd. of John Morris		
Thomas Money .	8	8	for 2 graves . 13	13	4
Mr. Morgan . .	14	9	Rd. at Easter wase a		
Thomas Knight .	2	6	twellmunth bred		
Thomas Jennaway .	4	3	and wine . . 17	17	2
Robert Pickman .	1	0	Rd. at Christmas last		
William Dickason .	2	6	for bred and wine	4	6
William Blesoe .	4	3	Rd. at Ester last for		
Robert Wright . .	4	0	bred and wine . 17	17	8
Thomas Plowman .		2	Rd. of Henry Barnes		2
Richard Dickason .		2	Rd. of William Brook	4	0
Francis Bland . .		7			

XXXIX.

Manerii de Kingesthorpe supervisus ibm̄ fact' xvi die Aprilis anno regni Dom' n̄ri Jacobi Dei grat̄i Anglie Scotie ffrancie et Hibernie Regis fidei defens' viz. Anglie ffrancie et Hibernie quinto et Scotie quadragesimo per Willm̄ Samwell mil', Willm̄ Tate mil' Johēm Henry Armʳ Thomam Mulsho arm' et Willm̄ Blake gen' virtute Commissionis dcti d̄ni Rs ext' sum' dct' Regis eis et aliis direct' sup' sacrum tenēn ibm̄

Nichī Walker	Francesci Manly de Spratton
Robtī Pirkmer	—— Haddon de ead'
Symōn Wallis	Robtī Clarke de ead'
Georgii Hilliar de Bucton	Thome Pearson de Spratton
Hugon' Stanton de ead'	Johnnis de ead'
Hugon' Lucas de ead'	Willī Dunckly de Wilton
Willī Smythe de Billinge magna	John Scot de Dallington
Johanis Harrys de ead'	

Qui dicunt sup' sacr̄m quod.

Robtus Pirkmer claim tener' p' copīa rottulor' cur' manerii de Kyngesthorpe has pcell' terr' territor' et hereditamentor' in Kingesthorp predict' ut sequitur.

coit' voc' } Domum mansionale p^r estim' vi
coticell' et di } spac'[1] unu horr' vii spac unu al-
teru horr' 5 spac unu alt' horr iii spac' unu
kille house ii spac i mault house ii spac unu
stabul' ii spac' un kow house iii spac unu
pidgeon house i spac ii pomar' et unu gar-
dinu le backside continens per estim' . i acr. dim'.

coit' voc { Pratum in combus pratis viz.
xviii quarterons { northward and southward . vi acr.

Terr' arabil' et lesur' in le Northfield in divsis
pcellis p' est' . . . . xxiv acr.

Terra arabil' in le Woodfield in divsis pcellis p'
est' . . . . . xx acr.

Ter' arab' in le Brookefelde in divsis pcells per est' xvi ac.

Hend' sibi et heredibus suis sedm conss manii pdti per ann xxviii*s*.

. . . Brooke clam tener' p' copia rottulo ut sup has pcell' terr' tentor et hereditamentor nuper in tenura Thomæ pris sui, viz. :

Dom mansionale continen' p' estim' viii spac',
unu horreu cont' iiii spac et stabull' et i
kowhouse ii spac unu maulthouse ii spac,
unu pomar' le backside eisdem adjacen' et
claus eisdem adjacen' cont' p' estim' . i ar. et dim.

Pratum in coibus pratis viz., southwarde et north-
warde per est' . . . ii acr. et dim.

terre arabil' et terre in le Northfield . . xiv ac.

terre ar' in le wood field . . . xii ac.

[1] 'Spac',' *i.e.*, spatia, 'bays.' The size of a house or barn seems to have been estimated by the number of interspaces between the rafters of the roof. In the Claims of Tenants, No. XL., which is written in Latin, the writer has in one instance introduced the word 'bay' instead of spac', evidently by inadvertence.

terre ar' in the Brookefield . . x ac.
       per ann. xviii*s.* iv*d.* et sect.

* * * * * *

Idem Francs' Morgan cl$\overline{am}$ ten' ut sup' un$\overline{u}$ capitle mes-
suagium c$\overline{u}$ pt̄iis voc' A ffarme House nuper patris sui et
ante.
   d$\overline{om}$ mansionale   spac, un$\overline{u}$ horr'   spac' alt horr
      spac' un$\overline{u}$ stabull i le killehouse et maulthouse spac
pomar' gard$\overline{in}$ et curtilag'.
claus' pastur' adjacen' cont' p' estim .   .   . ii acr.
claus' pastur' voc Nene Close in Woodfield p' est' . iii ac.
   habend' sibi et hered' su' ut sup' redditus per ann, xl*s.*

Idem Fra$\overline{nc}$ cl$\overline{am}$ ut sup' cert' terr' in co$\overline{ibus}$ campis de
Kyngesthorpe nuper Clement Welsted et aute   Wel-
sted et   Welsted de antiquo terr' arr' in $\overline{coibus}$
campis $\begin{cases} \text{Northfield.} \\ \text{Woodfield.} \\ \text{Brookfield.} \end{cases}$ hab^d ut sup redd' per ann iii*s.* ix*d.*

Idem Ffranciscus Morgan cl$\overline{am}$ ut sup^d unum cottagium
cum pt̄n suis voc' Batman's house p'ope Conegens well
nuper Thomæ Coles ante agnete Barbore et Barbory ex antiquo, viz. :
— domum mansionalem ii spac' ho$\overline{rr}$ ii spac et cur-
    tilag' voc le grasseyard modo in occupatione
    Georgii Sporley cont' p^r est . . . i rodd.
   habend' sibi et hered' suis sed$\overline{m}$ co$\overline{nss}$ maner p^r reddit
a$\overline{nn}$ xiiii*d.*, a$\overline{nn}$ val demittend xxx*l.* iii*s.* iiii*d.*

   —on. cl$\overline{am}$ ut sup^d cottagium mo' voc' Burchull's house
cu pt$\overline{nen}$ juxta le Kings well, viz. :
domum mansional i spac' et curtilag p^r est .   iiii pertic.
    modo in occupacione Rich. Pitman.
   hab$\overline{end}$ ut sup^d p^r redd per ann xiii*d.*, ann val dimitt xxx*s.*

Idem Ffranciscus clam ten' ut sup^d cottagium et cert terr modo voc Trusses ante Thomæ Coles et Orpyn ex antiquo.

*   *   *   *   *   *

Awdrey Bett vid' nup^r uxor Sylvester Bett ante uxor Thomæ Parker defunct clam tener' p^r copiam dat   die anno Rs   cert terr', viz. :

prat in le Moore Southward p^r est   .   .   } i rodd.
prat in le Moore Northward p^r est   .   .   }

Terr' arabil' in Woodfield p^r est   . iii acr. i rodd et di rod.

Terr' arab' in Northfielde p^r est   .   . iii acr. i rod.

Terr' arab' in Brookefield p^r est   .   . i ac. i rod.

     habend sibi p^r termino vite sue remaner' Johanne Knipe et hered' suis p^r redd ann iiis. vid. ann val demit.

Henry Weston clam tener' ut sup^d has pcell' terr' tentor' et hered^{tor} sequen^d, viz. :

Domum mansionalem modo in tenura ipsius Henry
    nuper Simon Cooke le backside et clausum, &c.,
    eidem adjacen cont per est   .   . i acr.

Pratum in coibus pratis southward p' est   . i ac.

Terr arab in le Northfield p' est   .   . iii ac.

Terr arab in le Woodfield p' est   .   . iiii acr.

Terr arab in le Brookfield   .   .   iii ac. et dd.

    hend sibi et heredibus sm conss manii p' redd per ann ivs. iid., et sect cur'.

Johannes Smyth clam ten' ut sup^d has pcell' terr' et tentor' ut sequitur, viz. :

Domum mansional in tenur' ipsius Johannis nuper
    patris sui iii spac i horr iii spac i stabul i spac
    le backside adjacen' .   .   .   . i rod.

Terr' arab' in diversis pcell' in le north field   . iii rod.

Terr arab' in le Woodfield   .   . dim acr.

    hend sibi et heredi' suis ut sup^d p' reddit ann xviiid. et sect cur.

Gardianus Ecclesiæ de Abington in cōm Northfield clam
tener' ut dic x cert' terr' in campis de Kingsthorpe, pd', viz. :
terr' arab' in Manwellfield p' estm . . dm ac.
ter arab' in Brookfield p' estm . . . ii acr.

      pr reddit ann vs. et sect cur.

Hugo Weston clām tener' divss terr in Kingsthorpe voc
Denton's.

   *   *   *   *   *   *

Hugo Hayward et Elizabeth uxor ejus clām tener' pr copīa
rotlor ut in jure ipsius Elizabeth et hered ipsius Elizabeth
cert' terr' et tēnta in Kingsthorpe nup Wilmer Mace et ante
Hopkyns, viz. :
Unūm Cottagium vi spac i horreu decar' iii spac
    cum le backside x yards pr estm . . i rod.
pratum in coibus pratis northward pr est . . di ac.
Terr' arabilis in le Northfield pr est . . iv acr.
Terr arab. in le Woodfield pr est . . . iv acr.
Terr' arab. in le Brookfield pr est . . . vii acr.

    hend' sibi et hered' suis ut supd pr redd ann viis. viid. et
sect cur.

Thomas Williams clām ut supd cert' terr' et tēntā in
Kingsthorpe nup' prīs sui et ante Orpyn ut sequitur.
Unūm cottagīu ii spat et Člm eidem adjacen' pr est   i rod.
Terr' arabil in le Brookefield . . i acr. et dim.
Terr' arabil in le Woodfield pr est   i ac. iii rod et dim.
Terr' arabil in le Northfield pr est . . iii acr.

    per redd p ann iiis. ivd. et sect cur.

Simon Morrys clām tener' sibi et hered ut supd cert' terr'
et tēnta in Kingsthorpe nuper Wilhelmi Morrys prīs sui de-
functi et avi &c., viz. :
Domum mansional v spac' i horr v spac' i stabull
    ii spac' le yard backside et clm eidem adiacen'   i acr.
Pratum in coibus pratis de Kingsthorpe pd south-
    ward . . . . . ii acr.

Terr' arabil in le Woodfeld   . xvi acr. xiii rod.
Terr arabil in le Northfeld p^r est .   . xiv acr.
Terr arabil in Brookfield p^r est   .   .   .   x acr.
    hend et tenend sibi et hered su p^r redd ann xixs. viii$d$. et sect cur.

[Morr]ys clamat tener' ut sup^d sibi et hered' suis cert' terr' et ten' ut sup^d antea pris sui et antea avi sui.
Unum cottagium in occupacion hugonis Draper
     cum clo, eidem adjacent'   .   .   .   i rod.
terr' arabil in le Northfeld p^r est .   .   i acr. iii rod.
terr arabil in le Woodfield p^r est .   .   .   ii acr.
terr arabil in le Brookfield p$_r$ est .   .   .   ii acr.
    hend et tenend sibi et hend suis p^r redd p' ann iiish. id. o.

     *   *   *   *   *   *

    Magister hospitalis de Savoy clam tener unu messuagium terr tentor et hereditament' modo in tenura Francisci Morgan, viz. :

Domum mansionalem vi spac, horr' ii spac iii clausm
     adjac' p' estim'   .   .   i acr. dim.
Terr' arr' in le Northfeld p' estim   .   . xii ac.
Terr' arr' in le Woodfeld p' estim   . xix ac. iii rod.
Terr' arr' in le Brookefeld p' estim .   . xx ac.
Prat' in coibus prat' cont' p' estim northward et
     southward   .   .   .   iv ac.
iii clausus inclusus cont' in toto per estim . iv acr.

                                             xxxiv$s$.

    But whether the said messuage and lands be holden of the manor of Kyngesthorpe accordynge to the custome, we knowe not.
    Tria molend' aquat', viz., unu molend' aquat' voc' le North-mill cont per estim' iiii spac et vestur'[1] unius le holme cont' p' estim' ii ac in occupacione Francisci Barnard, gen, annual' reddit', ls.

          [1] 'Vestura'=produce, crop.

Ūnu molend' aquat' vocat' Nether Mill cont' p' estim' iiii spac et unū le holme cont' p' estim' i ac in occupat' Thome Knapp.

Unu molend' aquat' voc' the South Mill cont' p' estim' iiii spac et ūnu le holme contin' p' estim' i ac in occupat' Francisci Morgan, armig, v*li.* xviii*s.* iv*d.*

Dicunt ulterius jur pdti sūp sācr sū p̄d qd met' et bounds manēr de Kingesthorpe pdte tendunt se modo et forma sequenti.

Incipient apud ter' voc' Sindering juxta Boughton meadowe et abinde per meta voc Boughton mere usque le heath et abinde usque le Westcorner de Moulton parke orientaliter spac mille pass et abinde usque et infr' capital' messu voc le great Lodge de moulton parke, et sic per eundem murum (?) usque Abbington dike et sic per foss (?) pdt usque regiam viam voc Molton way et abinde usque quandam meta voc Abbington mere sup' quendam fonte voc Swarbrick (?) head orientaliter pr estmac' mille passu et abinde usque quandam metam de Abbington pdt voc Monksparke et per furcas voc le gallowes quæ sunt infra metas de Kingesthorpe et abinde usque meta adjungend' sup' Northn heath et abinde usque quendam locum voc longlands sic abinde usque quendam locum voc' Theavedale et sic ex dorso cujusdam loci voc' Walbacke jxta Northampton et abinde p' regiam viam retro essu[1] usque quandam venellam voc Walbacke lane australiter pr estim' mille passu et abinde p' candam venella usque metas ville Northampton adjacent cuidam loco voc' Southmill wong et per easdem . : .

et sic retro esu usque et infra quædam . . .

Southmille holme . . . current a villa de Kingesthorp

. . . flumen illud usque quodda molendu voc

. . . p estm mille passim et ab

. . . locum voc Sindering borealiter.

---

[1] Probably retrocessu.

XL.

[The following list of Claims of Copyhold Tenants, with their payments, is in so mutilated a condition that only a portion of the names
can be deciphered. It is without date, but is probably anterior to the
'Supervisus,' No. XXXIX., and from the occurrence of many of the
names in both the lists it might seem to be of about the same date as the
'Trew Rental,' No. XXXIII.]

Names of Tenants.

				s.	d.
Edmund Wallis	.	.	.	20	4
Richard Walker	.	.	.	24	
William Lambart	.	.	.	20	4
Simon Smith	.	.	.	7	10
Richard Lawrence	.	.	.	2	8
— Yonger	.	.	.	6	1
Thomas Knapp	.	.	.	4	10
Symon Wallis	.	.	.	36	0
Anthony Smith	.	.	.	8	9
Robert Porter	.	.	.		6
Richard Gardiner	.	.	.		16
William Gulliver	.	.	.		5
Katerine Mewes	.	.	.	2	
Roger Cosby	.	.	.		16
Simon Camp	.	.	.	2	3
George Hilliar	.	.		18
Christopher Hatton	.	.	.		5
Edward Whitsey	.	.	.		5

				s.	d.
Francis Terringham	.	.		10	0
John Bosworth	.	.	.		3
John Harris	.	.	.		7
William Gardiner	.	.	.		16
Thomas Yonger	.	.	.		4
Thomas Pilmer	.	.	.		16
Henry Draper	.	.	.		14
Simon Else	.	.	.	15	
Richard Mottershed	.	.	.		10
Philip Jeffs	.	.	.	2	7
Thomas Yonger	.	.	.	6	9
Richard Dickinson	.	.		8	4
Cicely Cooke	.	.	.	12	0
Robert Cooke	.	.	.	37	0
Izacar Brooke	.	.	.	36	8
William Mottershed	.	.	.	50	6
Thomas Wiseman	.	.	.		9
Thomas Child	.	.	.	9	6
Anthony Rowell	.	.	.	3	4
John White	.	.	.		12
Anthony Morgan, sr	.	.	.	6	8
John Wright	.	.	.		18
— Friers	.	.	.		12
Georgius Thorley	.	.	.	4	2
William Harcourt	.	.	.		3
John Wilson	.	.	.		3
Robert Sheppard	.	.	.	5	8
John Pye	.	.	.	18	8
Alexander Jennings	.	.	.	4	1

The following extracts illustrate the meaning of certain words :

Ricardus Lawrence clam' tener' ut supr' has pcell' terr' ten' et hereditr' ut sequitr nuper Oliv'i Latham.

Domum mansional' iii spac'¹ unū horr' ii spac' unū atreū²
et clm eisdem adiacen', etc.

*   *   *   *   *   *

Robtus Cooke clam' tener' p' rotul' maner' ut sup' unū
tent' et cert' terr' et cotag' nup' Simonis Cooke ante Robti
Cooke.

Dom' mansional' vi spac' duo horr' vi spac' duo stabul' et
le heyhouse v bayes unū le Kilnhouse ii bayes unū yarde et
pomar', etc.   Quatuor cotecell' prat' pastur' inclus' cont' p'
estim' iii acr di.

*   *   *   *   *   *

coiter³   (Prat' in coi prat' voc' Wistersholme p' est' i ac. di.
voc' xxviii { Prat' in coi prat' voc' le North meadow p' est' ii acr.
qterns.   (Prat' in coi prat' voc' South meadow p' est iii ac. di.

*   *   *   *   *   *

Wm. Mottershed gen' clam' tener', etc., etc.

Prat' in coi prat' voc South mead p' est'	. .	ii ac.
Prat' in coi prat' voc Walbank p' est	. .	di ac.
Prat' in coi prat' voc le Gulch p' est	. .	ii ac.
Prat' in coi prat' voc Worsterholme p' est'	. .	i ac.

*   *   *   *   *   *

¹ 'Spac'': for *spatia*, Anglice 'bays.' In the next extract the English
word is used by inadvertence instead of the Latin.

² 'Atreu': for *atrium*, Anglice 'yard,' as in the following extract.

³ This would seem to show that the word 'quarteron' is equivalent
to 'rood.'

On the other hand, we find in another part the words 'prat in coi
prat' iii rod,' with the marginal note 'coiter voc ii quartrons.' But possibly the words 'coiter voc' may have indicated the reputed quantity,
which might not have been accurate in every case.

XLII.

This indenture, made the 10th day of July, Anno Dm. 1633, and in the ninth year of the reigne of o^r most gratious soverigne lord Charles, by the grace of God of England, Scotland, France, and Ireland, King, Defendr of the Faith. Between John Readinge, of the Inner Temple, London, Esqr., Richard Mottershedde, of Kingsthorpe, in the county of Northampton, gent., etc., etc. . . . of the one part. And Thomas Mottershedde, of Kingsthorpe aforesaid, son and heir of William Mottershedde, of Kingsthorpe, aforesaid, gent., deceased, son and heir of John Mottershedde, late also of Kingsthorpe aforesaid, deceased, of the other part.

Whereas our late soveigne Lord King James, of famous memory, by his Highness' letters patent under the great seal of England, bearing date at Westmr the 13th day of April, in the 14th year of his Highness' reign over the realm of England, France, and Ireland, and of Scotland the nine and fortith, of his special grace certaine knowledge and mere mocon, and for the consideracons conteyned and specified in the said letters pattent, hath for him, his heirs, and successors given and graunted unto Francis Morgan, late of Kingsthorpe aforesaid, Esqr., deceased, Francis Barnard, of Kingsthorpe aforesaid, esqr., deceased, the said William Mottershedde, of Kingsthorpe aforesaid, gent., deceased, etc., etc. . . . parties to these presents men and tenants of

the said town of Kingsthorpe, and to their heirs and assigns
for ever, all that the said town and village of Kingsthorpe or
Thorpe, in the said county of Northampton, with all and
singular the rights, members, and appurtenances whatsoever
to the said town and village apperteyning, and also the reversion and reversions whatsoever of the said town, with all
the members and appertenances to the same belonging, and
all rents and yearly profits belonging to the same town, and
all others the lands, tenements, hereditam^{ts}, and premises
in the said recited letters patent mentioned, and all rights,
jurisdictions, liberties, franchises, customs, privileges, profits,
commodities, advantages, emoluments, and hereditaments
whatsoever to the said town belonging, fully, freely, and
wholly, and in as ample manner and form as the men and
tenants of Kingsthorpe aforesaid at any time heretofore
ever had, held, used, or enjoyed the said town and other
the premises in the said recited letters patent mentioned to
be graunted by force of any charter, gift, grant, or confirmation, for any term of years or by reason of any lawful pre-
scription, use, or custom heretofore had or used, or by any
other lawful way or means whatsoever, *to have, hold, and*
enjoy the said town and all and singular other the premises
before in the said recited letters pattent mentioned . . .
unto the said Francis Morgan, Francis Barnard, John Readinge, etc., etc. . . . *now witnesseth this present indenture* that
the same John Readinge, Richard Mottershedde, Simon
Morris, etc., etc. . . . have for divers good causes and consideration them thereunto especially moving, and for and
to the intent to make sure and confirm unto him the said
Thomas Mottershedde, his heirs and assigns, the messuage
or tenement, lands, tenements, and hereditaments hereafter
in these presents mentioned, granted, released, and confirmed, being heretofore copyhold land and holden by copy
of court roll of the said manor and town of Kingsthorpe,
and to the intent to make the same fee simple in the said

Thomas Mottershedde and his heirs, do by these presents
for them and every of them grant, release, and confirm, etc.,
etc. . . . *all that messuage, tenement, or farmhouse, and all
that dovehouse thereunto belonging*, with the appurtenances
situate, lying, and being in Kingsthorpe aforesaid, and also
all the close of pasture, with the appurtenances, in Kingsthorpe aforesaid, near or adjoining unto, and now or late
used or occupied with the said messuage or tenement, and
now or late in the tenure or occupation of the said Thomas
Mottershedde . . . and also all the arable land, *leyland, and
pasture ground lying and being in the parish and field of
Kingsthorpe, containing by estimation four score and eleven
acres, part whereof were heretofore* taken in exchange from
the said Francis Morgan, deceased, for other lands of the
said William Mottershedde, deceased, and the said fourscore
and eleven acres are lying and being dispersed within the
field and precincts of Kingsthorpe, and both said messuage
or tenement belonging and extending, and therewith now
or lately used, occupied, or belonging, and were heretofore
in the occupation of the said William Mottershedde . . .
to have and to hold the said messuage or tenement, close or
pasture, arable lands, leyes, meadows, pastures, and commons,
etc., to the only and proper use and behoofe of him the said
Thomas Mottershedd and of his heires and assigns for ever,
yielding and paying yerely unto the s^d John Readinge, Rich^d
Mottershedd, Simon Morris, etc., etc., to be collected and
gathered by the said Bayliff of the said Towne of Kingsthorpe for the time being yerely for ever the some of *Forty-
six shillings and 4 pence* of good and lawful money of England, being the ancient coppicholde rent and now the Fee
Farm rent of and for the said messuage and tenement, close
of pastures, and premisses, or some part thereof, and *Twelve
pence*, chiefe rent for the same premisses yerely at the Feasts
of S. Michael Tharchangel and annunciation of o^r blessed
Lady Saint Mary the virgin, or withine twenty dayes next

before either of the said Feast days, by equal porcons at or in the Court house or Town house of Kingsthorpe aforesaid . . . and the said Thomas Mottershedde, for himself, his heirs, execut^rs, adminis^rs, for every of them doth covenant, graunt, promise, and agree to and with the said John Readinge, Richd Mottershedde, etc., etc., etc., and every of them and every of their several heirs and assigns, by these presents, that he the said Thomas Mottershedde, his heirs, etc., etc., shall and will yearly for ever hereafter pay or cause to be paid unto the said John Readinge, Richd Mottershedde, etc., etc., etc., that be or shall be lords of the manor of Kingsthorpe, the said sum of ffortie six shillings and four pence, being the said coppyholde rent or ffee ffarm rent of the premises, or some part thereof, and the said twelve pence chief rent before expressed at the days and times before lymitted . . .

* * * * * *

and the said John Readinge, for him, his heirs, execut^rs, etc., etc., and the said Richd Mottershedde, for him, his heirs, etc., and the said Simon Morris, for him, his heirs, etc. . . . and not one for another, do respectively graunt and covenant to and with the said Thomas Mottershedde, his heirs, etc., that he, the said Thomas Mottershedde, his executors and administrators, and every of them, at all and every time and times from and after thensealing and delivering of these presents, shall or may for evermore then after lawfully and quietly and peaceably have, hold, use, occupy, possess, and enjoy, to the proper use and behoof of him the said Thomas Mottershedde, his heirs, etc., the said messuage or tenement, close of pasture, etc., etc., and premises before mentioned . . . and every part and parcel thereof, without any lawful lett, disturbance, interruption, etc., of or by him the said John Readinge, his heirs, etc., or of or by him the said Richd Mottershedde, his heirs, etc.,

etc., etc. . . . and that they, the said John Readinge, Richd Mottershedde, Simon Morris, etc., etc., have not done, made, or committed any act or things whatsoever to charge, encumber, or impeach the aforesaid-mentioned premises, in witness whereof the parties first above named have to these present indentures interchangeably set their hands and seals the day and year first above written.

XLIV.

(Some parts of this document are destroyed, as indicated by the lacunæ.)

Inquisition into Charities, etc., by Comm under Great Seal.   Anno 1683.

To all Christian people to whom the present writing shall come, we, Richard Raynsford, Walter Littleton, Edward Saunders, Esquire, and Charles Tyrell, Gent., being four of the Comm^rs amongst others authorized by vertue of the King's Maties Comm^n under the great seal of England, issuing out of the high Court of Chancery, bearing date at Westm^r the two and twentieth day of Feby last past before the date of these presents, to the Revd Father in God William, Lord Bp. of Peterbro', Thomas Pinfold, Doctor of Laws, and Chancellor to the said Bp., and also to Thomas Cox and John Stephens, Esquire, and John Raynsford, gent., and divers other persons directed according to a certain statute made in the high court of Parliament, holden at West^r, in the seven and twentieth day of Oct^r, in the three and fortieth year of the reigne of our late soveraigne lady of famous memory Elizabeth, late Queen of England, and entituled an act to redress the misimployment of lands, goods, and stocks of money heretofore given to charitable uses, send greeting in our Lord God everlasting.

Whereas by an inquisition indented taken at the Guildhall, in the town of Northampton, in the county afore said, on the sixteenth day of August last past, before the date of these presents before the said Thomas Cox, John Stephens, John Raynsford, and Charles Tyrrell, by vertue of the Comm[n] aforesaid, by the oaths of Thomas Sergeant, of the said town of Northampton, gent., Richard Ebrall, of the same, gent., Theophilus Wiston, of the same, gent., Robert Foes the elder, of the same, gent., Robert Stiles, of the same, gent., John Clifford, of the same, gent., Robert Addys, of the same, gent., Thomas Dunkley, of the same, Thomas Hanson, of the same, Daniel Singleton, of the same, Edward Hilliar the elder, of the same, Edward Boddington, of the same, and John Dunkley, of the same, honest and lawful men of the said county of North[ton], who being duly returned, impannelled, sworne, and charged to inquire of and upon the matters contained in the said statute by vertue of the comm[n] aforesaid, it was found by the said Jurors, in and by the said inquisition, that one Thomas Knapp, heretofore of Kingsthorpe, in the said county of North[ton], long since deceased, did by his last will and testament in writing, which was proved in the Ecclesiastical Court held for the Dyoces of Peterbro', on or about the six and twentieth day of May, which was in the year of our Lord 1613, give unto the poor of Kingsthorpe aforesaid a certain yearly rent of 5 shillings per annum, to be paid out of the rent of his house in Kings thorpe aforesaid, called the Bakehouse, upon S. Thomas' Day, and then to be distributed to the said poor by the discretion of the parson and Churchwardens of Kingsthorpe aforesaid, and that Francis Cooke, of Kingsthorpe afores[d], gent., was at the time of taking the said inquisition owner of the said house, and that the said house was then in the occupation of Mary Morris, widow, and that the said yearly rent of 5 shillings had heretofore been duly paid according to the said will of the donor thereof; but that the said

[marginal note: Thos. Knapp, gift of 5s. per ann.]

10

Francis Cooke having for divers years permitted a poor inhabitant of the said town of Kingsthorpe to dwell in another house of him the said Francis Cooke there without paying any rent for the same, the inhabitants of the said Town of Kingsthorpe have been content, in consideration thereof, to permit the said Francis Cooke to detain the said yearly rent of 5 shillings during such time as he so suffered the said poor inhabitant to dwell in his said other house, and that the said poor inhabitant being then lately dead, he, the said Francis Cooke (as appeared by credible evidence then given thereof), was willing and desirous that the said yearly rent of 5 shillings should for ever hereafter be duly paid and distributed to the poor people of Kingsthorpe afores[d], on S. Thomas' Day yearly, according to the said mind and will of the said donor thereof.

And it was further found by the jurors afores[d], in and by the said inquisition, that one Walter Burnell, heretofore of Kingsthorpe afore[d], did, being owner of a certain room or building in Kingsthorpe afore[d], then being used as a shopp, and in the occupation of Francis Billingham, standing on the east side of the high road leading to the town of Northampton, the dwellinghouse then of Clement Darlow, gent., standing on the north side, and the dwelling house of William Brooks, on the south side thereof, did heretofore give the yearly rent or summe of six shillings and eightpence to be paid out of the said shopp to the overseers of the poor of the town of Kingsthorpe, for the time being, on Good Friday yearly for ever, for the use of the poor people of Kingsthorpe aforesaid. And that the said yearly rent or summe of 6 shillings and 8 pence had from time to time been paid to the said charitable uses, and ought to be for ever hereafter according to the mind and direction of the said donor thereof. And that the said Clement Darlow had been owner of the said shopp, and received the rent and profit thereof, for the space of

Wal[r] Burnell, gift of 6s. 8d. p. ann.

8 years last past and upwards, and ought to be accountable for the said yearly rent or summe of 6 shillings and 8 pence for all such time as he had been owner of the said shopp.

And it was further found by the jurors aforesaid, in and by the said inquisition, that one Simon Rogers, long since dead, being heretofore owner of a certain messuage, tenement, or dwellinghouse,

Sim. Rogers, gift 5s. per ann.

situate in Kingsthorpe aforesaid, on the east side of the high road leading to the town of Northampton, on the north side of the above mentioned shopp, which said messuage, tene- ment, or dwellinghouse the abovenamed Clement Darlow now (occupies), did give or grant a rent charge or summe of 5 shillings per annum, to be issuing and paid out of the said messuage or dwellinghouse on S. Thomas' Day for ever, to the use of the poor of Kingsthorpe aforesaid. The said messuage . . . house did afterwards descend and come to one Simon Childe . . . and was about 18 years since or some what . . . Childe by the said Clement Darlow, who had ever since be . . . that the said rent charge or sum of 5 shillings per annum . . . upwards being paid for many years together, and so downwards during such time as the said messuage, tenement, or dwellinghouse was in the pos- session of the said Simon Childe, and until the same was purchased of the said Simon Childe by the said Clement Darlow as aforesaid, and that the said Clement Darlow was privy to the said gift or rentcharge, and ought to give an account to the Church wardens or overseers of Kingsthorpe aforesaid how he had paid and employed the same, and forthwith to pay all such money as he was in arrear for the said rentcharge to the overseers of the poor of Kingsthorpe, for the use of the said poor of Kingsthorpe, and that the said rent charge or summe of 5 shillings per annum ought for ever hereafter to be duly paid on the Feast day of Saint Thomas the Apostle yearly to the overseers of the poor of Kingsthorpe afores^d for the time being, and by them to be

distributed to and among the poor people of Kingsthorpe
aforesaid, according to the mind and intent of the said donor
thereof.

And it was further found by the jurors aforesaid, in and
John Smith, by the said inquisition, that one John Smith,
gift of 4s. per heretofore of Kingsthorpe aforesaid, deceased,
ann.   being seized in his demeasne as of ffee and in a
certain dwelling house and some lands in Kingsthorpe aforesaid, did by his last will and testament in writing, bearing
date on or about the 17th day of October, in the year of our
Lord 1637, give the rent or summe of 4 shillings per annum
to the poor of Kingsthorpe aforesaid, in these words following: I give to the poor of Kingsthorpe the summe of
4 shillings to be yearly paid them on the Feast of S. Thomas
for ever, and my will is that my wife Elisabeth during her
life shall discharge the said four shillings yearly, and after
her decease William Billingham and Samuel Rider shall pay
out of my house and land 2 shillings apiece yearly for ever
upon the aforesaid Feast.

And that the said house was situate in Duck End in
Kingsthorpe aforesaid, and that one William Butlin, miller,
then was and for the space of 12 years last past had been
owner, and received the rent and profit thereof, and was
privy to the said gift of 2 shillings per annum out of the
same, and ought to give a good account how he had paid
the same during such time as he had enjoyed the said house,
and (ought) forthwith to pay all arrears thereof to the overseers of the poor of Kingsthorpe afore[d] for the use of the
said poor, and that the abovenamed Clement Darlow had
about one year since purchased and was then owner of the
said lands, being likewise privy to the said gift of 2 shillings
per annum out . . . to pay forthwith to the overseers of the
poor of Kingsthorpe . . . said use, and that the said yearly
summe of four shillings . . . into 2 several summes of
2 shillings per annum ought . . . out of the said house and

lands respectively on . . . of the poor of Kingsthorpe aforesaid for the time being for the use of the poor of Kingsthorpe aforesaid.

And it was further found by the jurors aforesaid, in and
by the said Inquisition, that one Henry Weston,
being heretofore seized in his demeasne as of
ffee of and in one house and some meadow
ground and ten acres of land and leys in Kingsthorpe aforesaid, did by his last will and testament in writing, bearing
date the 29th day of April, 1611, did give the two several
yearly rents of 12 pence to be paid out of the same to the
use of the poor of Kingsthorpe aforesaid, namely, 12 pence
out of his house and meadow and 12 pence out of his said
ten acres of land and leys ; and that one Dorothy White was
then owner of the said house, and did confess before the
said Commissioners and jurors, at the time of the taking of
the said inquisition, that she was privy to the said gift and
ought to pay the said rent of 12 pence per annum for the
use of the said poor.

Hen. Weston, gift of 2s. per ann.

And that one John Mewes, of Kingsthorpe afore[d], was
then the owner of the said ten acres of land and leyes, and
did likewise confess to the said comm[rs] and jurors that he
was privy to the said gift, and ought to pay the said rent of
12 pence per annum out of the said land and leys for the
use of the said poor, and that he is 5 years in arrear for the
said rent, which the said jurors did find and say he ought
forthwith to pay to and for the charitable use aforesaid.

Mayden Hooke. And it was further found by the jurors aforesaid, in and by the said inquisition, that it did
appear to them by good evidence at the time of the taking
the said inquisition that they did find that a certain piece of
meadow ground, called by the name of Maiden Hooke,
lying in the parish of Kingsthorpe afore[d], in a certain place
called Worsters Holme, was heretofore given and appointed
to the use following, viz., that the rent and profit thereof

should yearly for ever be laid out, employed, and disposed in buying bread and drink for . . . passengers through Kingsthorpe aforesaid.

Mr. Clark, And it was further found by the jurors afore[d], gift of £20. in and by the said inquisition . . . George Clarke . . . Doctor Clarke heretofore . . . did give . . . 20 pounds of lawful . . . aforesaid with direction . . . and overseers of the poor of Kingsthorpe . . . to be distributed to the poor on S. George's . . . said money was at the time of taking the said inquisition lent unto and in the hand of Edward Foster, of Kingsthorpe aforesaid, upon security, and that the interest thereof had been from time to time duly paid and disposed according to the will and mind of the said donor, and ought so to be and continue for ever here-after, as, in, and by, before recited inquisition (and which is hereunto annexed), whereunto for more certainty relačon being had it doth and may more plainly and at large appear.

Now know ye that wee the said Com[rs], taking upon us the execution of the said statute by virtue of the said com-mission so to us and others directed as aforesaid, and by virtue of the power and authority to us and others in that behalf, in and by the said statute and Commission given and remitted, having duly called before us, and the said jurors duly sworn at the time of the taking the said inquisi-tion, all persons interested or concerned, or that pretend to be interested or concerned in or about the premisses or any part or parcel thereof, and having heard or examined all witnesses on either side produced, and heard what was alleged by the parties or their agents, or any of them, and having well weighed their allegations and proofs, and the said verdict and inquisition, doe this present 8th day of Feb-ruary, in 6 and 30th year of the reign of our Sovereign Lord Charles the second, by the grace of God of England, Ire-land, France, and Scotland, King, Defender of the Faith, etc., annoq d[m] 1683, adjudge, determine, and decide, as

followeth, and first we do order, adjudge, determine, and
decree that all the several annuities or rent charges mentioned in the above certified inquisition, and every of them
and every part and parcel of them and every of them, and
also all the rent issues and proffitts of the said piece of
meadow ground lying in the parish of Kingsthorpe aforesaid
called the Maiden Hooke, and also the interest, increase,
and product of the above mentioned sum of 20 pounds, so
as aforesaid given by the said George Clark, dec^d, shall
from time to time for ever hereafter be laid out, distributed,
disposed, and employed to and for the aforesaid pious and
charitable uses respectively to and for which the same were
found by the jurors in and by the same inquisition to have
been given, limited, assigned, or appointed, and according
to the will, direction, and intent of the donors thereof respectively, and not otherwise.

And we do further order, adjudge, determine, and decree
that Francis [Cooke], of Kingsthorpe aforesaid, Esqre.,
Edward Reynolds, of Kingsthorpe aforesaid, ·Doctor ot
Divinity, William Atkins, of Kingsthorpe afore^d, gent. . . .
and the survivor of them . . . of the poor of Kingsthorpe
afore^d, from . . . trustees of and for all and every the above
. . . piece of meadow ground called Maiden Hooke . . .
every of them, and shall take care to se the same . . .
proffitts thereof faithfully employed and disposed to the
uses aforesaid respectively, and according to the mind, will,
direction, and intent of the donors thereof respectively, and
we do further order, adjudge, determine, and decree that
the said Clement Darlow shall within the space of 30 days
next after he shall have notice of this our decree give a true
account to the abovenamed trustees, or the major part of
them, how, when, and to whom he hath paid the above-
mentioned annuities or rentcharges of 6 shillings and 8
pence and 5 shillings so as aforesaid issuing and payable
out of his said messuage and shopp in Kingsthorpe afore-

said, and what arrears of them or either of them are behind
and unpaid respectively since the purchase of the said messuage and shopp out of which the same are payable, and
also that he, the said Clement Darlow, shall forthwith pay
under the said trustees, or under such persons that they or
the major part of them shall appoint to receive the same, all
and every such summe and summes of money as he shall
be found to be in arrear of said rentcharge . . . which he
cannot by sufficient proof . . . have duly paid according to
the donor's will . . . determine and decree that the above
named . . . [4 lines] . . . [shall be reduced] to two, that
then those two surviving trustees shall by some writing under
their hands and seals elect, choose, constitute, and appoint
so many more of the most discreet, honest, and substantial
inhabitants of Kingsthorpe afores^d, to be trustees with them
of and for the said premisses, to and for the charitable uses
aforesaid, do such . . . shall therein be fit, and so from
time to time, as the like occasion shall require, and these
our decrees, determinations, judgements, and orders, which
the said court do hereby humbly certify into his Majesty's
High Court of Chancery under our hands and seals, dated
the said 8th day of January, in the 6 and 30th year of the
reign of our Sovereign Lord Charles the 2nd, by the grace
of God of England, Scotland, France, and Ireland, King,
Defender of the Faith, Anno D^m 1683, Ri. Raynsford,
Wal. Littleton, Edw. Saunders, Charles Tyrrell.

　　　　　　　　　　　　　　Examined by . . .

[The Charities referred to in this document no longer exist under the
names of the respective donors, but probably most of them have been
absorbed in a Fund now in the hands of the Charity Commissioners,
producing £6 0s. 2d. per annum, and which is distributed in weekly
doles of bread to certain poor women of the place.]

XLV.

This indenture, made in the 29th day of September, in the 4th year of our sovereign lady Anne, by the grace of God, etc., etc., and in the year of our Lord 1705, between John Morgan, Esqre., Henry Milward, gentleman, Wm. Atkins, gentleman, and John Billingham, yeoman, all of Kingsthorpe, in the county of Northampton, of the one part, and Francis Cooke, Edmund Morgan, Hatton Atkins, gentlemen, Wm. Green, junior, Wm. Morris, senior, Wm. Morris, junr., Richd Hollis, John Cooch, Samuel Crick, and Edward Atkins, yeomen, all of Kingsthorpe aforesaid, of the other part. Whereas our late sovereign lord King James, by his letters pattents bearing date at Wstmr the 13th day of April, in the 14th year of his said reign, did grant to Thomas Hollis, Richd Morris, Francis Morgan, Francis Barnard, and others therein named, since deceased, the town of Kingsthorpe, with its members and appurtenances, and did thereby also grant that the said grantees therein named, and their heirs, should and might have all rights, jurisdictions, liberties, etc., etc., within the said town as fully, freely, and entirely as any the men and tenants of Kingsthorpe aforesaid then before had used, held, or enjoyed by any charter, gift, etc., at the ffee ffarm of forty pounds per an., as by the said letters pattent, etc., may appear, and Whereas since the making the said letters pattents the said

town of Kingsthorpe hath been granted to the several tenants
and their heirs in ffee ffarm at several yearly rents, and such
part thereof as was not granted away as aforesaid, together
with the manor, lordship, or seignory of Kingsthorpe, and
all other franchises, liberties, etc., thereunto belonging, did
lawfully come unto the said Thomas Hollis and Rich^d
Morris and their heirs by right of survivorship, and Whereas
the said Thomas Hollis and Richd Morris, by their indenture bearing date the one and twentieth day of January, in
the year of our Lord 1650, and enrolled in his Majesty's
High Court of Chancery, did grant, bargain, sell, aliene,
enfeoff, and confirm unto Wm. Morris and Wm. Billingham
and Thos. Morgan, and others therein named, and their
heirs, the manor, lordship, or seignory of Kingsthorpe,
with the rights, royalties, members, and appurtenances of
the same, together with profits of courts goods and chatles
waived and strayed goods and chatles of felons, and all other
profits, etc., etc. And whereas the same was lawfully vested
in the said Wm. Morris and Wm. Billingham, and their heirs
by right of survivorship. And whereas the said Wm. Morris
and Wm. Billingham, by their indenture bearing date the
thirteenth day of October, in the year of our Lord 1684, did
grant, sell, aliene, etc., unto Francis Morgan, Esquire, John
Morgan, Henry Milward, etc., etc., the manor, lordship, and
seignory of Kingsthorpe aforesaid, with the rights, etc., etc.
Now this indenture witnesseth that the said John Morgan,
Henry Milward, Wm. Atkins, and John Billingham, for the
good and benefit of the said town, and in performance of
the original trust in the said letters pattent and in the said
recited indenture devolved upon them by survivorship, and
for the better ordering and governing the said town, and
also for and in consideration of the sum of 5 shillings apiece
of lawful English money to them in hand paid by the said
Francis Cooke, Edmond Morgan, Hatton Atkins, etc., etc.,
etc., before the ensealling and delivery of these presents,

have granted, bargained, sold, aliened, etc., unto the said Francis Cooke, Edmond Morgan, Hatton Atkins, etc., etc., all that the manor, lordship, or seignory of Kingsthorpe aforesaid, with the rights, royalties, privileges, etc., etc., etc., and all lands, tenements, and hereditaments, parcells of the said manor, conteined in the letters pattents, and not granted to themselves or to some or any of them, or to any other person in ffee ffarm as aforesaid, and the reversion and reversions, remainder and remainders of all and singular the premises, and all the estate, right, title, interest, claim, and demand what soever of the said John Morgan, Henry Milward, Wm. Atkins, John Billingham, or any of them, of, in, and to the same, To have and to hold the said manor or seignory of Kingsthorpe, lands, tenements, hereditaments, etc., etc., unto the said Francis Cooke, Edmund Morgan, Hatton Atkins, etc., etc., To the use of the said Francis Cooke, Edmund Morgan, Hatton Atkins, etc., etc., and of the said John Morgan and Henry Milward, Wm. Atkins, and John Billingham, and of their heirs, etc., for ever, And the said John Morgan and Henry Milward, Wm. Atkins, and John Billingham . . . do hereby covenant, promise, grant, and agree to, and with the said Francis Cooke, Edmund Morgan, Hatton Atkins, etc., etc., that the aforesaid manor, lands, tenements, etc., and all other the premisses herein before granted or mentioned . . . shall remain, continue, and be to the uses herein before mentioned, etc., etc., and it is lastly mutually agreed by and between all the said parties to these presents, and so hereby declared, that when and as often as there shall be but four of the grantee parties to these presents surviving, that then such four surviving grantees, or more of them in case they should think fit sooner to renew their said estates, shall at the request of the best or most considerable freeholders of the said town and inhabitants for estates, and at the cost and charges of the said town, make such new grant or conveyance of the said

manor of Kingsthorpe, and other the before granted premisses, to such of the then freeholders and inhabitants of
the said town and their heirs as the said surviving grantees,
with the best and most considerable freeholders of the said
town and inhabitants for estates, shall nominate and think
fit, to the end that the same may continue in grant for ever,
that the said town may be better governed and ordered,
that the ffee ffarm rent may be duly collected and paid, and
that the profits arising out of the same may be employed
for support of government and for the best advantage of the
said town.   In witness whereof the parties first above-named
to these present indentures interchangably have put their
hands and seals the day and year first above written.

A SELECTED LIST

OF

STANDARD PUBLICATIONS & REMAINDERS

Offered for Sale at remarkably low prices by

JOHN GRANT, BOOKSELLER,

25 & 34 George IV. Bridge,

EDINBURGH.

Robert Burns' Poetical Works, edited by W. Scott Douglas, with Explanatory Notes, Various Readings, and Glossary, illustrated with portraits, vignettes, and frontispieces by Sam Bough, R.S.A., and W. E. Lockhart, R.S.A., 3 vols, royal 8vo, cloth extra (pub £2 2s), 16s 6d. W. Paterson, 1880.

Dryden's Dramatic Works, Library Edition, with Notes and Life by Sir Walter Scott, Bart., edited by George Saintsbury, portrait and plates, 8 vols, 8vo, cloth (pub £4 4s), £1 10s. Paterson.

Large Paper Copy—Best Library Edition.

Molière's Dramatic Works, complete, translated and edited by Henri Van Laun, with Memoir, Introduction, and Appendices, wherein are given the Passages borrowed or adapted from Molière by English Dramatists, with Explanatory Notes, illustrated with a portrait and 33 etchings, India proofs, by Lalauze, 6 magnificent vols, imperial 8vo, cloth (pub £9 9s), £2 18s 6d. Wm. Paterson.

—— The same, 6 vols, half choice morocco, gilt top (pub £12 12s), £4 18s 6d.

" Not only the best translation in existence, but the best to be hoped. It is a direct and valuable contribution to European scholarship."—*Athenæum.*

Richardson's (Samuel) Works, Library Edition, with Biographical Criticism by Leslie Stephen, portrait, 12 vols, 8vo, cloth extra, impression strictly limited to 750 copies (pub £6 6s), £2 5s. London.

Sent Carriage Free to any part of the United Kingdom on receipt of Postal Order for the amount.

JOHN GRANT, 25 & 34 George IV. Bridge, Edinburgh.

Choice Illustrated Works :-

Burnet's Treatise on Painting, illustrated by 130 Etchings
from celebrated pictures of the Italian, Venetian, Flemish, Dutch,
and English Schools. also woodcuts, thick 4to, half morocco, gilt
top (pub £4 10s), £2 2s.

Canova's Works in Sculpture and Modelling, 142 exqui-
site plates, engraved in outline by Henry Moses, with Literary
Descriptions by the Countess Albrizzi, and Biographical Memoir
by Count Escognara, handsome volume, imperial 8vo, half
crimson morocco, gilt top (pub at £6 12s), reduced to 21s.

Carter's Specimens of Ancient Sculpture and Painting now
Remaining in England, from the Earliest Period to the Reign of
Henry VIII., edited by Francis Douse, and other eminent antiquaries, illustrated with 120 large engravings, many of which are
beautifully coloured, and several highly illuminated with gold,
handsome volume, royal folio, half crimson morocco, top edges
gilt (first pub at £15 15s), now reduced to £3 3s.

Also uniform in size and binding.

Carter's Ancient Architecture of England, including the
Orders during the British, Roman, Saxon, and Norman Eras,
also under the Reigns of Henry III. and Edward III., illustrated
by 109 large copperplate engravings, comprising upwards of 2000
Specimens shown in Plan, Execution, Section, and Detail. best
edition, illustrated by John Britton (first pub at £12 12s), now
reduced to £2 2s.

Castles (The) and Mansions of the Lothians, illustrated
in 103 Views, with Historical and Descriptive Accounts, by John
Small, LL.D., Librarian, University, Edinburgh, 2 handsome
vols, folio, cloth (pub £6 6s), £2 15s.   W. Paterson.

Claude Lorraine's Beauties, consisting of Twenty-four of
his Choicest Landscapes, selected from the Liber Veritatis,
beautifully engraved on steel by Brimley, Lupton, and others, in
a folio cloth portfolio (pub £3 3s), 12s 6d.   Cooke.

Marlborough Gems—The Collection of Gems formed by
George Spencer, Third Duke of Marlborough, illustrated by 108
full-page engravings, chiefly by Bartolozzi, with Letterpress
Descriptions in French and Latin by Jacob Bryant, Louis
Dutens, &c., 2 handsome vols, folio, half crimson morocco, gilt
top (selling price £10 10s), £2 12s 6d.   John Murray, 1844.

The most beautiful Work on the " Stately Homes of England."

Nash's Mansions of England in the Olden Time, 104
Lithographic Views faithfully reproduced from the originals, with
new and complete history of each Mansion, by Anderson, 4 vols
in 2, imperial 4to, cloth extra, gilt edges (pub £6 6s), £2 10s.
Sotheran.

Choice Illustrated Works—*continued*:—

Lyndsay (Sir David, of the Mount)—A Facsimile of the ancient Heraldic Manuscript emblazoned by the celebrated Sir David Lyndsay of the Mount, Lyon King at Arms in the reign of James the Fifth, edited by the late David Laing, LL.D., from the Original MS. in the possession of the Faculty of Advocates, folio, cloth, gilt top, uncut edges (pub £10 10s), £3 10s.
Impression limited to 250 copies.

Also Uniform.

Scottish Arms, being a Collection of Armorial Bearings, A.D. 1370-1678, Reproduced in Facsimile from Contemporary Manuscripts, with Heraldic and Genealogical Notes, by R. R. Stodart, of the Lyon Office, 2 vols, folio, cloth extra, gilt tops (pub £12 12s), £4 10s.
Impression limited to 300 copies.

Several of the manuscripts from which these Arms are taken have hitherto been unknown to heraldic antiquaries in this country. The Arms of upwards of 600 families are given, all of which are described in upwards of 400 pages of letterpress by Mr Stodart.

The book is uniform with Lyndsay's Heraldic Manuscript, and care was taken not to reproduce any Arms which are in that volume, unless there are variations, or from older manuscripts.

Strutt's Sylva Britanniæ et Scotiæ ; or, Portraits of Forest Trees Distinguished for their Antiquity, Magnitude, or Beauty, drawn from Nature, with 50 highly finished etchings, imp. folio, half morocco extra, gilt top, a handsome volume (pub £9 9s), £2 2s.

The Modern Cupid (en Chemin de Fer), by M. Mounet-Sully, of the Comedie Français, illustrations by Ch. Daux. A Bright, Attractive Series of Verses, illustrative of Love on the Rail, with dainty drawings reproduced in photogravure plates, and printed in tints, folio, edition limited to 350 copies, each copy numbered. Estes & Lauriat.
Proofs on Japan paper, in parchment paper portfolio, only 65 copies printed (pub 63s), £1 1s.
Proofs on India paper, in white vellum cloth portfolio, 65 copies printed (pub 50s), 16s.
Ordinary copy proofs on vellum paper, in cloth portfolio, 250 copies printed (pub 30s), 10s 6d.

The Costumes of all Nations, Ancient and Modern, exhibiting the Dresses and Habits of all Classes, Male and Female, from the Earliest Historical Records to the Nineteenth Century, by Albert Kretschmer and Dr Rohrbach, 104 coloured plates displaying nearly 2000 full-length figures, complete in one handsome volume, 4to, half morocco (pub £4 4s), 45s. Sotheran.

Walpole's (Horace) Anecdotes of Painting in England, with some Account of the Principal Artists, enlarged by Rev. James Dallaway : and Vertue's Catalogue of Engravers who have been born or resided in England, last and best edition, revised with additional notes by Ralph N. Wornum, illustrated with eighty portraits of the principal artists, and woodcut portraits of the minor artists, 3 handsome vols, 8vo, cloth (pub 27s), 14s 6d. Bickers.

—— The same, 3 vols, half morocco, gilt top, by one of the best Edinburgh binders (pub 45s), £1 8s.

Works on Edinburgh :—

Edinburgh and its Neighbourhood in the Days of our Grandfathers, a Series of Eighty Illustrations of the more remarkable Old and New Buildings and Picturesque Scenery of Edinburgh, as they appeared about 1830, with Historical Introduction and Descriptive Sketches, by James Gowans, royal 8vo, cloth elegant (pub 12s 6d), 6s. J. C. Nimmo.

"The chapters are brightly and well written, and are all, from first to last, readable and full of information. The volume is in all respects handsome."—*Scotsman.*

Edinburgh University—Account of the Tercentenary Festival of the University, including the Speeches and Addresses on the Occasion, edited by R. Sydney Marsden, crown 8vo, cloth (pub 3s), 1s. Blackwood & Sons.

Historical Notices of Lady Yester's Church and Parish, by James J. Hunter, revised and corrected by the Rev. Dr Gray, crown 8vo, cloth (pub 2s 6d), 9d.

Of interest to the antiquarian, containing notices of buildings and places now fast disappearing.

History of the Queen's Edinburgh Rifle Volunteer Brigade, with an Account of the City of Edinburgh and Midlothian Rifle Association, the Scottish Twenty Club, &c., by Wm. Stephen, crown 8vo, cloth (pub 5s), 2s. Blackwood & Sons.

"This opportune volume has far more interest for readers generally than might have been expected, while to members of the Edinburgh Volunteer Brigade it cannot fail to be very interesting indeed."—*St James's Gazette.*

Leighton's (Alexander) Mysterious Legends of Edinburgh, illustrated, crown 8vo, boards, 1s 6d.

CONTENTS:—Lord Kames' Puzzle, Mrs Corbet's Amputated Toe, The Brownie of the West Bow, The Ancient Bureau, A Legend of Halkerstone's Wynd, Deacon Macgillvray's Disappearance, Lord Braxfield's Case of the Red Night-cap, The Strange Story of Sarah Gowanlock, and John Cameron's Life Policy.

Steven's (Dr William) History of the High School of Edinburgh, from the beginning of the Sixteenth Century, based upon Researches of the Town Council Records and other Authentic Documents, illustrated with view, also facsimile of a School Exercise by Sir Walter Scott when a pupil in 1783, crown 8vo, cloth, a handsome volume (pub 7s 6d), 2s.

Appended is a list of the distinguished pupils who have been educated in this Institution, which has been patronised by Royalty from the days of James VI.

The Authorised Library Edition.

Trial of the Directors of the City of Glasgow Bank, before the Petition for Bail, reported by Charles Tennant Couper, Advocate, the Speeches and Opinions, revised by the Council and Judges, and the Charge by the Lord Justice Clerk, illustrated with lithographic facsimiles of the famous false Balance-sheets, one large volume, royal 8vo, cloth (pub 15s), 3s 6d. Edinburgh.

Wilson's (Dr Daniel) Memorials of Edinburgh in the Olden Time, with numerous fine engravings and woodcuts, 2 vols, 4to, cloth (pub £2 2s), 16s 6d.

Sent Carriage Free to any part of the United Kingdom on receipt of Postal Order for the amount.

JOHN GRANT, 25 & 34 George IV. Bridge, Edinburgh.

Works on the Highlands of Scotland : -

Disruption Worthies of the Highlands, a Series of Biographies of Eminent Free Church Ministers who Suffered in the
North of Scotland in 1843 for the Cause of Religious Liberty,
enlarged edition, with additional Biographies, and an Introduction by the Rev. Dr Duff, illustrated with 24 full-page portraits
and facsimiles of the autographs of eminent Free Churchmen,
4to, handsomely bound in cloth, gilt (pub £1 1s), 8s 6d.

Gaelic Names of Plants, Scottish and Irish, Collected and
Arranged in Scientific Order, with Notes on the Etymology,
their Uses, Plant Superstitions, &c., among the Celts, with
Copious Gaelic, English, and Scientific Indices, by John Cameron, 8vo, cloth (pub 7s 6d). 3s 6d.   Blackwood & Sons.

" It is impossible to withhold a tribute of admiration from a work on which
the author spent ten years of his life, and which necessitated not only voluminous
reading in Gaelic and Irish, but long journeys through the Highlands in search
of Gaelic names for plants, or rather, in this case, plants for names already
existing."—*Scotsman.*

Grant (Mrs, of Laggan)—Letters from the Mountains,
edited, with Notes and Additions, by her son, J. P. Grant, best
edition, 2 vols, post 8vo, cloth (pub 21s), 4s 6d.   London.

Lord Jeffrey says :—" Her 'Letters from the Mountains' are among the
most interesting collections of real letters that have been given to the public :
and being indebted for no part of their interest to the celebrity of the names
they contain, or the importance of the events they narrate, afford, in their success, a more honourable testimony of the talents of the author. The great
charm of the correspondence indeed is its perfect independence of artificial
helps, and the air of fearlessness and originality which it has consequently
assumed."

Historical Sketches of the Highland Clans of Scotland,
containing a concise account of the origin, &c., of the Scottish
Clans, with twenty-two illustrative coloured plates of the Tartan
worn by each, post 8vo, cloth, 2s 6d.

" The object of this treatise is to give a concise account of the origin, seat,
and characteristics of the Scottish Clans, together with a representation of the
distinguishing tartan worn by each."—*Preface.*

Keltie (John S.)—A History of the Scottish Highlands,
Highland Clans, and Highland Regiments, with an Account of
the Gaelic Literature and Music by Dr M'Lauchlan, and an
Essay on Highland Scenery by Professor Wilson, coloured illustrations of the Tartans of Scotland, also many steel engravings, 2
vols, imperial 8vo, half morocco, gilt top (pub £3 10s), £1 17s 6d

*Mackenzie (Alexander)—The History of the Highland
Clearances,* containing a reprint of Donald Macleod's "Gloomy
Memories of the Highlands," "Isle of Skye in 1882," and a
Verbatim Report of the Trial of the Brae Crofters, thick vol,
crown 8vo, cloth (pub 7s 6d), 3s 6d.   Inverness.

" Some people may ask, Why rake up all this iniquity just now? We answer,
That the same laws which permitted the cruelties, the inhuman atrocities,
described in this book, are still the laws of the country, and any tyrant who may
be indifferent to the healthier public opinion which now prevails, may *legally*
repeat the same proceedings whenever he may take it into his head to do so."

*Stewart's (General David, of Garth) Sketches of the
Character, Institutions, and Customs of the Highlanders of Scotland,* crown 8vo, cloth (pub 5s), 2s.   Inverness.

Stewart's sketches of the Highlands and Highland regiments are worthy to
rank beside the Highland works of Sir Walter Scott, or even more worthy, for
facts are stronger than fiction. Every Scottish lad should have the book in his
hands as soon as he is able to read.

Scottish Literature :—

The genial Author of " Noctes Ambrosianæ."

Christopher North—A Memoir of Professor John Wilson,
compiled from Family Papers and other sources, by his daughter,
Mrs Gordon, new edition, with portrait and illustrations, crown
8vo, cloth (pub 6s), 2s 6d.

"A writer of the most ardent and enthusiastic genius."—HENRY HALLAM.
"The whole literature of England does not contain a more brilliant series of
articles than those with which Wilson has enriched the pages of *Blackwood's
Magazine.*"—Sir ARCHIBALD ALISON.

Cockburn (Henry)—Journals of, being a Continuation of
the Memorials of his Time, 1831-1854, 2 vols, 8vo, cloth (pub
21s), 8s 6d. Edinburgh.

*Cochran-Patrick (R. W.) — Records of the Coinage of
Scotland,* from the Earliest Period to the Union, numerous
illustrations of coins, 2 vols, 4to, half citron morocco, gilt top,
£4 10s. David Douglas.

Also uniform.

Cochran-Patrick (R. W.)—The Medals of Scotland, a
Descriptive Catalogue of the Royal and other Medals relating to
Scotland, 4to, half citron morocco, gilt top, £2 5s. David
Douglas.

Also uniform.

*Cochran-Patrick (R. W.)—Early Records relating to
Mining in Scotland,* 4to, half citron morocco, £1 7s 6d. David
Douglas.

"The future historians of Scotland will be very fortunate if many parts of
their materials are so carefully worked up for them, and set before them in so
complete and taking a form."—*Athenæum.*
"We have in these records of the coinage of Scotland not the production of a
dilettante but of a real student, who with rare pains and the most scholarly dili-
gence has set to work and collected into two massive volumes a complete history
of the coinage of Scotland, so far as it can be gathered from ancient records."—
Academy.
"Such a book . . . . revealing as it does the first developments of an
industry which has become the mainspring of the national prosperity, ought to
be specially interesting to all patriotic Scotsmen."—*Saturday Review.*

Crieff: Its Traditions and Characters, with Anecdotes of
Strathearn, Reminiscences of Obsolete Customs, Traditions, and
Superstitions, Humorous Anecdotes of Schoolmasters, Ministers,
and other Public Men, crown 8vo, 1s.

"A book which will have considerable value in the eyes of all collectors of
Scottish literature. A gathering up of stories about well-known inhabitants,
memorable local occurrences, and descriptions of manners and customs."—
Scotsman

*Sent Carriage Free to any part of the United Kingdom on
receipt of Postal Order for the amount.*

JOHN GRANT, 25 & 34 George IV. Bridge, Edinburgh.

Scottish Literature—*continued:*—

Douglas' (Gavin, Bishop of Dunkeld, 1475-1522) Poetical Works, edited, with Memoir, Notes, and full Glossary, by John Small, M.A., F.S.A. Scot., illustrated with specimens of manuscript, title-page, and woodcuts of the early editions in facsimile, 4 vols, beautifully printed on thick paper, post 8vo, cloth (pub £3 3s), £1 2s 6d. W. Paterson.

"The latter part of the fifteenth and beginning of the sixteenth century, a period almost barren in the annals of English poetry, was marked by a remarkable series of distinguished poets in Scotland. During this period flourished Dunbar, Henryson, Mercier, Harry the Minstrel, Gavin Douglas, Bellenden, Kennedy, and Lyndesay. Of these, although the palm of excellence must beyond all doubt be awarded to Dunbar,—next to Burns probably the greatest poet of his country,—the voice of contemporaries, as well as of the age that immediately followed, pronounced in favour of him who,
'In barbarous age,
Gave rude Scotland Virgil's page,'—
Gavin Douglas. We may confidently predict that this will long remain the standard edition of Gavin Douglas; and we shall be glad to see the works of other of the old Scottish poets edited with equal sympathy and success."—*Athenæum.*

Lyndsay's (Sir David, of the Mount, 1490-1568) Poetical Works, best edition, edited, with Life and Glossary, by David Laing, 3 vols, crown 8vo, cloth (pub 63s), 18s 6d.

———— Another cheaper edition by the same editor, 2 vols, 12mo, cloth (pub 15s), 5s. W. Paterson.

"When it is said that the revision, including Preface, Memoir, and Notes, has been executed by Dr David Laing, it is said that all has been done that is possible by thorough scholarship, good judgment, and conscientiousness."—*Scotsman.*

Lytteil (William, M.A.)—Landmarks of Scottish Life and Language, crown 8vo, cloth (pub 7s 6d), 2s. Edinburgh.

Introductory Observations; Cumbrae Studies, or an "Alphabet" of Cumbrae Local Names; Arran Studies, or an "Alphabet" of Arran Local Names; Lochranza Places; Sannox Scenes and Sights; Short Sketches of Notable Places; A Glance Round Bute; Symbols; Explanations, &c. &c.

M'Kerlie's (P. H., F.S.A. Scot.) History of the Lands and their Owners in Galloway, illustrated by woodcuts of Notable Places and Objects, with a Historical Sketch of the District, 5 handsome vols, crown 8vo, roxburghe style (pub £3 15s), 26s 6d. W. Paterson.

Ramsay (Allan)—The Gentle Shepherd, New Edition, with Memoir and Glossary, and illustrated with the original graphic plates by David Allan; also, all the Original Airs to the Songs, royal 4to, cloth extra (pub 21s), 5s. W. & A. K. Johnston.

The finest edition of the celebrated Pastoral ever produced. The paper has been made expressly for the edition, a large clear type has been selected, and the printing in black and red is of the highest class. The original plates by David Allan have been restored, and are here printed in tint. The volume contains a Prologue, which is published for the first time.

---

8 *John Grant, Bookseller,*

Scottish Literature—*continued:*—
The Earliest known Printed English Ballad.

Scottysche Kynge—*A Ballad of the*, written by John
Skelton, Poet Laureate to King Henry VIII., reproduced in
facsimile, with an Historical and Biographical Introduction, by
John Ashton, beautifully printed on thick paper, small 4to, cloth,
uncut edges (pub 16s), 3s 6d. Elliot Stock.

Southey says of him:—"The power, the strangeness, the volubility of his
language, the audacity of his satire, and the perfect originality of his manner,
made Skelton one of the most extraordinary writers of any age or country."

This unique ballad was printed by Richard Fawkes, the King's printer, in
1513, immediately after the battle of Flodden Field, which is described in it, and
is of great interest.

Every justice has been done to the work in this beautiful volume, the paper,
printing, and binding of which are all alike excellent.

One of the Earliest Presidents of the Court of Session.

*Seton (Alexander, Earl of Dunfermline, Chancellor of
Scotland*, 1555-1622) — *Memoir of*, with an Appendix contain-
ing a List of the various Presidents of the Court, and Genealogical
Tables of the Legal Families of Erskine, Hope, Dalrymple, and
Dundas, by George Seton, Advocate, with exquisitely etched
portraits of Chancellor Seton, and George, seventh Lord Seton,
and his family ; also the Chancellor's Signatures, Seals, and Book-
Stamp ; with etchings of Old Dalgety Church, Fyvie Castle, and
Pinkie House, small 4to, cloth (pub 21s) 6s 6d. Blackwood & Sons.

"We have here everything connected with the subject of the book that could
interest the historical student, the herald, the genealogist, and the archæologist.
The result is a book worthy of its author's high reputation."—*Notes and Queries.*

*Warden's (Alex. J.) History of Angus or Forfarshire, its
Land and People*, Descriptive and Historical, illustrated with
maps, facsimiles, &c., 5 vols, 4to, cloth (published to subscribers
only at £2 17s 6d), £1 17s 6d. Dundee.

Sold separately, vol 2, 3s 6d ; vol 3, 3s 6d ; vols 4 and 5, 7s 6d ;
vol 5, 3s 6d.

A most useful Work of Reference.

Wilson's Gazetteer of Scotland, demy 8vo (473 pp.),
cloth gilt (pub 7s 6d), 3s. W. & A. K. Johnston.

This work embraces every town and village in the country of any importance
as existing at the present day, and is portable in form and very moderate in
price. In addition to the usual information as to towns and places, the work
gives the statistics of real property, notices of public works, public buildings,
churches, schools, &c., whilst the natural history and historical incidents connected with particular localities have not been omitted.

The *Scotsman* says :—"It entirely provides for a want which has been greatly
felt."

*Younger (John, shoemaker, St Boswells, Author of "River
Angling for Salmon and Trout," "Corn Law Rhymes," &c.)*—
Autobiography, with portrait, crown 8vo (457 pages), cloth (pub
7s 6d), 2s.

"'The shoemaker of St Boswells,' as he was designated in all parts of Scotland, was an excellent prose writer, a respectable poet, a marvellously gifted
man in conversation. His life will be read with great interest ; the simple heart-
stirring narrative of the life-struggle of a highly-gifted, humble, and honest
mechanic,—a life of care, but also a life of virtue."—*London Review.*

---

*Sent Carriage Free to any part of the United Kingdom on
receipt of Postal Order for the amount.*

JOHN GRANT, 25 & 34 George IV. Bridge, Edinburgh.

Grampian Club Publications, of valuable MSS. and Works of Original Research in Scottish History, Privately printed for the Members :—

The Diocesan Registers of Glasgow—Liber Protocollorum
M. Cuthberti Simonis, notarii et scribæ capituli Glasguensis, A.D.
1499-1513; also, *Rental Book of the Diocese of Glasgow*, A.D.
1509-1570, edited by Joseph Bain and the Rev. Dr Charles
Rogers, with facsimiles, 2 vols, 8vo, cl, 1875 (pub £2 2s), 7s 6d.

*Rental Book of the Cistercian Abbey of Coupar-Angus,
with the Breviary of the Register,* edited by the Rev. Dr Charles
Rogers, with facsimiles of MSS., 2 vols, 8vo, cloth, 1879-80 (pub
£2 12s 6d), 10s 6d.

—— The same, vol II., comprising the *Register of
Tacks of the Abbey of Cupar, Rental of St Marie's Monastery,* and
Appendix, 8vo, cloth (pub £1 1s), 3s 6d.

*Estimate of the Scottish Nobility during the Minority of
'James VI.,* edited, with an Introduction, from the original MS.
in the Public Record Office, by Dr Charles Rogers, 8vo, cloth
(pub 10s 6d), 1s. 6d.

The reprint of a manuscript discovered in the Public Record Office. The
details are extremely curious.

Genealogical Memoirs of the Families of Colt and Coutts,
by Dr Charles Rogers, 8vo, cloth (pub 10s 6d), 2s 6d.

An old Scottish family, including the eminent bankers of that name, the
Baroness Burdett-Coutts, &c.

*Rogers' (Dr Charles) Memorials of the Earl of Stirling
and of the House of Alexander,* portraits, 2 vols, 8vo, cloth (pub
£3 3s), 10s 6d.   Edinburgh, 1877.

This work embraces not only a history of Sir William Alexander, first Earl of
Stirling, but also a genealogical account of the family of Alexander in all its
branches ; many interesting historical details connected with Scottish State affairs
in the seventeenth century ; also with the colonisation of America.

*Sent Carriage Free to any part of the United Kingdom on
receipt of Postal Order for the amount.*

JOHN GRANT, 25 & 34 George IV. Bridge, Edinburgh.

Histories of Scotland, complete set in 10 vols for £3 3s.

This grand national series of the Early Chronicles of Scotland, edited by the most eminent Scottish antiquarian scholars of the present day, is now completed, and as sets are becoming few in number, early application is necessary in order to secure them at the reduced price.

The Series comprises :—

Scoticronicon of John de Fordun, from the Contemporary MS. (if not the author's autograph) at the end of the Fourteenth Century, preserved in the Library of Wolfenbüttel, in the Duchy of Brunswick, collated with other known MSS. of the original chronicle, edited by W. F. Skene, LL.D., Historiographer-Royal, 2 vols (pub 30s), not sold separately.

The Metrical Chronicle of Andrew Wyntoun, Prior of St Serf's Inch at Lochleven, who died about 1426, the work now printed entire for the first time, from the Royal MS. in the British Museum, collated with other MSS., edited by the late D. Laing, LL.D., 3 vols (pub 50s), vols 1 and 2 not sold separately.
Vol 3 sold separately (pub 21s), 10s 6d.

Lives of Saint Ninian and St Kentigern, compiled in the 12th century, and edited from the best MSS. by the late A. P. Forbes, D.C.L., Bishop of Brechin (pub 15s), not sold separately.

Life of Saint Columba, founder of Hy, written by Adamnan, ninth Abbot of that Monastery, edited by Wm. Reeves, D.D., M.R.I.A., translated by the late A. P. Forbes, D.C.L., Bishop of Brechin, with Notes arranged by W. F. Skene, LL.D. (pub 15s), not sold separately.

The Book of Pluscarden, being unpublished Continuation of Fordun's Chronicle by M. Buchanan, Treasurer to the Dauphiness of France, edited and translated by Skene, 2 vols (pub 30s), 12s 6d, sold separately.

A Critical Essay on the Ancient Inhabitants of Scotland, by Thomas Innes of the Sorbonne, with Memoir of the Author by George Grubb, LL.D., and Appendix of Original Documents by Wm. F. Skene, LL.D., illustrated with charts (pub 21s), 10s 6d, sold separately.

In connection with the Society of Antiquaries of Scotland, a uniform series of the Historians of Scotland, accompanied by English translations, and illustrated by notes, critical and explanatory, was commenced some years since and has recently been finished.

So much has recently been done for the history of Scotland, that the necessity for a more critical edition of the earlier historians has become very apparent. The history of Scotland, prior to the 15th century, must always be based to a great extent upon the work of Fordun : but his original text has been made the basis of continuations, and has been largely altered and interpolated by his continuators, whose statements are usually quoted as if they belonged to the original work of Fordun. An edition discriminating between the original text of Fordun and the additions and alterations of his continuators, and at the same time tracing out the sources of Fordun's narrative, would obviously be of great importance to the right understanding of Scottish history.

The complete set forms ten handsome volumes, demy 8vo, illustrated with facsimiles.

Sent Carriage Free to any part of the United Kingdom on receipt of Postal Order for the amount.

JOHN GRANT, 25 & 34 George IV. Bridge, Edinburgh.

Campbell (Colin, Lord Clyde)—Life of, illustrated by Extracts from his Diary and Correspondence, by Lieut.-Gen. Shadwell, C.B., with portrait, maps, and plans, 2 vols, 8vo, cloth (pub 36s), 6s 6d. Blackwood & Sons.

"In all the annals of 'Self-Help,' there is not to be found a life more truly worthy of study than that of the gallant old soldier. The simple, self-denying, friend-helping, brave, patriotic soldier stands proclaimed in every line of General Shadwell's admirable memoir."—*Blackwood's Magazine.*

De Witt's (John, Grand Pensionary of Holland) Life: or, *Twenty Years of a Parliamentary Republic,* by M. A. Pontalis, translated by S. E. Stephenson, 2 vols, 8vo, cloth (pub 36s), 6s 6d. Longman.

Uniform with the favourite editions of Motley's "Netherlands" and "John of Barnveld," &c.

Johnson (Doctor): His Friends and his Critics, by George Birkbeck Hill, D.C.L., crown 8vo, cloth (pub 8s), 2s. Smith, Elder, & Co.

"The public now reaps the advantage of Dr Hill's researches in a most readable volume. Seldom has a pleasanter commentary been written on a literary masterpiece. . . . Throughout the author of this pleasant volume has spared no pains to enable the present generation to realise more completely the sphere in which Johnson talked and taught."—*Saturday Review.*

Mathews (Charles James, the Actor)—Life of, chiefly Autobiographical, with Selections from his Correspondence and Speeches, edited by Charles Dickens, portraits, 2 vols, 8vo, cloth (pub 25s). 5s. Macmillan, 1879.

"The book is a charming one from first to last, and Mr Dickens deserves a full measure of credit for the care and discrimination he has exercised in the business of editing."—*Globe.*

Brazil and Java—The Coffee Culture in America, Asia, and Africa, by C. F. Van Delden Lavine, illustrated with numerous plates, maps, and diagrams, thick 8vo, cloth (pub 25s), 3s 6d. Allen.

A useful work to those interested in the production of coffee. The author was charged with a special mission to Brazil on behalf of the coffee culture and coffee commerce in the Dutch possessions in India.

Smith (Captain John, 1579-1631)—*The Adventures and Discoveries of,* sometime President of Virginia and Admiral of New England, newly ordered by John Ashton, with illustrations taken by him from original sources, post 8vo, cloth (pub 5s), 2s. Cassell.

"Full of interesting particulars. Captain John Smith's life was one peculiarly adventurous, bordering almost on the romantic; and his adventures are related by himself with a terse and rugged brevity that is very charming."—ED.

Philip's Handy General Atlas of America, comprising a series of 23 beautifully executed coloured maps of the United States, Canada, &c., with Index and Statistical Notes by John Bartholomew, F.R.G.S., crown folio, cloth (pub £1 1s), 5s. Philip & Son.

Embraces Alphabetical Indices to the most important towns of Canada and Newfoundland, to the counties of Canada, the principal cities and counties of the United States, and the most important towns in Central America, Mexico, the West Indies, and South America.

Sent Carriage Free to any part of the United Kingdom on receipt of Postal Order for the amount.

JOHN GRANT, 25 & 34 George IV. Bridge, Edinburgh.

Little's (*J. Stanley*) *South Africa*, a Sketch-Book of Men and Manners, 2 vols, 8vo, cloth (pub 21s), 3s 6d. Sonnenschein.

Oliphant (*Laurence*)—*The Land of Gilead*, with Excursions in the Lebanon, illustrations and maps, 8vo, cloth (pub 21s), 8s 6d. Blackwood & Sons.

"A most fascinating book."—*Observer*.
"A singularly agreeable narrative of a journey through regions more replete, perhaps, with varied and striking associations than any other in the world. The writing throughout is highly picturesque and effective.—*Athenæum*.
"A most fascinating volume of travel. . . . His remarks on manners, customs, and superstitions are singularly interesting."—*St James's Gazette*.
"The reader will find in this book a vast amount of most curious and valuable information on the strange races and religions scattered about the country."—*Saturday Review*.
"An admirable work, both as a record of travel and as a contribution to physical science."—*Vanity Fair*.

Patterson (*R. H.*)—*The New Golden Age, and Influence of the Precious Metals upon the War*, 2 vols, 8vo, cloth (pub 31s 6d), 6s. Blackwood & Sons.

CONTENTS.

VOL. I.—THE PERIOD OF DISCOVERY AND ROMANCE OF THE NEW GOLDEN AGE, 1848-56.—The First Tidings—Scientific Fears, and General Enthusiasm—The Great Emigration—General Effects of the Gold Discoveries upon Commerce—Position of Great Britain, and First Effects on it of the Gold Discoveries—The Golden Age in California and Australia—Life at the Mines. A RETROSPECT.—History and Influence of the Precious Metals down to the Birth of Modern Europe—The Silver Age in America—Effects of the Silver Age upon Europe—Production of the Precious Metals during the Silver Age (1492-1810)—Effects of the Silver Age upon the Value of Money (1492-1800).

VOL. II.—PERIOD OF RENEWED SCARCITY.—Renewed Scarcity of the Precious Metals, A.D. 1800-30—The Period of Scarcity. Part II.—Effects upon Great Britain—The Scarcity lessens—Beginnings of a New Gold Supply—General Distress before the Gold Discoveries. "CHEAP" AND "DEAR" MONEY—On the Effects of Changes in the Quantity and Value of Money. THE NEW GOLDEN AGE.—First Getting of the New Gold—First Diffusion of the New Gold—Industrial Enterprise in Europe—Vast Expansion of Trade with the East (A.D. 1855-73)—Total Amount of the New Gold and Silver—Its Influence upon the World at large—Close of the Golden Age, 1876-80—Total Production of Gold and Silver. PERIOD 1492-1848.—Production of Gold and Silver subsequent to 1848—Changes in the Value of Money subsequent to A.D. 1492. PERIOD A.D. 1848 and subsequently. PERIOD A.D. 1782-1865.—Illusive Character of the Board of Trade Returns since 1853—Growth of our National Wealth.

Tunis, Past and Present, with a Narrative of the French Conquest of the Regency, by A. M. Broadley, Correspondent of the *Times* during the War in Tunis, with numerous illustrations and maps, 2 vols, post 8vo, cloth (pub 25s), 6s. Blackwood & Sons.

"Mr Broadley has had peculiar facilities in collecting materials for his volumes. Possessing a thorough knowledge of Arabic, he has for years acted as confidential adviser to the Bey. . . . The information which he is able to place before the reader is novel and amusing. . . . A standard work on Tunis has been long required. This deficiency has been admirably supplied by the author."—*Morning Post*.

JOHN GRANT, 25 & 34 George IV. Bridge, Edinburgh.

Burnet (Bishop)—*History of the Reformation of the Church of England*, with numerous Illustrative Notes and copious Index, 2 vols, royal 8vo, cloth (pub 20s), 10s. Reeves & Turner, 1880.

"Burnet, in his immortal History of the Reformation, has fixed the Protestant religion in this country as long as any religion remains among us. Burnet is, without doubt, the English Eusebius."—Dr APTHORPE.

Burnet's *History of his Own Time*, from the Restoration of Charles II. to the Treaty of the Peace of Utrecht, with Historical and Biographical Notes, and a copious Index, complete in 1 thick volume, imperial 8vo, portrait, cloth (pub £1 5s), 5s 6d.

"I am reading Burnet's Own Times. Did you ever read that garrulous pleasant history? full of scandal, which all true history is; no palliatives, but all the stark wickedness that actually gave the *momentum* to national actors; none of that cursed *Humeian* indifference, so cold, and unnatural, and inhuman," &c. —CHARLES LAMB.

Creasy (Sir Edward S.)—*History of England*, from the Earliest Times to the End of the Middle Ages, 2 vols (520 pp each), 8vo, cloth (pub 25s), 6s. Smith, Elder, & Co.

Crime—Pike's (Luke Owen) *History of Crime in England*, illustrating the Changes of the Laws in the Progress of Civilisation from the Roman Invasion to the Present Time. Index, 2 very thick vols, 8vo, cloth (pub 36s) 10s. Smith, Elder, & Co.

Globe (The) *Encyclopædia of Useful Information*, edited by John M. Ross, LL.D., with numerous woodcut illustrations, 6 handsome vols, in half-dark persian leather, gilt edges, or in half calf extra, red edges (pub £4 16s), £2 8s. Edinburgh.

"A work of reference well suited for popular use, and may fairly claim to be the best of the cheap encyclopædias."—*Athenæum.*

History of the *War of Frederick I. against the Communes of Lombardy*, by Giovanni B. Testa, translated from the Italian, and dedicated by the Author to the Right Hon. W. E. Gladstone. (466 pages), 8vo, cloth (pub 15s) 2s. Smith, Elder, & Co.

Freemasonry—Paton's (Brother C. I.) *Freemasonry and its Jurisprudence*, according to the Ancient Landmarks and Charges, and the Constitution, Laws, and Practices of Lodges and Grand Lodges, 8vo, cloth (pub 10s 6d), 3s 6d. Reeves & Turner.

—— **Freemasonry, its *Symbolism, Religious Nature, and Law of Perfection*,** 8vo, cloth (pub 10s 6d), 2s 6d. Reeves & Turner.

—— **Freemasonry, its *Two Great Doctrines*,** The Existence of God, and A Future State; also, Its Three Masonic Graces, Faith, Hope, and Charity—in 1 vol, 8vo, cloth (pub 10s), 2s 6d. Reeves & Turner.

The fact that no such similar works exist, that there is no standard of authority to which reference can be made, notwithstanding the great and growing number of Freemasons and Lodges at home, and of those in the British Colonies and other countries holding Charters from Scotland, or affiliated with Scottish Lodges, warrants the author to hope that they may prove acceptable to the Order. All the oldest and best authorities—the ablest writers, home and foreign—on the history and principles of Freemasonry have been carefully consulted.

Arnold's (Cecil) Great Sayings of Shakespeare, a Comprehensive Index to Shakespearian Thought, being a Collection of Allusions, Reflections, Images, Familiar and Descriptive Passages, and Sentiments from the Poems and Plays of Shakespeare, Alphabetically Arranged and Classified under Appropriate Headings, one handsome volume of 422 pages, thick 8vo, cloth (pub 7s 6d), 3s. Bickers.

Arranged in a manner similar to Southgate's "Many Thoughts of Many Minds." This index differs from all other books in being much more comprehensive, while care has been taken to follow the most accurate text, and to cope, in the best manner possible, with the difficulties of correct classification.

The most Beautiful and Cheapest Birthday Book Published.

Birthday Book—Friendship's Diary for Every Day in the Year, with an appropriate Verse or Sentence selected from the great Writers of all Ages and Countries, each page ornamented by a richly engraved border, illustrated throughout, crown 8vo, cloth, bevelled boards, exquisitely gilt and tooled, gold edges, a perfect gem (pub 3s 6d), 1s 9d. Hodder & Stoughton.

This book practically has never been published. It only requires to be seen to be appreciated.

Dobson (W. T.)—The Classic Poets, their Lives and their Times, with the Epics Epitomised, 452 pages, crown 8vo, cloth (pub 9s), 2s 6d. Smith, Elder, & Co.

CONTENTS.—Homer's Iliad, The Lay of the Nibelungen, Cid Campeador, Dante's Divina Commedia, Ariosto's Orlando Furioso, Camoens' Lusiad, Tasso's Jerusalem Delivered, Spenser's Fairy Queen, Milton's Paradise Lost, Milton's Paradise Regained.

English Literature : A Study of the Prologue and Epilogue in English Literature, from Shakespeare to Dryden, by G. S. B., crown 8vo, cloth (pub 5s), 1s 6d. Kegan Paul, 1884.

Will no doubt prove useful to writers undertaking more ambitious researches into the wider domains of dramatic or social history.

Bibliographer (The), a Magazine of Old-Time Literature, contains Articles on Subjects interesting to all Lovers of Ancient and Modern Literature, complete in 6 vols, 4to, antique boards (pub £2 5s), 15s. Elliot Stock.

" It is impossible to open these volumes anywhere without alighting on some amusing anecdote, or some valuable literary or historical note."—*Saturday Review.*

Book-Lore, a Magazine devoted to the Study of Bibliography, complete in 6 vols, 4to, antique boards (pub £2 5s), 15s. Elliot Stock.

A vast store of interesting and out-of-the-way information, acceptable to the lover of books.

Antiquary (The), a Magazine devoted to the Study of the Past, complete set in 15 vols, 4to, antique boards (pub £5 12s 6d), £1 15s. Elliot Stock.

A perfect mine of interesting matter, for the use of the student, of the times of our forefathers, and their customs and habits.

Chaffers' Marks and Monograms on European and Oriental Pottery and Porcelain, with Historical Notices of each Manufactory, preceded by an Introductory Essay on the Vasa Fictilia of the Greek, Romano-British, and Mediæval Eras, 7th edition, revised and considerably augmented, with upwards of 3000 potters' marks and illustrations, royal 8vo, cloth extra, gilt top, £1 15s. London.

Civil Costume of England, from the Conquest to the Present Time, drawn from Tapestries, Monumental Effigies, Illuminated MSS., by Charles Martin, Portraits, &c., 61 full-page plates, royal 8vo, cloth (pub 10s 6d), 3s 6d. Bohn.
In addition there are inserted at the end of the volume 25 plates illustrating Greek costume by T. Hope.

Dyer (Thomas H., LL.D.)—Imitative Art, its Principles and Progress, with Preliminary Remarks on Beauty, Sublimity, and Taste, 8vo, cloth (pub 14s), 2s. Bell & Sons, 1882.

Great Diamonds of the World, their History and Romance, Collected from Official, Private, and other Sources, by Edwin W. Streeter, edited and annotated by Joseph Hatton and A. H. Keane, 8vo, cloth (pub 10s 6d), 2s 6d. Bell & Sons.

Hamilton's (Lady, the Mistress of Lord Nelson) Attitudes, illustrating in 25 full-page plates the great Heroes and Heroines of Antiquity in their proper Costume, forming a useful study for drawing from correct and chaste models of Grecian and Roman Sculpture, 4to, cloth (pub £1 1s), 3s 6d.

Jewitt (Llewellyn, F.S.A.) — Half-Hours among some English Antiquities, illustrated with 320 wood engravings, crown 8vo, cloth gilt (pub 5s), 2s. Allen & Co.
CONTENTS:—Cromlechs, Implements of Flint and Stone, Bronze Implements among the Celts, Roman Roads, Temples, Altars, Sepulchral Inscriptions, Ancient Pottery, Arms and Armour, Slabs and Brasses, Coins, Church Bells, Glass, Encaustic Tiles, Tapestry, Personal Ornaments, &c. &c.

King (Rev. C. W.)—Natural History of Gems and Decorative Stones, fine paper edition, post 8vo, cloth (pub 10s 6d), 4s. Bell & Sons.
"Contains so much information and of so varied a nature, as to make the work . . . by far the best treatise on this branch of mineralogy we possess in this or any other language."—*Athenæum.*

Leech's (John) Children of the Mobility, Drawn from Nature, a Series of Humorous Sketches of our Young Plebeians, including portrait of Leech, with Letter on the Author's Genius by John Ruskin, 4to, cloth, 1841 (pub 7s 6d), 3s 6d. Reproduced 1875, Bentley & Son.

Morelli (G.) — Italian Masters in German Galleries, translated from the German by L. M. Richter, post 8vo, cloth (pub 8s 6d), 2s. Bell & Sons.
"Signor Morelli has created nothing less than a revolution in art-scholarship, and both by precept and example has given a remarkable impulse to s und knowledge and independent opinion.'—*Academy.*

Sent Carriage Free to any part of the United Kingdom on receipt of Postal Order for the amount.

JOHN GRANT, 25 & 34 George IV. Bridge, Edinburgh

Exquisitely beautiful Works by Sir J. Noel Paton at a remarkably low price.

Paton's (*Noel*) *Compositions from Shakespeare's Tempest*, a Series of Fifteen Large Outline Engravings illustrating the Great Drama of our National Poet, with descriptive letterpress, oblong folio, cloth (pub 21s), 3s. Chapman & Hall.

Uniform with the above.

Paton's (*Noel*) *Compositions from Shelley's Prometheus Unbound*, a Series of Twelve Large Outline Engravings, oblong folio, cloth (pub 21s), 3s. Chapman & Hall.

Smith (*J. Moyr*)—*Ancient Greek Female Costume*, illustrated by 112 fine outline engravings and numerous smaller illustrations, with Explanatory Letterpress, and Descriptive Passages from the Works of Homer, Hesiod, Herodotus, Æschylus, Euripides, and other Greek Authors, printed in brown, crown 8vo, cloth elegant, red edges (pub 7s 6d), 3s. Sampson Low.

Bacon (*Francis, Lord*)—*Works*, both English and Latin, with an Introductory Essay, Biographical and Critical, and copious Indices, steel portrait, 2 vols, royal 8vo, cloth (originally pub £2 2s,) 12s. 1879.

"All his works are, for expression as well as thought, the glory of our nation, and of all later ages."—SHEFFIELD, Duke of Buckinghamshire.

"Lord Bacon was more and more known, and his books more and more delighted in; so that those men who had more than ordinary knowledge in human affairs, esteemed him one of the most capable spirits of that age."

Burn (*R. Scott*)—*The Practical Directory for the Improvement of Landed Property*, Rural and Suburban, and the Economic Cultivation of its Farms (the most valuable work on the subject), plates and woodcuts, 2 vols, 4to, cloth (pub £3 3s), 15s. Paterson.

Martineau (*Harriet*)—*The History of British Rule in India*, foolscap 8vo (356 pages), cloth (pub 2s 6d), 9d. Smith, Elder, & Co.

A concise sketch, which will give the ordinary reader a general notion of what our Indian empire is, how we came by it, and what has gone forward in it since it first became connected with England. The book will be found to state the broad facts of Anglo-Indian history in a clear and enlightening manner; and it cannot fail to give valuable information to those readers who have neither time nor inclination to study the larger works on the subject.

Selkirk (*J. Brown*) — *Ethics and Æsthetics of Modern Poetry*, crown 8vo, cloth gilt (pub 7s), 2s. Smith, Elder, & Co.

Sketches from Shady Places, being Sketches from the Criminal and Lower Classes, by Thor Fredur, crown 8vo, cloth (pub 6s), 1s. Smith, Elder, & Co.

"Descriptions of the criminal and semi-criminal (if such a word may be coined) classes, which are full of power, sometimes of a disagreeable kind."—*Athenæum.*

Southey's (*Robert*) *Commonplace Book*, the Four Series complete, edited by his Son-in-Law, J. W. Warter, 4 thick vols, 8vo, cloth (pub 42s), 14s. Longmans.

Warren's (*Samuel*) *Ten Thousand a Year*, early edition, with Notes, 3 vols, 12mo, cloth (pub 18s), 4s 6d. Blackwood, 1853.

Jones' (Professor T. Rymer) General Outline of the Organization of the Animal Kingdom, and Manual of Comparative Anatomy, illustrated with 571 engravings, thick 8vo, half roan, gilt top (pub £1 11s 6d), 6s. Van Voorst.

Jones' (Professor T. Rymer) Natural History of Animals, Lectures delivered before the Royal Institution of Great Britain, 209 illustrations, 2 vols, post 8vo, cloth (pub 24s), 3s 6d. Van Voorst.

Hunter's (Dr John) Essays on Natural History, Anatomy, Physiology, Psychology, and Geology, to which are added Lectures on the Hunterian Collection of Fossil Remains, edited by Professor Owen, portrait, 2 vols, 8vo, cloth (pub 32s), 5s. Van Voorst.

Forestry and Forest Products — Prize Essays of the Edinburgh International Forestry Exhibition, 1884, edited by John Rattray, M.A., and Hugh Robert Mill, illustrated with 10 plates and 21 woodcuts, 8vo, cloth (pub 16s), 5s. David Douglas.

COMPRISES :—

BRACE'S Formation and Management of Forest Tree Nurseries.

The same, by THOMAS BERWICK.

STALKER'S Formation and Management of Plantations on different Sites, Altitudes, and Exposures.

The same, by R. E. HODSON.

MILNE'S Afforesting of Waste Land in Aberdeenshire by Means of the Planting Iron.

MACLEAN'S Culture of Trees on the Margin of Streams and Lochs in Scotland, with a View to the Preservation of the Banks and the Conservation of Fish.

CANNON'S Economical Pine Planting, with Remarks on Pine Nurseries and on Insects and Fungi destructive to Pines.

ALEXANDER on the Various Methods of Producing and Harvesting Cinchona Bark.

ROBERTSON on the Vegetation of Western Australia.

BRACE'S Formation and Management of Eucalypus Plantations.

CARRICK'S Present and Prospective Sources of the Timber Supplies of Great Britain.

OLDRIEVE on the best Method of Maintaining the Supply of Teak, with Remarks on its Price, Size, and Quality; and on the Best Substitutes for Building Purposes.

On the same, by J. C. KEMP.

ALEXANDER'S Notes on the Ravages of Tree and Timber Destroying Insects.

WEBSTER'S Manufacture and Uses of Charcoal.

BOULGER'S Bye-Products, Utilisation of Coppice and of Branches and other Fragments of Forest Produce, with the View of Diminishing Waste.

STONHILL'S Paper Pulp from Wood, Straw, and other Fibres in the Past and Present.

GREEN'S Production of Wood Pulp.

T. ANDERSON REID'S Preparation of Wood Pulp by the Soda Process.

CROSS and BEVAN'S Report on Wood Pulp Processes.

YOSHIDA'S Lacquer (*Urushi*), Description, Cultivation, and Treatment of the Tree, the Chemistry of its Juice, and its Industrial Applications.

Sent Carriage Free to any part of the United Kingdom on receipt of Postal Order for the amount.

JOHN GRANT, 25 & 34 George IV. Bridge, Edinburgh.

Johnston's (W. & A. K.) Instructive Series :—

Scientific Industries Explained, showing how some of the important Articles of Commerce are made, by Alexander Watt, F.R.S.S.A.. First Series, containing Articles on Aniline Colours, Pigments, Soap-making, Candle-making, Paper-making, Gunpowder, Glass, Alcohol, Beer, Acids, Alkalies, Phosphorus, Bleaching Powder, Inks, Vinegar-making, Acetic Acid, Fireworks, Coloured Fires, Gun-cotton, Distillation, &c. &c., crown 8vo, cloth (pub 2s 6d), 1s.

" Mr Watt discourses of aniline pigments and dyes ; of candles and paper ; of gunpowder and glass ; of inks and vinegar ; of fireworks and gun-cotton ; . . . excursions over the whole field of applied science ; . . one of the best is that on ' gilding watch-movements. A systematic arrangement of the subjects has been purposely avoided, in order that the work may be regarded as a means of intellectual recreation."—*Academy.*

Scientific Industries Explained, Second Series, containing Articles on Electric Light, Gases, Cheese, Preservation of Food, Borax, Scientific Agriculture, Oils, Isinglass, Tanning, Nickel-plating, Cements and Glues, Tartaric Acid, Stained Glass, Artificial Manures, Vulcanised India-rubber, Ozone, Galvanic Batteries, Magnesia, The Telephone, Electrotyping, &c. &c., with illustrations, crown 8vo, cloth (pub 2s 6d), 1s.

Mechanical Industries Explained, showing how many useful Arts are practised, with illustrations, by Alexander Watt, containing articles on Carving Irish Bog-oak, Etching, Galvanised Iron, Cutlery, Goldbeating, Bookbinding, Lithography, Jewellery, Crayons, Balloons, Needles, Lapidary, Ironfounding, Pottery and Porcelain, Typefounding, Bread-making, Bronze-casting, Tile-making, Ormolu, Papier-maché, &c. &c., crown 8vo, cloth (pub 2s 6d), 1s.

"It would form a useful present for any boy with mechanical tastes."— *Engineer.*

Science in a Nut-Shell, in which rational Amusement is blended with Instruction, with numerous illustrations, by Alexander Watt, crown 8vo, illustrated boards (pub 1s), 6d.

CONTENTS :—Absorption of Carbonic Acid by Plants. —The Air-Pump. — Amalgams.—To Produce Artificial Ices.—Attraction : Capillary Attraction.— Carbon.—Carmine.—How to Make Charcoal.—To Prepare Chlorine.—Contraction of Water—Crystallisation.—Distillation.—Effect of Carbonic Acid on Animal Life.—Electricity.—Evaporation.—Expansion by Heat, &c. —Heat.—Hydrogen Gas.—Light.—To Prepare Oxygen.—Photographic Printing.—How to Make a Fountain.—Refractive Power of Liquids.—Refrigeration.—Repulsion.—Solar Spectrum.—Specific Gravity Explained.—Structure of Crystals —Sympathetic Ink, &c. &c.

Sent Carriage Free to any part of the United Kingdom on receipt of Postal Order for the amount.

JOHN GRANT, 25 & 34 George IV. Bridge, Edinburgh.

Stewart's (Dugald) Collected Works, best edition, edited
by Sir William Hamilton, with numerous Notes and Emendations,
11 handsome vols. 8vo, cloth (pub £6 12s), the few remaining
sets for £2 10s.   T. & T. Clark.

Elements of the Philosophy of the Human Mind, 3 vols,
8vo, cloth (pub £1 16s), 8s 6d.

Philosophy of the Active Powers, 2 vols, 8vo, cloth (pub
£1 4s), 6s 6d.

Principles of Political Economy, 2 vols, 8vo, cloth (pub
£1 4s), 5s.

" As the names of Thomas Reid, of Dugald Stewart, and of Sir William Hamilton will be associated hereafter in the history of Philosophy in Scotland, as
closely as those of Xenophanes, Parmenides, and Zeno in the School of Elea, it
is a singular fortune that Sir William Hamilton should be the collector and
editor of the works of his predecessors. . . . The chair which he filled
for many years, not otherwise undistinguished, he rendered illustrious."—
Athenæum.

Dante—The Divina Commedia, translated into English
Verse by James Ford, A.M., medallion frontispiece, 430 pages,
crown 8vo, cloth, bevelled boards (pub 12s), 2s 6d.   Smith,
Elder, & Co.

" Mr Ford has succeeded better than might have been expected: his rhymes
are good, and his translation deserves praise for its accuracy and fidelity. We
cannot refrain from acknowledging the many good qualities of Mr Ford's translation, and his labour of love will not have been in vain, if he is able to induce
those who enjoy true poetry to study once more the masterpiece of that literature
from whence the great founders of English poetry drew so much of their sweet-
ness and power."—*Athenæum.*

Pollok's (Robert) The Course of Time, a Poem, beautifully printed edition, with portrait and numerous illustrations,
12mo, 6d.   Blackwood & Sons.

"'The Course of Time' is a very extraordinary poem, vast in its conception,
vast in its plan, vast in its materials, and vast, if very far from perfect, in its
achievement."—D. M. MOIR.

Monthly Interpreter, a New Expository Magazine, edited
by the Rev. Joseph S. Exell, M.A., joint-editor of the "Pulpit
Commentary," &c., complete from the commencement to its close,
4 vols. 8vo, cloth (pub £1 10s), 10s 6d.   T. & T. Clark.
Vols. 1, 3, 4, separately, 2s each.

The aim of *The Monthly Interpreter* is to meet in some adequate way the
wants of the present-day student of the Bible, by furnishing him in a convenient
and accessible form what is being said and done by the ablest British, Ameri-
can, and foreign theologians, thinkers, and Biblical critics, in matters Biblical,
theological, scientific, philosophical, and social.

Parker's (Dr Joseph, of the City Temple) Weaver Stephen:
or, The Odds and Evens of English Religion, 8vo, cloth (pub
7s 6d), 3s 6d.   Sonnenschein.

" Dr Parker is no repeater of old remarks, nor is he a superfluous commentator
His track is his own, and the jewels which he lets fall in his progress are from
his own casks; this will give a permanent value to his works, when the produc-
tions of copyists will be forgotten."—C. H. SPURGEON.

*Skene (William F., LL.D., Historiographer-Royal for
Scotland)*—The Gospel History for the Young, being Lessons on the
Life of Christ, adapted for use in Families and in Sunday Schools,
3 maps, 3 vols, crown 8vo, cloth (pub 15s), 6s.   Douglas.

" In a spirit altogether unsectarian provides for the young a simple, interesting, and thoroughly charming history of our Lord."—*Literary World.*
" The 'Gospel History for the Young' is one of the most valuable books of
the kind."—*The Churchman.*

By the Authoress of " The Land o' the Leal."   £ s. d.

Nairne's (Baroness) Life and Songs, with a
Memoir, and Poems of Caroline Oliphant the Younger, edited
by Dr Charles Rogers, *portrait and other illustrations*, crown
8vo, cloth (pub 5s)   Griffin   0 2 6
"This publication is a good service to the memory of an excellent and gifted
lady, and to all lovers of Scottish Song."—*Scotsman.*

Ossian's Poems, translated by Macpherson,
24mo, best red cloth, gilt (pub 2s 6d)   0 1 6
A dainty pocket edition.

Perthshire—Woods, Forests, and Estates of
Perthshire, with Sketches of the Principal Families of the
County, by Thomas Hunter, Editor of the *Perthshire Consti-
tutional and Journal, illustrated with 30 wood engravings,*
crown 8vo (564 pp), cloth (pub 12s 6d)   Perth   0 4 6
"Altogether a choice and most valuable addition to the County Histories of
Scotland."—*Glasgow Daily Mail.*

Duncan (John, Scotch Weaver and Botanist)
—Life of, with Sketches of his Friends and Notices of the
Times, by Wm. Jolly, F.R.S.E., H.M. Inspector of Schools,
etched portrait, crown 8vo, cloth (pub 9s)   Kegan Paul 0 3 6
"We must refer the reader to the book itself for the many quaint traits of
character, and the minute personal descriptions, which, taken together, seem to
give a life-like presentation of this humble philosopher. . . . The many incidental notices which the work contains of the weaver caste, the workman's
esprit de corps, and his wanderings about the country, either in the performance
of his work or, when that was slack, taking a hand at the harvest, form an interesting chapter of social history. The completeness of the work is considerably
enhanced by detailed descriptions of the district he lived in, and of his numerous
friends and acquaintance."—*Athenæum.*

Scots (Ancient)—An Examination of the An-
cient History of Ireland and Iceland, in so far as it concerns
the Origin of the Scots: Ireland not the Hibernia of the
Ancients; Interpolations in Bede's Ecclesiastical History and
other Ancient Annals affecting the Early History of Scotland
and Ireland—the three Essays in one volume, crown 8vo, cloth
(pub 4s)   Edinburgh, 1883   0 1 0
The first of the above treatises is mainly taken up with an investigation of the
early History of Ireland and Iceland, in order to ascertain which has the better
claim to be considered the original country of the Scots. In the second and
third an attempt is made to show that Ireland was the ancient Hibernia, and
the country from which the Scots came to Scotland; and further, contain a
review of the evidence furnished by the more genuine of the early British Annals
against the idea that Ireland was the ancient Scotia.

Traditional Ballad Airs, chiefly of the North-
Eastern Districts of Scotland, from Copies
gathered in the Counties of Aberdeen, Banff, and Moray, by
Dean Christie, and William Christie, Monquhitter, with the
Words for Singing and the Music arranged for the Pianoforte
and Harmonium, illustrated with Notes, giving an Account of
both Words and Music, their Origin, &c., 2 handsome vols,
4to, half citron morocco, gilt top, originally published at
£4 4s by Edmonston & Douglas, reduced to   1 10 0

---

*Sent Carriage Free to any part of the United Kingdom on
receipt of Postal Order for the amount.*

JOHN GRANT, 25 & 34 George IV. Bridge, Edinburgh.

www.ingramcontent.com/pod-product-compliance
Lightning Source LLC
Chambersburg PA
CBHW030606040726
47497CB00008B/2871